IF LOOKS COULD KILL

Also by Olivia Kiernan

The Killer in Me
Too Close to Breathe

IF LOOKS COULD KILL

Olivia Kiernan

riverrun

First published in Great Britain in 2020 by

riverrun

An imprint of
Quercus Editions Ltd
Carmelite House
50 Victoria Embankment
London EC4Y 0DZ

An Hachette UK company

A CIP catalogue record for this book is available
from the British Library

HB ISBN 978 1 52940 105 9
TPB ISBN 978 1 52940 106 6
EBOOK ISBN 978 1 52940 107 3

10 9 8 7 6 5 4 3 2 1

Typeset by CC Book Production
Printed and bound in Great Britain by Clays Ltd, Elcograf S.p.A.

Papers used by Quercus are from well-managed forests and other responsible sources.

For Grace and Matthew

CHAPTER 1

You'll find the Gardens buried in the heart of Dublin, away from the grey Liffey waters and the stiff smile of the Ha'penny Bridge, on down, beyond Grafton Street's red-brick road and the old ghosts of Trinity College. Somewhere around a corner, up a narrow street, is the entrance, framed with concrete pillars set into an old stone wall. Inside, winged angels stand watch over dark pools and sunken lawns. The trees form hidden avenues, follow-me trails that lead to fountains, tumbling waterfalls and neat box-hedge mazes. The rusted iron arm of a sundial observes time here and, on this day, it is casting its shadow to one o'clock. The late February sun is a scream of cool light in the sky and slowly the park, whose waiting trees are full of bright new foliage, begins to fill.

First, a couple of teenagers: a boy dressed in loose jeans and a school shirt, his sweater tied low on his hips, his arm around a girl. She's maybe fourteen, thin and small, her school blazer is over one arm, her skirt rolled up at the waist comes to mid-thigh. Thick black tights cover her legs, a pair of black slip-ons on her feet, the backs folded under her heels.

She bumps along next to the boy, her head forced a little forward by the weight of his arm. They make their way towards one of the fountains, where the boy's arm drops away and they both take the time to shuffle free of their schoolbags. The boy sits on the fountain's edge, the girl next to him. She has to lift herself up onto the stone and when she sits, only the tips of her toes skim the ground. She looks up at the boy and he looks down at her. Then they are kissing, at first only faces turned to one another, but after a few moments, the boy's hand goes to the girl's and she turns more fully to him.

In this time, a woman enters the park, a toddler in hand. The toddler, despite the brightness of the day and the slow climb of the temperature, is wearing a thick padded coat, a scarf and round fluffy earmuffs. They walk down one of the little paths, then the toddler breaks free, wellied feet pumping towards one of the benches that looks out on the lawn. She throws herself at it, using her padded middle to lever herself onto the seat. The woman joins her and promptly reaches into a bag to remove a blanket, which she spreads on the bench between them. She passes a juice box to the toddler then arranges the rest of the bag's contents of Tupperware on the blanket. The toddler brings the juice to her lips, her legs kick a beat beneath her and the woman unwraps a sandwich and sits back, her face tipped to take in the most of the sun's warmth.

It's filling up now. Not packed, but enough of a sprinkling of visitors to signal lunch hour. A young woman carries a take-away coffee to a favourite spot to read a book. A group of suits cradling paper lunch-bags, energy drinks and crisps pass her. The woman watches the men settle around a bench on the

2

opposite side of the park. They're loud with banter carried out of the office. Something, a shared joke perhaps, sets one of them off and there's a roar of laughter. The sound makes the kissing teens look up.

It is around this moment that Rory McGrane stops briefly outside the park gates. Pedestrians, racing against the thin slice of their lunch hour, bump up against him as they move by, on to cafés, corner shops or pubs to meet friends, lovers or escape work colleagues. Rory steps a little to the side to let a group of people pass. He takes a moment to watch them, observing their walks, the ease of their movements: relaxed, hands in pockets, the occasional pat of a back or shoulder, the friendly squeeze of a forearm.

Rory's hot, but he barely notices. In an unconscious movement, he lifts a hand to his throat and runs a strong finger around the neck of his shirt. He took his time ironing the shirt this morning. Pressing creases along the arms like he'd been taught to do. In his other hand, he feels the weight of his navy holdall. He tightens his grip around it then turns into the park, away from the manic din of the traffic and the quiet tinkle of the Luas as it snakes through Dublin city.

The park is not as busy as he thought it would be, but it will be enough, he thinks. It has to be because he's not sure he'll be able to face another attempt. But what choice would he have? None, he thinks. He walks down the pavement; last year's leaves cling in dry brown clumps to the borders, but there's fresh growth all around and above him. It's a good day, not raining, and he's glad about that if nothing else.

He walks across the lawn and looks around. A little way off, a young woman looks up from her reading. Her coat is spread out on the grass to protect her work clothes. She takes a sip from a takeaway cup then returns to her book, but he can see her focus has been thrown and every now and then she looks in his direction as if waiting for him to make his move.

He can feel the heat coming over him now. The sweat gathering down his back. His mouth turned dry. He puts down the bag then straightens, wiping the back of his hand across his lips and swallowing. He's surprised at the emotion he's feeling. Fear. He had thought once he was here he would feel relieved, almost free, and he experiences a jolt of disappointment that he's still stalked by his weaknesses.

There's a young couple holding hands at the fountain. He spies the boy's thumb moving over and back on the girl's wrist, sees the soft smile creeping across the girl's face. And he thinks what it might feel like to be young once more. To have his chance again. Avoid the mistakes. He swallows again. Focuses. There is only forward. That is all that's left to him.

He squats down and opens the zip of his bag. He pushes his documents aside until he finds the small triangular case. He unclips it and removes his gun. It's been some time since he's had to use it but he won't need much skill to do what he needs to today. When he straightens again, he takes another look around. Too late he notices the toddler on the bench, the mother with her face tipped back in the sun. He hadn't thought about children. The woman with the book is watching him again and he sees her eyes drop to the weapon in his hand. Her mouth makes an 'O' shape and she scrambles to her feet, knocking the cup into the grass, her book pressed to her chest but she doesn't run and he wonders at her hesitation. He lifts the gun, his finger suddenly steady on the trigger. A light breeze trembles over his face and he thinks he probably should have shaved this morning, then he places the gun to his temple and pulls the trigger.

CHAPTER 2

When I look back, it comes to me, that there's one event, upon which rests the decision about the type of person you believe yourself to be. And although every step from then on, you're attempting to discover who you are, you've already become one thing or another, all hinged on that single event. As if you'd only been stretching the elastic of your existence from that point. That moment, long since passed, but living on behind every action, every choice, forming you over and again.

For me, it was nothing grand. No drama. I was happy. Content. Safe. Where it didn't matter who I was because I didn't know then, I was shaped by bigger people around me, my horizon kept comfortably close, set behind the walls of my home. My parents' bedroom. The light cool but not cold. Maybe spring. I think it was morning. The room still held the scent of my mother's moisturizer, a sweet floral magnolia. I'm watching my dad – pulling the blazer of his uniform closed. His fingers, long and thin, adjusting the collar. His wedding band glinting on his pale skin.

He works up the buttons on his uniform. When he's done, he threads the belt around his waist, pulls it tight, sets it so that the buckle sits in line with the buttons. Then he tugs his blazer down. And I see him rise a little, his shoulders pulling back through the thick navy wool of his uniform. My eyes follow him as he reaches out to the dresser, takes up his hat. He places it on his head, pushing it down firmly, smoothing a hand over the back of his hair, the other hand straightening the peak.

He's transformed. More than Dad. A symbol of righteousness and good. He catches my eye in the mirror and winks. And I can remember the feeling I had. Of warmth. A secret pride that my dad helped people. That he was a hero.

I'd watched him do this often. Enjoying the ritual, the patience he took as he turned from Dad to guard. And maybe it was the look in my eye that he saw, or the sudden realization that the reason I watched was because I wanted the same path as himself. But that day he moved towards me and kneeled, so that I had to look down into his face.

He took my hands in his and I felt the warm comfort of his wedding ring against my skin. 'It's important to know who you are, love, but more important to know how others see you.'

'What do you mean, Daddy? I am who I am.'

He smiled. Eyes closing briefly. 'That you are,' he said.

He got up and I followed him out of the room. The darkness of his uniform stark against the light cream walls of our hallway. The foreignness of him moving through our home had never struck me before, but in that moment I saw it: as if his words had cracked softly against the image I had of him and split it neatly in two. Two halves of my father, now weighing evenly in each hand. The person he was and the person he presented to others.

In the days after, I watched everyone, searched for their other selves, noticed when my mum rushed us, stressed and late, out the door for school, then turned her smile to a neighbour, changing the tone of her voice. And on the obsession grew, a secret study to detect the changes, to discover the person behind smiles, tears, make-up, confidence. Then through my training, and on to detective, where I learned that some people were better at hiding their true selves than others but, in their wake, left evidence, where I could see their tells, read their behaviours and finally see all the faces a person can wear.

I push the back of the earring onto its post. Simple silver studs that stand out against my deep navy satin dress that falls to the floor. I'm wearing my hair up, swept off my face in a loose knot, my fringe arranged to the left so that it covers the shining scar on the side of my forehead and temple. There are other scars too, hidden beneath my clothes. A thin white one in my abdomen where a knife once found a home, a bone fragment chipped free from the back of my neck, suspended deep in the soft tissues just above the neckline of my dress. There are other tells that might be noticed if someone were to look closely enough: a limp I've trained myself to walk free of but still pulls if I sit too long; the time I take to cross a room, counting tables, obstacles, one, two, three . . . the paces required to leave quickly, safely. In the dark. Should I need to.

Taking up my bag, I reach for my perfume. Then I slip into my coat and leave the flat. Baz waits with the engine running and, eager to escape the biting cold of the evening, I open the door and get into the passenger seat.

'Thanks for this,' I say, settling my bag on my lap.

Baz Harwood, my partner at the Bureau for Serious Crime, friend and all-round putter-upper, although he gives as good as he gets in that department too, is dressed in jeans and a green hoodie. It's a studied casualness he's going for but his hair is still damp from the shower, the smell of his aftershave fills the car. A tiny fragment of tissue sticks to the corner of his jaw where he's run his razor too close.

He sweeps his gaze over me, eyes widening. Fucker.

I look at him squarely. 'What?'

His eyebrows lift a fraction, he smiles then turns his attention to the street ahead. 'Nothing.'

'I can't go in work gear,' I say, plucking the dress free of my ankles, thankful I haven't caught it in the door. 'If I wasn't giving out one of the awards, I would be at home, having a bloody rest.'

He laughs at that because he knows I wouldn't. Instead I'm attending the annual Gardaí awards. Although I'm using the word 'annual' in the lightest of ways, being as it's the first. A new little initiative dreamed up by our ever-inventive commissioner, Donna Hegarty, to help throw some good publicity at our not-so-good-publicity-winning force.

I pull down the sun visor. Slide over the mirror and frown in at my reflection. 'The food will be good.'

'You're selling it to me.' He flicks his eyes in my direction again. 'Relax. Clancy will be there. Just try not to spend the evening talking shop.'

I groan. 'I'm not great at small talk.'

9

'I noticed.'

'You sure you can't come?'

His face draws into a smug smile. 'I've had this weekend trip in the diary for ages.'

I flip the visor back up. 'Three weeks.'

'Still.'

Baz is in love. Two months' worth. He mentions his girlfriend more often than it rains. Like a soppy teenager, he shoe-horns her name into as many conversations as he can. *Chief, we've a body down near the Liffey. Christ, myself and Gemma had a takeaway coffee there last weekend.* The staff draw bets on the number of times per shift she comes up. Even if he never said her name, you'd tell from the perpetual smile on his face. Everything makes him happy. There are detectives who when they get in deep with someone ease up. You can see them throwing covetous eyes at the desk jobs going. Requesting positions or departments that don't feature shift work. Nice nine-to-fives. And they squirrel away in the background until they're up for pension and then it's see ya later. But Baz is not one. If anything, he's more hungry. I'm guessing his relationship is still at the stage where the badge is a turn-on. Reality will come soon enough. There's no better litmus test of a relationship than being a detective, and I feel a pang on Baz's behalf when I think of it.

'We got the best place on this new holiday site. Little cottage near Clogherhead. Can you believe Gemma's never been there?' he says to me.

I try not to roll my eyes. 'That's a shocker.'

He shoots me an irritated look.

'Sorry. I'm jealous. I hope you have a lovely time.'

10

He glowers out the window. The traffic is deathly slow. Never the quickest in Dublin at the best of times, navigating the merry-go-round of one-ways and the Luas commanding all to stay clear until she swoops by. The tram, from the moment of its conception, was met with irritation by commuters – whether in car, on foot, bus or taxi – even though everyone's happy enough to use it when it suits. Now antipathy towards it is maintained by numerous strikes, travel disruption and the cost of development. It probably doesn't help that the odd person or bike seems to get sucked under it on occasion.

We turn onto the Southside quays and roll slowly to a stop near O'Connell Street. The light is dropping from the sky. Friday night calling people home or out. The street is a hustle of dark coats, heels, slick-haired men, shoulders up against the sharp tongue of the wind coming off the river, the odd person pushing through the crowds in trackies, clasping white-bagged takeaways like cherished bairns in their arms, the homeless stacked up and still in cardboard and sleeping bags in the dark crevices of the street, life turning around them.

Baz lets the car roll on another few inches. Taps his hand on the steering wheel and strains his neck to try and see what the hold-up is. Could be one of myriad problems that choke up the city: a delivery van pulled up on the pavement, set on hitting his delivery window; a rear-end shunt from one impatient commuter to another or simply a car in the wrong lane attempting to turn; exhausted drivers refusing to give over a metre of hard-won road. To the right are the dark waters of the Liffey. On the other side of the river, the traffic is heavy but moving.

'I think you'll be late,' Baz says.

'We've time yet. Clancy will save me a seat. I'm not presenting until after the dinner. What the fuck is going on though?' I push down the window and look out beyond the rows of red lights ahead of us. The tell-tale violet of garda lights wavers on the buildings ahead. 'Hang on. Let me see.'

I step out of the warmth of the car and the cold wind that sweeps through the squat stone balustrades of O'Connell Bridge hits me full in the face.

'I can phone in,' Baz shouts across at me, indicating that I should get back in.

'Half the force is out, remember? I won't be a minute,' I say. 'By the way, you've a little something there.' I point to my chin. He frowns then scrambles for the visor to examine his face.

I close the door then step up on the pavement. Ahead, garda cars, traffic cones sealing off the road, an officer in a high-vis jacket waving through the odd vehicle. Beyond the roadblock, the dark silhouette of Daniel O'Connell standing high above his bevy of angels crying out for liberty and peace to past and future Ireland. I'm about to turn back, assuming it's an accident that's brought Dublin to a halt when I notice the small gathering accumulating on the pavement. People stopping, some with phones out.

I hear a shout, 'get back', coming from the direction of the monument. The crowds have that feeling of anticipation like an audience in a theatre waiting for the fat lady to sing. My coat flaps open in the stiff breeze as I move down the street towards the commotion, icy air snapping at my ankles.

'I'll fucking do it. Don't come any fucking closer,' a man's voice screams. The words slurring over the din.

The crowd stills, in a way that feels like they might want him to do whatever it is he's saying. Clearly not something catastrophic enough for them to worry about their own safety but you never bloody know. It never fails to surprise me how long it takes people to run from danger.

I push my way towards the voice. A few shoulders attempt to close in around me as if I was skipping a queue at a checkout, but eventually I get through to see for myself what the ruckus is.

A bloke, maybe mid-twenties, on his side, on the ground, in front of old Daniel there, his hand over his abdomen, and what looks like blood seeping out from between his fingers. A beanie hat pushed back on his head, face white, a scatter of acne over his jaw. Standing over him, another bloke, in his twenties or maybe younger: rake-like physique, his neck so slim I'd guess that even I'd get both hands clear around it; a large bobble of an Adam's apple working up and down in his throat like a yo-yo. He too is clutching his abdomen, less blood though, and in his hand a knife that looks like it's come straight from his mammy's kitchen drawer.

Four uniforms in high-vis are trying to keep the crowds back.

'Drop the knife, mate,' one of the officers says, and he puts out a gloved palm, motions towards the ground.

I step up beside him. 'DCS Sheehan. What's going on?'

The guard looks me over, not altogether convinced and I don't blame him. I find my badge in my coat pocket, show it to him.

'Meet Gar and Mark here. Both fucking eejits. Both fucking flying. One took the other's score so Mark here stabbed him, now he's stabbing himself if we come near.' He says it as if he's reporting on the weather.

'Normal day then so.'

13

''Tis that alright,' he remarks.

The uniform nearest Mark takes another step forward.

And Mark turns the knife towards his stomach and jabs the blade through his thin white T-shirt. The crowd give an involuntary whoosh of groans, as if they could feel it. I wince on his behalf. He makes a low moaning sound and clutches his abdomen again. He waves the bloodied knife at the encroaching guards. 'I said I'd fucking do it now get back.'

'This is going to be some comedown for our man Mark,' I say to the guard. 'You got ambulances on the way?'

'They're about a minute out.'

'Mark,' Gar pants from the ground. 'Man, I didn't take it.'

'Shut up,' Mark says. He wipes the back of his hand under his nose.

I move forward. 'Mark?'

He looks up, shifts from foot to foot, like the ground is moving beneath him. 'Who the bleedin' hell are you?'

'My name's Frankie. I'm a guard. What's happened?'

'Fucking stole my hit.'

'Who?'

He looks at me as if I'm blind, points the knife at the bloke on the ground. 'Him!'

'I didn't, mate,' Gar replies. Although the fixed-eyed stare on his face says otherwise. Could be shock, loss of blood making him looked stoned, but I'm thinking it's mostly drugs.

'He says he didn't,' I say to Mark.

'He did.'

Gar raises his head a bit then coughs. 'I didn't mate, I swear on May's grave I didn't.' His head falls back. 'Fucking 'ell.'

14

The guard behind me moves a foot more and Mark's head twitches in his direction. 'I said don't come closer.' He rewards himself with another gut-punch of the knife at his abdomen.

This one looks deeper and a few spatters of blood hit the ground around him, the white toes of his trainers.

'Jesus.' I shake my head at the guard. Don't move. Stay back. Although a part of me is thinking maybe these two finishing each other off mightn't be the worst thing to happen in the world. 'That looks like a bad one.' I say and nod at the blood staining Mark's T-shirt.

He bends over his stomach, pants. 'Yeah, well, stay back. This is between me and him.'

'I knew a fella once who did similar. Not to himself like but someone stabbed him just where you're stabbed right there.'

Mark grimaces, shakes his head as if he doesn't care but he looks out from beneath his brow, his eyes blinking away sweat. 'What happened to him, then?'

I point towards his gut. 'That's right through the colon I'd say. Same as this friend of mine. He was lucky though, he got to hospital so they could do something. But they said a couple of minutes more and he would've been shitting into a bag for the rest of his life.'

The knobble bobs in Mark's throat. He folds at the middle again for a moment, his forehead growing wet, lips paling.

'Mate, I'm in a bad way here,' Gar moans.

'You stole from me, man,' Mark grumbles. A new rage bubbling up inside of him. He wipes sweat or tears away from his eyes with the hand holding the knife, then spits onto the street.

The knife falls to his side, taps against his leg. And it's hard to tell if he's relenting or about to go at his mate again.

I can sense the guards want to try and rush in. But as much as I'd rather Mark and Gar didn't finish each other off here, in front of half of Dublin, I don't want a colleague getting hit if I can help it.

'Mark, there's an ambulance coming,' I shout out to him, pulling his attention away from the injured man on the ground.

'Stay back!' He takes a moment to look down at his T-shirt. Sways a bit on his feet and I will him to pass out. 'If you didn't take it then where is it, ha? You were right there. I left it in my shoe then it was gone.'

Gar lets out a loud moan, coughs, rolls over and back. Then he seems to rouse himself a bit. His head comes up. 'You put it in your bleedin' pocket,' he roars.

'Liar,' Mark shouts at him and takes a shuffling couple of lunges towards him. The guards tense.

'Mark!' I shout.

He pulls back, skinny chest puffing in and out as if it was on a string.

'Have you checked your pockets?' I ask. Nothing like this job to make you sound like your own mother.

'Course I checked my fucking pockets,' he sniffs. But he pats his hands over his jeans anyway, knife between thumb and forefinger. His expression changes, anger wiped away and a smile erupts across his face.

He pulls out a small clear bag. Holds it up. 'Fuck yeah, mate. Sorry. It's right here.' He drops the knife. And the guards move in. Mark is on his front next to his mate just as the paramedics pull up.

I turn back through the dispersing crowds, wind stinging my eyes and feeling ever so slightly sorry that the road will clear after all. I get into the car.

'What was that?' Baz asks.

'Dublin,' I say.

He gives me a bemused look, puts the car in gear and waits for the traffic ahead to clear.

CHAPTER 3

I ease out of the bed, find my T-shirt on the floor and pull it on. Slowly, I stand up. The room is warm, too dry. A piercing slice of sunlight breaks through a gap in the curtains; a finger of trembling warmth that makes me wince. I go to the window, jerk the drapes closed. The room is a mess of discarded clothes, a glass on the locker shows the sticky residue of bourbon. I swallow. Look over the still shape in the bed.

The covers have slipped down his back, his head pitched to the side, mouth open; a leg hangs off the edge of the bed. Light brown hair, which has turned to a curl in the night, falls over his temples. His hand rests palm-up near his face and I remember the feel of it at the back of my head, then my hands at his waist, pulling his shirt free, at his chest, working buttons down. Our faces pressed together, nose to nose. On the floor his clothes. The gardaí badge has fallen out of his pocket and I have the urge to pick it up, check his name against my memory but it's right next to the bed and out for the count as he is, I don't want to risk waking him. Yet. I leave the room and head for the shower.

Standing under the hot jets of water, the awards ball flashes in highlighted sequences behind my closed eyes. Clancy, my boss, the assistant commissioner, reaching out to top up my glass for the third time before filling his own, his blue eyes softened with alcohol, slouched on his chair, his tie pulled loose, a skeptical eye on the stage as Donna Hegarty rounds off a congratulatory speech on the number of new garda joining the force this year. Later, us helping Clancy into a taxi, a crooked rendition of 'She Walks through the Fair' slurring from his lips. I smile, imagine his head this morning. I don't think he'll be bothering the office today.

I get dressed, make some coffee, toast and take it to the window. I pull it open and the roar of Dublin swoops inside, breathes reality into my face; the low growl of buses, the sigh and hiss of articulated lorries as they stop and start in the streets.

Below me, Grafton Street, pedestrianized, red-surfaced; the shops, lights on, but not quite open. A couple of women sharing a cigarette, waiting for their manager or some superior to arrive and let them into their working day. I gaze at the blue haze of smoke that spreads out around them before slowly dissolving in the bright morning air, finding myself drawing a long breath in through my nose as if I could pull the smoke towards me. I throw a longing look at the ashtray on the low sill. It's clean, empty, has been for a month now.

Times are changing. I'm changing. Becoming more cautious, less reliant on instinct rather than evidence. That's what I'm aiming for. In the past, I would have said a good detective is led by their instincts but the more cases you work, the greater the urge to take that shortcut, to weed out other possibilities too quickly, let the gut take over. It's not a bad thing to be reminded to look again. Sometimes what you see in front of you is not what's in front of you, and no one's above reminding themselves of that. Clancy is delighted with this turnabout. He doesn't say it but I can tell. It's the first time since I've known him that he's not watched me with that wariness in his expression, as if he'd always been half-wondering, *What's she going to do now?*

I check the time. Eight-thirty. I find my phone in my bag. Battery dead. I plug it in then sit at the breakfast bar and open my laptop. Three documents expand on my desktop. A submission from Harcourt Street Garda Station on a request for new policy to deal with gang crime. A pilot programme in conjunction with our own forensics department that will see criminal analysts, profilers and archaeologists adding their skillset to new DNA evidence in order to assist in a review of Ireland's cold cases. The last document, almost completed and ready for launch in the next twelve months, an anti-corruption policy. Local to each district. Taking another mouthful of coffee, I look over the last document. I'm pleased it's finished and it can be sent through to headquarters. I'll be glad to see the back of it. I've never enjoyed this part of policing, dealing with a faceless entity, systems and red tape, even if it's our own. I like to feel the results of my job, on the front line, in the pursuit of justice. A justice that feels personal. Give me a name, a person, a victim that I can see.

'Hey,' a voice rasps from behind me. 'Working already?'

I turn. 'Hey,' I say, closing the laptop. I get up, go to the sink and rinse out the cafetière. 'Some paperwork is all. How'd you sleep?'

20

'Oh, you know,' he says. 'Like the dead.'

He's dressed. Jeans and shirt, and I remember that this is the reason I started talking to him the night previous. Some joke about him not conforming by not wearing a suit. I see him look around for his jacket. He spots it squashed up against the sofa, picks it up, shakes the creases out then puts it on.

'You want coffee?' I ask.

He rubs both hands over his face. 'Actually, you know, I probably should be getting off.' He checks his phone, his thumb scrolling quickly over the screen. When he looks up at me, he gives me a rueful smile. 'You know when you can sense it's going to be one of those days?'

I smile again, try to hide my relief. Leave the cafetière on the draining board. 'Oh yes.'

He pockets his phone and glances around again. 'Ah,' he says, reaching for the empty glasses and bottle on the table. 'The usual suspects,' he says, holding them up. He pauses, grimaces. 'Sorry, bad joke.' He brings them to the kitchen and leaves them on the breakfast bar.

'Thanks,' I say, 'You don't have to do that.'

He nods, stands awkwardly, hand taps on the counter. 'Some night, right? I mean the party.'

'I'm glad it'll only happen once a year,' I say, reaching up to massage my temple.

'Right,' he says. He moves across the room, stops a pace or two in front of me. His hand lifts, then drops to his side, as if he's unsure of what move to make next. 'Sorry, I do genuinely need to go. I've got a case. Media already running it. Local media, but still. And *I'm not available to comment*,' he says, mimicking

21

the journo speak. He hesitates for a beat, takes a breath and eyes me cautiously. 'But I'd really like to see you again.'

I can smell the sleep on him, mixed with the faint scent of his aftershave. It's not unpleasant. For a flash, I imagine the moving parts of my life more balanced. Professional and personal vying for equal weight; a voice through the door of my flat when I open it after a shift. In the morning when I leave. Something to return to. Someone. I feel a clutching tightness in my chest. Another person taking up space. Space and time that I leave open for victims. Cases. Hungry cases that consume all emotion and energy, and me free to give it as needed. Selfishly. Selflessly. I guess there is truth in the saying that if you want something enough, you'll make it happen and to be honest, I don't want to share my life, it's complicated enough as it is.

'Thanks, I—' I begin.

But he gets there before me, something on my face giving my answer away before I can speak it. 'Look, don't worry.' He smiles. 'It would have been nice but it's okay.'

I match his smile. Nod.

He's silent for a moment, his eyes moving around the room, back to the counter, then me. 'Okay. Well, I guess I'll see ya,' he says, lifting his hand at me before leaving.

The main floor of the Bureau for Serious Crime is tellingly empty for a Saturday morning. Some of the team being wily enough to put in for the time off well in advance of last night's celebrations, others preferring the sniffle and cough down the phone early this morning, but both camps deciding not to suffer through their hangovers under the flare of fluorescent light and the shrill call of the ever-chiming phone lines. Not that you could tell this morning but we're the first stop for all serious crime that may be of national interest. Namely murder. All my team have earned their position here; even if some of them are lacking in experience they each have a valuable skillset, whether it's managing the media or being able to extract a suspect's digital history from a rain-soaked hard drive.

It's normal for a detective working murder to not give up until their case is solved but the team we've built have a particularly relentless determination. There are the usual tensions, in-house playground problems that sometimes makes me wonder how some of them manage to feed and dress themselves of a morning but on a case they are highly motivated, each one combing their portion of the investigation for some critical piece of evidence to drop at my feet. Dependent on budget, of course.

I stand inside the door, take off my coat, fold it over my arm and take a look at what I've got. Detective Inspector Helen Flood, reliable as rain on a bank holiday, is at her desk; hair smoothed back, eyebrows plucked into impossibly thin arches – so narrow, it's hard when I'm close up not to focus on them, to marvel at their construction, literally not one hair out of place. Her face is round but not fat. What my mother would call, 'strong'.

Helen works the logistics of our cases, searches the backgrounds of suspects, witnesses and victims' families, draws up uniforms, specialists and calls in our team as needed. Her enthusiastic efficiency has no off button. Every case, every task is met with the same high level of commitment. It's wearing – particularly on days like today, where most are simply wanting to survive their shift – but increasingly her constant pushing in the background is what's turned cases around for us.

'Good morning, Chief,' she says from her desk. She lifts up a sports bottle, gives it a shake and flips open the top. 'Pretty quiet today, thank God.' She takes a quick gulp of her drink, clicks the lid closed and places it carefully at the back of her desk. She gathers up a set of papers. 'Here's what's come in.' She hands me the bundle.

Paul, DI Collins, is on the other side of the room. Handset to his ear, absorbing the bulk of our queries and calls, he is bent over his desk, so that all I can see are the few wisps of hair that lie flat over his smooth, shining scalp. He glances over at me, nods a nervous hello then returns to the phone.

'Thanks,' I say to Helen. I flick through the papers, a summary of the darker events that have happened in the last twelve hours in the country. 'Coffee first then I'll be in my office.'

'Okay, Chief. It was a good night, right?' she says, a hint of a smile playing at the corner of her mouth.

I look around the empty room. 'A bit too good,' I say. 'Any word from Clancy?'

'Nothing yet.'

Small mercies. I go to my office. Set down a fresh coffee and the crime reports on my desk. I go to the window and push it open then lift a small jug of water from the sill and tip it into the base of the bonsai. It's showing off a fresh wave of green leaves, the branches maturing, twisted and curled like arthritic hands beneath the foliage. I take up the clippers and cut away a wiry straggle of new growth, then remove my jacket, hook it on the back of my chair and sit down.

I look through the reports. Most of the cases are already well through the system, prosecutions imminent and requiring only a signature. Nora and Graham Sweeney, charges of slavery and trafficking. Chris Trainer, twenty-nine, of Mullingar, Westmeath on charges of cyber crime. Terry Mantle, car theft and murder. Then the cases of interest, active or soon to be active and waiting for the decision on which department might be best suited to investigate. Each one laid out, the number of witness transcripts collected, evidence submitted, trial or pre-trial dates confirmed or expected: Anya Smith, forty-six years, murdered in her home, suspect in custody, partner Andy Cross. Shane Adams, twenty-three, murdered, bottled outside the Lucky Susan pub off Lower Leeson Street. Debbie Nugent, fifty-five, Wicklow, missing.

I pause at the last one, not sure how the case has found its way into my office – the other end of Helen's overthinking habit, perhaps. Missing persons should go to the station at Harcourt Street. But looking over the report, I see what's brought this case to my office: a crime scene at the house, bloody enough to suspect murder. And then the list of websites that are already running the story of her disappearance.

I look at the address, five kilometres outside of Ballyalann in Wicklow. I'm not familiar with it. Helen, anticipating my ignorance, has attached notes. A small town buried in the wide green clefts of the mountains almost eighty kilometres from Dublin city centre. I sense straight away that Debbie's face will be on every paper in the province before tomorrow evening. Here's the thing about murder: in the city it never captures the imagination as much; sadly, people expect it. What's a knifing among enemies

25

in a packed street? But murder in a small community, there's nothing surer to make people shift uncomfortably in their seats as they chew down on their buttered toast and leaf through the morning papers. Murder, without the faceless anonymity of a big city, feels very personal indeed.

The summary says Debbie Nugent was last seen by her daughter three days ago. The report came to us at nine this morning. If it is a murder scene, locating the body is paramount, but the breadth of the location will be an obstacle. Three days of decomposition. Body temperature lost. Time of death lost. Bruising, fingerprints, flesh. Memories. Gone. And if she's still alive, the pressure is greater. We know that every hour missing means an hour closer to death. The team will need volunteers and officers for a search and considering the location, extensive forensic analysis. I pick up the phone, dial out to Helen.

'Do we have the call-in for the Wicklow case?'

'I can pull it up,' she says.

'Thanks,' I say. 'And can we get any CCTV of her last sighting? There's a comment here that she was travelling to Dublin on that day. Did she go by car? Bus? Get a lift?'

'I'll look into it,' Helen replies, eager.

There's a photo attached for Debbie Nugent. Two daughters it says. Both grown. One living at home. The photo shows a steady face, reddened over the cheeks, wind-burn, dark-hair, thick and fuzzy to just below her jawline. She is perhaps thirty in the picture. I check the age against the report. The photo is over twenty years old.

Helen knocks lightly on the door of my office then steps inside with a transcript of the callout.

'We don't have a more recent photograph to circulate?' I ask her.

'I can't seem to get anything from the local station. I've run a search on social media and this is the only image that comes up.'

I sigh. Sometimes even getting the basics of a case down is like trying to push an elephant through the eye of a needle. 'Okay.'

I take the transcript of the call and flick through the pages. 'Let's get the playback,' I say, returning the pages to her. I want to hear the degree of urgency from the caller. Listen for breathing changes. Crying. The stillness of disbelief. I want to hear emotion. And sometimes we can pick up small leakages of information around what's really happened: *she's been stabbed* becomes a sight more telling when we get out to a scene and discover the victim's stab wounds are not visible to anyone until the body is moved. The callout is our first description of what's happened by a potential suspect. And there's not a detective worth their salt that would begin an investigation without listening to it first.

'No problem,' she says and reaching across me, clicks through to the station's database of calls.

'Ballyalann has its own station?'

She doesn't look up from the screen. 'Yep. They've someone on the desk on weekdays,' she continues. 'A visiting sergeant one day a week and two floating uniforms who cover some of the other villages and Ballyalann. There you go,' she says, pointing to the screen where the call is waiting to play.

'Thanks.' I click play.

A female voice, officious and matronly, trills out into the cold room. 'Ballyalann Garda Station. How can we help you?'

Then a man's voice: 'I think you need to get out here. To the Nugent house.'

'Who's calling, please?'

'It's David Sutton. Debbie's missing.'

'Missing?'

'Yeah, it's like there's been some kind of attack, there's blood. Lots of it.' His voice raises to a squeak at the end, breath fast down the line.

'Okay, we're sending someone out there now. Who's with you, David?'

'Margot. Kristen. She came in this morning.'

'Could there be anyone else on the property?'

'No, I don't think so.'

'We'll be out to you as soon as we can.'

'Please hurry,' then a pause before his voice drops: 'It looks like she's been killed.'

I listen to it again, trailing after every word looking for indicators of guilt. The last line from the caller is the only one that sticks out: 'It looks like she's been killed.' There is no mention of a body.

'I'm going down to it,' I say to Helen. 'Are Crime Scene already there?'

'Keith Hickey arrived with his team about an hour ago. You want me to call in Detective Harwood?'

Baz is likely walking the length of the beach in Clogherhead right now, a post-breakfast breath of air, hand-in-hand with his girlfriend. I feel a stab of guilt for knowing that I'm about to drag him away, but he's my partner and if he's to work this case by my side, it's best he's here from the get-go. Really, I'm

28

weighing up in my mind what will piss him off most: that I call him in and he doesn't get his money's worth from the cottage he's paid for, or that I don't and he's on the back foot of a murder investigation. Detectives, the ones with the hunt in their gut anyways, live in a hybrid state, ticked off that your work never leaves you alone while simultaneously being ticked off when it does. There's always a vague feeling that you should really be getting your personal life in order, a nagging pressure to strike what modern therapists might call a work–life balance, but there's no such thing when dealing with murder. When that call comes in, nothing stirs the blood more. You're on the clock, a race against time and time can't win.

'Yeah. Call him. Tell him to meet me in a couple of hours at the scene.'

CHAPTER 4

Rain follows me all the way to Wicklow, sheets of grey dropping in wide veils across the dull horizon. The road gradually narrows as it rises and falls through the hills and mountains. I pass through the occasional village, but apart from that the remoteness of the countryside is such that it's hard to believe I'm barely two hours from the Bureau.

I drive slowly over the crest of another hill and the road breaks away to my right, widens. A lookout point where a tourist bus has parked. People stand facing a dark cleft between the mountains; one has climbed on top of a boulder, posing for a photograph – hood up, face turned up to the pelting rain. A few are descending through the shivering ridges of heather and waving yellow grasses. There are paths and walking trails all over the hills and mountains here. On some of those trails you'll find posters stapled to trees or tied to signposts. Posters showing the faces of missing persons.

I move down a gear, ease the car down the other side. Immediately, the view changes; the rounded shadow of the hills give way to a dark avenue of fir, so dense I reach for my lights. I think of what the location can offer us in terms of searching for Debbie Nugent. A small rural community; people rely on each other in these places. The word 'neighbour' has a different meaning. Your nearest could be a quarter mile away but closer to you than if you'd lived side by side. Local pubs, churches, shops are important points of connection where stories and gossip are peddled out and, true or not, become impossible to shake. That could work to our advantage. Debbie may not be here to tell us what happened but the locals should be able to give us some of the puzzle. But the advantages of investigating in remote countryside are also its disadvantages. If there has been foul play, a glance out my window tells me how likely it is that we'll find Debbie's body. And as reliant on each other as they are, in my experience, an isolated rural community like this can hide some very big secrets.

However, our first reach out to the town seemed positive. Helen's hunt for CCTV footage of Debbie's last movements looked like it turned up gold with the first strike. A jolt of hope that this would be simple, a lead to Debbie's whereabouts. Some investigations are like that, get on the right path from the get-go and hop, skip and jump all the way down that road where the solution is waiting without an obstacle in your path. A woman at a local newsagents recalled seeing her waiting for the Dublin bus one morning. They'd a camera over the shop. However, when she thought on it further she remembered it was likely a few weeks ago. She'd been taking in a delivery and the confectionery order was wrong. But she found us the footage and sent it on. It was from three weeks ago. Old.

We watched it anyway. Anything that can tell us about our victim is valuable. We've a blank copybook on Debbie Nugent and we need to fill it. In the end, to know the victim is to know their killer. The camera was lodged over the awning of the newsagent's, taking in the top of an old fuel pump and capturing the bus stop at an angle. The shop manager remembered seeing her. Was sure of it but it took her a while to get the right clip. On the footage, bright, early afternoon sunshine flickers over the street. A white car passes, shoots out of view and a figure settles against the narrow bench to wait for the bus. Her back is to the camera, thick dark hair, light blue jeans, a purple fleece coat, trainers. Debbie.

More cars pass and she turns her head after each one, resettling her backpack on her lap. Another person approaches. A young man, late teens maybe early twenties. There is a nodding of heads as hello, a quick verbal exchange before the young man fishes his headphones out of his pocket, puts them in his ears. A lorry hurtles by, too fast. Then Debbie gets up as the bus pulls into view. Set for Dublin city centre. The young man gets on first. Then Debbie. She stands in the door of the bus, then after a moment moves away, down the aisle, only a vague shadow of herself visible on the camera. The bus pulls off and disappears out of shot.

I drive out that road now but in the opposite direction, following the route Helen's given me to Debbie's house. Her home. I find the turning, not so much a lane as a track, the ground eaten into the sides by poor weather and run-off from the hills above. The car bumps along slowly, hitting ridges of cracking tarmacadam where the weight of the hills

32

has caused it to fold like a wrinkled carpet. There's a loud grinding scratch from beneath me. 'Fuck,' I mutter and slow even more, trying not to think of what parts of my car I've left behind on the road.

To the left, the entrance to the house. Or access at least. Another track. I turn onto it and the ground descends for a hundred yards before ascending again, and the house comes into view. I crawl forward through mud and rough stone.

Ahead, there are three vehicles pulled up, among them a squad car and Baz's BMW, mud coating the wheel hubs and up the panels. I imagine his ire at having his new wax spoiled. Behind the blue-and-white crime-scene tape that bounces and ripples in the wind, I see Keith Hickey's Berlingo, the word FORENSICS white and loud on the side.

I pull up behind Baz and turn off the ignition. He unfolds out of the driver's side, ducking his head against the fat gobs of rain that drop through the trees overhead.

'Hey,' I shout when I get out. I peer up the driveway then reach back into the car for my coat.

'Howya,' Baz replies.

'Not much of a mini-break?'

'It was nice while it lasted,' he says, a hiss of frustration in his voice. 'How was last night?'

'Watching your superior throwing shapes on a dance floor in the small hours might have been worth the sufferance.'

'Clancy?'

'The rhythm got him. Or didn't.' I squint at him through the rain. 'You didn't have to come out, you know. You should have taken your weekend.'

He wipes a hand over his face, clearing raindrops from his forehead and eyes. 'Gemma understands. It's the job.'

'Right. You been inside?'

'Not yet. Any chance it'll be a quick job and I can get back to Gemma before the weekend closes?' he asks, his voice rises against the incessant patter of the rain. He watches a scene-of-crime officer carrying a box out to the forensics van then answers his own question. 'I'm thinking no such luck.'

We walk up the drive, sidestepping rivulets of water and soft patches of mud. The house is two-storey, an old farmhouse. Grey stone with a pleasant red-brick edging, but I can see the modern touches. Already a blue tarp porch has been erected at the front door by forensics.

To the side of the house, a parked hatchback, a light blue Focus. We pause, both of us, thinking the same thing. Wherever Debbie Nugent is, she hasn't taken her car.

'What do we know about the suspected victim? The family?' Baz asks.

'Unmarried, two children. Both grown: Kristen, eldest. And Margot. Debbie works in a garden centre in town. Full-time, but not weekends. The eldest daughter lives with her husband in northern France and had returned for a two-week stay this morning. The victim was last seen on Wednesday morning, the twenty-seventh of March, by her daughter Margot, who lives with her.'

In the squad car, two male officers crammed inside, a sheet of crumpled foil spread out on the dash on which there's a stack of sandwiches that could feed an army. The windows are half-fogged with steam from a Thermos that they're passing between them. I knock on the window. It comes down and the smell of cheese and pickle hits me full in the face. The driver is still wearing his hat; a shock of soot-black hair bursts out around the brim, eyebrows you could rest a book on meet in a dark shelf above his eyes, knees halfway up the sides of the steering wheel. He must be edging on six five. I can hear his parents now telling him he's fit for the guards with height like that. The guard closest to us, in the passenger seat, chews quickly over a mouthful of his sandwich. He's younger, late twenties maybe. Blue eyes and light fair hair, good show of muscles tight under his shirt.

'Alright, lads,' Baz says.

The tall one chews quickly, wipes more crumbs from his front. 'Yis must be the crew from Dublin, ha?'

'Detective Harwood and Detective Sheehan,' Baz replies.

The guard slides his hand over his trouser leg, cleaning off whatever sticky residue the sandwich has left on his fingers and reaches across his colleague, arm extended for Baz to shake. 'Timothy Morris,' he says. 'Or Timmy, if you like. And this here is Joe.'

'Joe Kaminski,' the younger one says, face flushing slightly.

'You were the first on the scene?'

'We were, yeah,' Timmy says, relinquishing his lunch to the foil on the dash. 'Got the callout at about ten this morning from David Sutton.'

'David Sutton?'

'The daughter's boyfriend. Margot's that is. A good lad.'

'And they were all here when you arrived?'

'Self and Joe here came out first. The sarge was out in an hour or so, came from Wicklow. We then took the sisters to the station so they wouldn't be troubled. They were upset. Understandably.'

35

'You touch anything?'

Timmy leans on the door of the car, attempts to shift his weight so he can turn in the seat to face us. 'No, no. Took a look in the room and knew that it'd have to be called in straight away. We did a quick sweep of the rooms on the off chance that Debbie herself might be in one of them, but the girls had already checked everywhere and sure the younger one had been living in the house and said she'd not seen the mother for a few days.'

'How about outside?'

He shakes his head. 'Thought it was best, now, to leave well enough alone until the experts got here. We wouldn't be used to this kind of investigation here, you know. It's normally speeding, drunks and the likes.'

I squint against the rain and look out beyond the car. 'Who was it that said it looked like murder?'

They glance at one another before Timmy answers. 'Both of us really. There's a lot of blood and she being missing. It looks like she was killed in the house and taken out, God knows where but there's plenty of places to dump a body in these parts.'

'Any trouble with the family before? Callouts, reports of violence, has Debbie gone missing prior to this?'

He's shaking his head but his eyes are already drifting towards the sandwiches on the dash. 'Never known a spot of trouble between them, isn't that right, Joe?'

Joe turns wide blue eyes to me. 'No Ma'am, I mean, yes, there was no trouble.'

I straighten away from the car and Joe seems to wilt back into the seat with relief. 'Okay, thanks.'

We leave the guards to their food and walk towards the house.

36

I hold up a ribbon of garda tape for Baz to duck under then follow suit.

A guard stands at the front door. Sleeves of her jacket dark with rain, water dripping from her hat. She touches the brim when we approach. Under her arm, a clipboard, covered in loose clear plastic.

'Detectives,' she says, a solemn look on her face. 'Garda Catherine Coyne.' She passes the clipboard and pen to us.

Baz signs us in. 'Have they searched the perimeter yet?'

Catherine takes the clipboard from him, straightens the plastic over the form and tucks it back under her arm. 'Not yet, Detective.'

'Have you had any media here yet?'

She nods out in the direction of the road, and through the trees I see a van and a couple of motorbikes parked up. I almost pity the journos sitting out in this weather waiting for a snap worthy of print.

'You might want to get a unit to the road. Keep the extended scene clear.' I look down the garden. 'We don't want reporters climbing all over the property until we know what we're dealing with.'

'Yes, Ma'am.'

'What about the car?' I nod at the Focus.

'I think the Sarge wants it taken in,' she says. 'I'm not sure. We've searched high and low for the keys though and no sign.'

'We know who it belongs to?'

'The vic—' she catches herself. 'It's registered to the suspected victim, Deborah Nugent.'

'Okay,' I say. I pull the lip of my hood forward, walk to the car, shield my reflection from the window and peer in. Inside, to the naked eye, it looks clean enough. The driver-side seat is pushed back. There's dirt and leaves in the footwell. Nothing more than you'd expect from a car driven on country roads. The hubs and tyres are thick with mud and debris. Splash marks up the side panels and over the doors. Other than that, the rest of the car is spotless.

I return to the house where Baz is already inside the forensics tent. 'Might be worth getting our own auto experts on the car,' I say. Out of habit, I check the integrity of the locks on the front door. Sturdy, unbroken, no damage.

Baz threads his legs into a white plastic suit and pulls it over his shoulders. 'I'll get Helen on it,' he says, then draws up his hood. I do the same then we turn to enter the house, pausing for a moment before going inside; a small ritual of sorts, an unconscious gathering up of our guts. Something you find yourself doing before stepping into any crime scene.

Metal plates have been put down inside the door and arranged like clinical lily pads through the house. In front of us, a single orange marker picks out some invisible artifact on the floor.

I look to Baz, whose eyes are on the marker too. I can't see anything. Can't make out why crime scene have marked this area out. The stone floor appears clean but both of us know there's one substance that can linger on surfaces even after it has been cleaned so thoroughly the naked eye is unable to pick it up. Blood. I feel a slight shiver. The hope of finding Debbie Nugent alive funnelling away like sand through an hourglass.

The house opens out into a good-sized reception space, which

38

is separated from the kitchen and dining area by a stone archway. Wooden units line the kitchen walls, an Aga is between the cupboards. At the sink and over the counters, dishes, pots, mugs; used, waiting to be washed. To the side, a tall stainless-steel pedal bin, crammed full and open-mouthed. The smell of slightly off food reaches across the room.

Three scene-of-crime officers are picking their way over the flagstone floor, white suits rustling every time they bend to place down another marker. Slightly to the right, a cosy living area, a TV, a sofa and low coffee table. A cold breeze filters in behind us and turns a page of a magazine left open on the table. There are bags next to the sofa. A small suitcase, one of those pull-along ones that fit in the overhead compartments in planes. Kristen, the oldest daughter's luggage.

From somewhere to the left I hear Keith, telling someone to 'get that' and imagine him pointing a finger at some fragment of evidence he's spotted on his walkthrough. Keith, short and with an off-key punch to his loud voice, is our lead SOCO. On his best day I can just about tolerate him, on his worst, I try to focus on the fact that he knows our rhythms and understands the limits of our budget.

He appears in the main room and waves at the SOCOs, who are quietly opening and closing kitchen cupboards and making notes. 'You two, get your outdoor gear on and get a walkthrough of the garden before this rain washes everything into the ground,' he says.

'Keith,' I say, alerting him to our presence and he looks over, a smile on his small mouth, pushing up tight round cheeks.

'Well,' he drawls.

'We okay to come through?'

'All and sundry have walked through it, bleedin' officers when they got here, though they say they didn't touch anything. And, of course, the daughter has been living here.'

'Body?'

'No sign. And I'd say whoever got done in that room is gone. Drag marks over the floor right through to the door that came up with luminol.' He points to the markers laid out on the ground.

'Where are we looking then?' Baz asks.

'The living room,' Keith says. 'First door on the left.'

We move carefully around the markers in the hallway and head for our scene. The door is open on the living room. We step inside and it's like we've crossed into another house. A lamp is on in the far corner. The curtains are partially closed, white light glows out from between the heavy folds of soft grey fabric. Even though my eyes are taking in the complementing shades of cream on the walls, on the deep twin sofas, the clean white marble of the mantelpiece, nothing about this room feels welcoming. The room is dull and cold. The air has a damp quality, musty, sweaty and heavy with the rusty tang of blood.

In the middle of the room, in front of the sofas, there is a wide bloodstain. It curves outwards before narrowing to an arm's width towards the sharp corner of the fireplace, where there is the unmistakable smear of a palm print. Over the stark white marble, more blood, large droplets that have run and dried into thin dark veins. The crime-scene officers have placed small plastic triangles around the stain. Numbers 3, 4, 5 and 6. Splashes of dried blood spot the pale fabric of the sofa, spatter the walls. Above, what could easily be taken as mildew blooming on the paintwork, a

40

fine spray of blood freckles the white ceiling. And I understand now why the first officer suspected homicide.

I swallow. Baz is watching the stain on the carpet as if a body might materialize from the floor. His mouth turns down at the corners. I can hear the sharp exhale of his breath over the rustle and thump of the crime-scene officers outside. David Sutton's voice rings through my head. *It looks like she might have been killed.*

'We should get search teams organized,' he says.

'Yes.'

He moves back, bends at the waist, hands still in his pockets. If you don't touch, you were never here.

'She trusted whoever was in here,' he nods to where the cream skirt of the sofa brushes the carpet, where a mug is caught in the folds: *World's Best Mum,* in curling letters on its side.

No forced entry. Did Debbie Nugent invite her attacker, her killer inside? I see another mug, upended near the skirting board. A light yellow tea stain just visible on the carpet. I picture her making tea, throwing conversation over her shoulder, making her killer feel comfortable. Anger fizzes beneath my skin.

'We need to know more. What her routines were, where she worked, what she was doing on Wednesday before she went missing,' I stop myself, my eyes catching on the lamp glowing in the corner.

I cross the room, move away from the dark stain on the floor. There's a bookshelf near the window, half empty, the books scattered over the floor, games, a folding chess board, pawns and bishops, queens and kings spilled out over worn boxes of Monopoly, as if someone had grabbed the top of the unit and tipped it forward until the contents slipped free of their shelves; the mess is the only indication that whoever was here wanted something from Debbie Nugent. But it's too soon to leap ahead. All we can do at this stage is add brushstrokes to the canvas. The shelves might have been toppled by her attacker. A flash of rage at their own lack of control. Look what you made me do. Or it could be staged, someone who wants us to believe that Debbie had something to hide, something to discover. All answers come around to our victim. All questions. And to answer them, we need her timeline so that we can work out who was with her, who had the opportunity, who would want her dead.

CHAPTER 5

'This is the SIO,' Keith announces from the doorway, before turning to face one of the walls to examine an area dusted for prints, his face pressed up close to the wallpaper.

A man steps into the living room but stops short when he sees me, a flush of pink rising on his face. He pushes his hands back on his hips, his forensics suit widening at the neck where I see the rumpled collar of his shirt, the same one he was wearing this morning. He puts on a smile, makes a show of ease but the effect he's looking for does not quite translate through his body; his shoulders have edged upwards, his smile too sharp. His discomfort is palpable.

Keith continues around the scene, scouting for anything that may have been missed by his team.

I swallow down the tightness in my throat, cross the room, remove a glove and put out a hand. 'DCS Frankie Sheehan.' I meet the SIO's eyes and he shakes my hand.

'Hello again,' he says.

Baz looks up. 'You know each other?'

'A little,' I say.

'Detective Sergeant Alex Gordon. Wicklow station, but I run the barracks in town,' he says and shakes Baz's hand too. 'So,' he turns.

I pull the glove back onto my hand. 'Phones?'

'No mobile. Only a landline.'

Keith chimes in. 'No Internet connection either.' He takes out his mobile, studies the screen with frustration. 'Been hell trying to get our images back to process. Or send off our prints. Slowed things right down. But we got her handbag, still in what looks like her bedroom. A purse, some clubcards, a debit card and a twenty-euro note. Other items, hairbrush, hand cream but no phone. You know,' he adds thinking on it, 'we couldn't get a print from inside it.'

'Her bedroom?'

'Yes.'

'It was wiped?'

'It'd be a fastidious person who managed to not leave a single print of their own in their room. The closest I've gotten was a victim who suffered from that disorder,' he clicks his fingers trying to bring forth the right words. 'OCD, that's the one. Wore gloves all the time. We found boxes of latex gloves in every room, bins just inside and outside the room doors, where they'd use one set to go through then deposit them in the bin outside. Fecking nightmare trying to get anything but we still got some, from the inside of the gloves.' He gives Alex the full benefit of his pride in that, chest rising, a too-pleased-with-himself look on his face, before adding: 'It was bloody hard though. We tested forty-two pairs before we got a viable one.'

'Interesting,' I say.

'Head-wrecking. These people, disorder aside – they don't think about what we might need if the worst happens. Leaving a handy set of tools about the house for God knows who to use as they strangle you in your bed.'

I drag a long breath in, make myself count to ten, push my irritation down. 'I'm not sure it's a choice for some people.'

He huffs at that.

'A David Sutton called it in?' I ask Alex, changing the subject.

'Yes, he went with Margot early this morning to collect her older sister Kristen from the airport. Came back and found this.'

'Where is he now?'

'He had a shift at work,' Alex replies.

'You've questioned him already?' Baz asks.

'He gave a statement. Said he needed to get going. I mean, we don't have a body, we couldn't make him stick around.'

Baz opens his mouth to speak and I can sense what's coming. I give him a look that tells him to keep his trap shut. No need to be setting ourselves out to be the city-know-it-alls quite yet.

'How about the daughters? What did they say?'

He touches his tongue to his lips, looks down. 'Nothing that explains all this. They were pretty silent, to be honest. Shocked, I think. But after some coaxing we managed to get that Margot had last seen her mother Wednesday morning. She said her mother had a trip away, to Dublin, but she didn't seem altogether sure of that. Couldn't tell us what she was doing there. If she visited anyone.' I think about the footage I watched earlier, of Debbie waiting in the town for the bus to Dublin and wonder why, if

45

the newsagent picked that out why they didn't give us footage of her leaving on Wednesday.

'Did she drive?'

Alex shakes his head. 'Margot says no, she tended to take the bus if she travelled into Dublin. She doesn't like driving in the city.'

I stare down at the fallen mug on the floor. 'How about where she was, Margot, on Wednesday evening?'

Alex removes a notebook from his pocket. Wanting to get things right. 'She was with David. Mr Sutton. At his house.'

'Not the tightest of alibis.'

'We can verify it easily enough. He lives with his mother,' Alex replies.

I study the blood on the carpet. Brown, dry. Old. I squat down, look over the stain, a deep red in the centre, drying to dirty browns and yellows on the fringes.

'We got a good collection of hair from that,' Keith's voice says behind me. 'A bone fragment too, skin, more hair attached. Someone really went at her,' he says, scanning the blood spatter on the walls, ceiling with a sickening look of marvel on his face. 'You've seen the window?' he asks.

I go back to the window, lift the edge of the curtain. The window is set deep into the wall, a wide wooden ledge packed with soft, tartan-covered cushions. There's a good view of the garden: the pointed shapes of the trees that border the property, the lilac shades of the mountains beyond. There's a yellow marker on the sill. The window has been smashed. Not all the way through. The glass webs outwards in a series of wide cracks. There is blood at the centre.

46

'The curtains were closed when we arrived,' Keith says. 'Not a chink of light coming in. We harvested two strands of hair from the glass there. Stuck right in the centre of where it's smashed,' he says. Then adds, 'Long, dark.'

'She hit the window?' Baz asks. 'Fell against it?'

'I don't think so,' Alex says. 'There'd be more blood, surely.' He motions over the window making a downward movement with his hand, indicating where he'd expect more blood if Debbie Nugent had hit her head or been pushed against the pane. 'I'd think she was struck down over there and this,' he points at the crack in the pane, 'came from the murder weapon. Transfer.'

'The curtains would have been open then?' Baz says. 'They pulled them closed after, perhaps to search the room. You know, so as they wouldn't be seen from the garden?'

'That would explain the lamp being on,' Keith says. A SOCO appears at the door, waves a gloved hand at him. 'Shout if you need me,' Keith says to us then follows the crime-scene officer out into the hallway. I hear him natter all the way up the stairs.

'Anything up there?' I ask Alex.

He shakes his head. 'Not like the mess in this room.'

'On the report it mentioned Debbie works at a local garden centre?'

Alex looks up from his notebook. 'Yeah. Yes. Monday through Friday. I've already checked in and she'd taken a week's holiday. They did mention that she'd been ill the week previous.'

'She called in?'

'I assume so.'

'You assume so?'

He swallows, rolls his bottom lip over the top. 'We don't know.'

He sighs. 'Look, I'm sorry. Mrs Ross at the station made the calls to the centre. Your best detective couldn't extract more information than that woman so I'm guessing the centre didn't know.'

I keep a rein on my frustration. 'Guessing won't get us through this case, Detective.'

He knows they've screwed up. 'I'll find out.'

'Thank you.'

Baz is quiet. He's watching Alex and every now and then he throws a glance in my direction as if he could read the events of the last twenty-four hours on my face.

'Margot went to work as usual Thursday and yesterday,' Alex continues, reading from the notebook. 'She does breakfast and lunch at a hotel near Greystones. She stayed at David's Wednesday and Thursday night, was home on Friday night but assumed her mother was already in bed. She thought they'd just missed each other. She said that sometimes happens.' I can hear the soft sound of doubt in his voice. And I can tell he doesn't want to say it but he's already picking out Margot as a person of interest. 'She says', he adds, 'she didn't go into this room or see it until her sister arrived this morning.'

It's possible. One glance around the room shows it's at odds with the rest of the house. It's fancy. Cold. The damp air telling me it's rarely heated. A good room. My mam used to be the same, a single room where all the good furniture was housed, cushions cellophane-wrapped until we had guests when it would be aired for a few days. Didn't matter if you'd thirteen children desperate for space in an Irish household, you could expect at least one room left fallow for special occasions. Except my mam

48

has changed now. She's not one for saving things for a better day or better things for other people.

'I don't see it,' Baz says.

Alex frowns, not sure which part of what Baz is not seeing. 'Don't see what?'

'He doesn't think it could be Margot,' I say.

Baz pushes the curtains aside. 'That.' He makes a backhanded upward sweep of his arm towards the window. And I can almost hear the crunch of glass, my teeth press together in anticipation of the sound. 'That's pure anger, there. And it was hit after the attack. Someone really got wound up about having to do this. Margot lives here.' He points to the books over the floor. 'Why would she kill her mother to go through these books? To search this room. She could do that in her own time. And why would Debbie be making tea for her daughter to have in the good room?'

Alex's frown deepens. 'The good room?'

I hide a smile behind a cough. 'Let's not narrow things down too quickly. The books could be staging. And we don't know the victim well enough to work out a motive. That leaves both Debbie's daughters, yes, that includes Kristen, at least until we have her flight details confirmed, and anyone else we know who has a connection, still in the frame. And they remain there until we can rule them out.'

'Your guy, Mr Hickey, took up a sample of the carpet. Said it would be difficult to date as it was, "dry as a tortilla chip".' Alex gives a pained smile so I know he's using Keith's words. 'But he thinks they might be able to get something. To date the scene.'

49

'Where's the father?' Baz asks.

Alex blinks at the change in direction. 'Never been on the scene, as far as I know. Debbie moved here, must be close to two decades ago now.'

I take in this information. Make a mental note for Helen to track down the daddy. I turn the idea around in my head that the father of Debbie's children might have decided to make an appearance in his kids' lives. Was this house a bolt-hole, an escape, a hideout that a violent ex-partner had discovered? If Debbie left him and took the kids, maybe he returned and decided there was payback. The ransacking of the room could be consistent with a fit of rage, a struggle, or maybe she had something on him that he needed to find and destroy.

'We'll need to speak to him, if he can be found.' Another question for Kristen and Margot. 'Murder weapon?' I ask. 'Have we anything?'

Alex shakes his head. 'Nothing.'

'Do you have a recent photograph?' I ask. 'Of Debbie?'

Alex steps around the sofa, 'I saw an album in here earlier,' he explains. 'He goes to a sideboard that runs along the far wall of the room. Squats down and opens it. He pushes a few boxes aside and pulls out a navy leather-bound album. He carries it to us, balancing it on one arm and lifts the cover. The first images are slightly out-of-focus family shots, but as he turns through the album, we get more of Debbie on her own. Young Debbie, stud through her nose, braids down her long hair. Gold hoops in her ears. Long, flowing skirts, denim waistcoats. Boots, sometimes sandals, depending on weather. Debbie at the beach, paddling in gentle, shallow waves, the bundle of her skirts clutched in her hand, her hair wild and wavy, half covering a smiling face. Then later, Debbie in the garden, a trowel in hand, her children sitting on the lawn stirring mud and water in plastic buckets. More of her walking, shots of the Wicklow mountains. Debbie, in grubby dungarees, an overcoat, a thick scarf and a lumpy bobble hat pulled down over her head, her arm pressing one of her daughters to her side.

I rest my finger over the young girl, her face round and full, skin dotted with light freckles, red hair trailing in a thick plait over her shoulder. 'Margot?'

'Yes.' He turns another page. 'Here. This is more recent, I think. Dated Christmas just gone.' He removes the photo from behind the acetate and hands it to me, closing the album and tucking it under his arm.

The photo shows Debbie smiling. Behind her, red and green ropes of tinsel hang over a kitchen dresser. She's wearing a woolly red sweater. The stud in her nose is gone. Grey streaks run through her dark hair. Her face has narrowed a little, her skin a little loose around her jawline, deep lines at each side of her mouth. But she looks happy; a gleam of merriment shining out from behind a pale grey.

'It's not everyone who keeps an album up to date, nowadays,' Baz remarks, taking the picture and studying it. 'Seems a bit on the hippy side,' he says, 'maybe less so in this picture.' He passes it back and I look down at it.

'When we begin the search, we'll start three miles out,' I say. 'We could go out further but we don't want to spread the search too thin. If there is a body, we need to find it quickly.'

'If our perp had a vehicle—'

51

'They'll have wanted to get rid of it quickly.'

'We're calling it murder?' Alex asks.

I survey the room. 'I think that's a given. We'll keep an open mind but it's best to treat it as we see it for now so we don't miss anything.'

'Okay, we'll start with the extended premises this after-noon, maybe move out a little, then a full-on search first thing tomorrow.' Alex gives us both a brief smile of apology then says, 'I'd best get back to the station, try and summon up that search team.' He leaves us to it, stepping carefully through the room until he's gone.

The back door is locked. Key in the door. I open it, step out into the garden. I can tell it isn't used often. The grass is a little long. The hedges growing limbs upwards and outwards. There's a wooden garden shed almost buried in the bushes; a dull green, the door held shut by a can of paint. I reach for my torch, head towards it. I move the tin out of the way and the door sags open a fraction.

I pull the door open wide, the hinges stiff and groaning, flick on the torch. The shed is full. A family's collection of past toys and equipment, the scent of foliage and earth mixed with a slight chemical scent – oil, paint, petrol. At the front, the lawnmower, pushed in nose first. I cast the beam of my torch around the floor. A few dried-up clumps of cut grass, fallen from the wheels of the mower. No one could get far into the shed. Not without serious shifting of the collection of junk inside. But above, on either side: shelves. Old shoeboxes. Rusted bean cans. I stand on my toes, careful not to disrupt the area too much. The light of the

52

torch picks up the disturbance in the layer of dust. Fingerprints white on the edge of the boxes, lids loose.

I pull one of the boxes forward, lift it down from the shelf. Inside, a set of keys, a mobile phone, not new but not old neither, a smartphone – I try to turn it on but the battery is dead – a purse, a yellow plastic wallet with a heart stitched in bright red on the front. Inside are bus tickets, about three-euros' worth of coins, a bank card. I ease it out of its casing. Margot Nugent. Debit card. I take out my phone, photograph the contents then take a close-up of the card and send it through to Helen. Then, pocketing my phone, I sift through the remaining items in the box. A silver chain with a flat round disc pendant; on the back, a name inscribed in swirling italics: *David.* A silver ring with a cloudy grey stone embedded in the centre. A mood ring. A strange place to keep a collection of trinkets. I return the items to the box, reverse out carefully, go back to the house.

Passing the box to a SOCO, I point through the kitchen window towards the shed. 'This is from the top shelf on the right. There's a mobile inside, get it to Detective Steve Garvin at the Bureau for Serious Crime. There are more boxes on the shelves. We'll need them taken in and dust the door for prints.'

'I'll let Mr Hickey know,' he says.

Baz is sifting through the drawers and cupboards. I tell him about the box of what looks like Margot's possessions in the shed.

'It could be that she wanted to throw them out but couldn't bring herself to,' he says.

'Since when would you throw out your house keys?'

'Good point. If they are her house keys,' he says and opens

CHAPTER 6

The local garda station is a small low building set behind black gloss railings. If it weren't for the blue lamp displaying the Garda Síochána crest you could mistake it for someone's well-kept bungalow. It's situated at the end of the main street, among the row of colourful residences that make up the tiny community of Ballyalann.

We arrive in convoy, Baz then me. Myself and Baz park up along the kerb, there being room for only the squad car in the car park off the side of the station.

Baz is on the phone to the Bureau, trading information with Helen and Paul, giving them our list of requests: put out a missing-persons alert to hospitals, details of possible head injuries to look out for among their patients. There is still the possibility that she never returned from Dublin and that the blood at the scene is not hers and we need to rule it out but, as good as an open mind is, I think there's no mistaking what happened at the scene we've just come from.

He also requests a check of hotels, B&Bs, hostels in Dublin

where Debbie might have stayed over the last few days. We want to look for her extended family, any mention of her on social media, calls to and from her landline over the last few weeks, searches for marriage announcements, birth certificates, local and in the Dublin area. Anything that might lead us towards the name of Margot and Kristen's father. We need as many avenues as possible into Debbie's life. Into her last movements in the run-up to her disappearance.

When Baz hangs up, he squints out at the swollen skies. 'Apart from what we got off her handbag, none of the prints found in the house are Debbie's. They got sets from Kristen, Margot and another from a person unknown but they anticipate they belong to David. They found Debbie's car keys. In a coat upstairs. Margot's wardrobe.'

Baz looks to me. I nod. Both of us understanding that no matter the result of this case, there'll be no winners.

'Come on,' I say. 'Let's see what she has to say.'

We get out of the car. I stand at the car door for a moment, look down the main street of the town. A truck is parked across from the newsagent, a man runs towards it, wellies slapping on the wet pavement, head ducked against the spit of rain. Jeans stained with mud and manure. He climbs into the cab of the truck and revs out the road towards us, a smiling border collie sitting in the passenger seat next to him. A woman stands in the doorway of the newsagent. She's watching us. Her arms folded high on her chest, presider of town and store. In front of the newsagents, the bus stop where Debbie Nugent caught her bus to Dublin three weeks ago, now occupied by a woman with a round pregnant belly, her backside perched on the narrow bench, a red-faced toddler squalling at her side.

I close the car door. Wait for Baz to get himself together then head into the station. Inside, a grey-haired lady in her sixties throws a smile up at us, stands, flustered. At her shoulder she wears the stripes of her years in service and I make a mental note that if there is a person to talk to about the Nugent family, this woman could be the one.

Alex appears from an office behind the desk. 'These are the detectives helping with the Nugent case, Mrs Ross.'

'Oh.' The woman rubs her hand over her hip before she extends it. I shake it, feel its softness envelop mine. 'Deirdre Ross,' she says.

'Detective Sheehan and this is Detective Harwood.'

She eyes us with a flat stare as if she is sure that we're not up to the job. 'You're taking the case, then?' she asks, voice rising with enough cynicism to make me straighten my spine. I have a brief flashback to a damp sports day at school where I volunteered to bat in a final game of rounders. My teacher's eyebrow nearly lost itself in her hairline when I raised my hand, her eyes staying on her clipboard when she ticked off my name, the line of her mouth barely parting as she said, 'You can try.'

'Yes,' I say.

Alex has paused in the small space of the reception at Mrs Ross' back. He smiles over her shoulder; a hint of indulgence in his eyes, telling us that whatever reaction this woman has to us, it's not personal.

He leans over the counter, takes a stack of printouts from a pigeonhole to Deirdre's left. 'These today's minors?'

'Yes, Sarge,' she says. 'Well,' she nods to us, starting over. 'If you need anything, I'm here to help. I'm sure we'll find poor Debbie soon enough with you on board.'

'We need to speak to Kristen and Margot. And it would be good to talk to David Sutton.'

She flicks a look at her watch. 'Is it necessary to bring David in this late in the afternoon?'

'He phoned it in,' Baz says. 'We absolutely need to speak to him.'

There's a brief stubborn pout of her lips. 'His mam is ill,' she mutters. 'Terminal.'

'I see,' I say in my best understanding voice, wanting to keep on Deirdre's good side. I rest a hand on the desk. 'Perhaps if you get us his address, we can go out to him instead.'

Deirdre sniffs her disapproval but she nods. 'You'll find the Nugent girls in the Family Room.'

To the left of the reception there's a door with a rectangular gold sign on it, declaring it 'The Family Room'. We step inside. Baz already pulling a notebook from his pocket.

Kristen Nugent is curled up on a tan-coloured two-seater. When I close the door she rolls off, scrambles to her feet, her face full of expectation, her hands smoothing over a long, pleated skirt then pushing hair off her face. She has her mother's looks. Dark, fit build, round face and tall. She looks like she belongs in the country, she has that earthy look about her, her fingers dressed in silver rings, bangles chiming on her wrists as she straightens her clothing.

Her voice is cracked and tired when she speaks, the tell-tale ache of crying in her throat.

'Any news?' she asks, her eyes intense on our faces.

'Nothing yet,' I say. 'Please, sit. It's Kristen, right?'

She runs her hands over the back of her skirt, sits. 'Yes,' clears throat, 'sorry, yes.'

'I'm Detective Sheehan and this is Detective Harwood. Would you mind answering a few questions?'

Her face turns pale, colour dropping from her dry lips.

'All very standard, I promise,' Baz adds.

A nod, barely there.

Standing at the window is Margot. The youngest Nugent. She looks like she's barely grown since that photograph was taken with her mother on the hills of Wicklow. The only difference, instead of the boyish wiriness that accompanied childhood she now wears a slight curve around the hips and chest, her face more narrow than her sister's, her nose slim and neat, her cheeks rising to a gentle arch.

She moves quickly to the sofa, sits next to her sister, her knees pressed tight against clasped hands, her body rigid and bent slightly over her middle as if she's in pain. The long braid from that photograph has become a shoulder-length spring of loose waves and is now a deep shade of red, which reflects the light above in stripes of coppers and gold when she moves.

'Margot,' I begin. Clear, grey eyes fix on me. 'When was the last time you saw your mum?'

She looks up through pale lashes. 'Wednesday. Wednesday morning.'

'That's the twenty-seventh of March?'

The date makes her pause, she looks up arranging days of the week in her head. 'Yes. Wednesday.'

Baz moves to the other side of the room, his expression slowly drifting into a frown.

'Are you sure?'

She drags in a breath and it straightens her a little. 'Yes. She was going to go to Dublin, I think for the night.' Her voice scratches low, to a whisper, so that I have to lean closer. I can see Baz out of the corner of my eye. His hand moving quickly over his notebook. Margot's gaze is looking inwards, her eyes unfocused, as if she's reliving those final moments with her mother. 'She was teasing me. I'm not a morning person,' she explains, 'and the house was cold, too early for the heating. She—' she frees a hand from her waist, touches her fingers against her right cheek. 'She said, "Wednesday's child" and then she kissed me goodbye.'

I watch her hand move slowly back to her waist, where it tightens around her middle again. Wednesday's child is full of woe.

I swallow. 'Then what happened?'

She looks up. 'She went out, I think.'

'She didn't have breakfast with you?'

She shakes her head. 'She'd already had hers by the time I came downstairs. A boiled egg, toast, tea.'

'You saw her eating it?'

'She has the same every morning.' She looks to Kristen, who nods in agreement.

'Okay. She left. Did she take the car?'

'Yes.'

I save this detail for later. Margot told Alex her mother didn't like to drive in the city. 'What time was it?'

61

She unhooks her hands, rolls the palms over her knees. 'Seven-thirty.'

'You're sure. That's early.'

'Yes. It was around the same time she leaves for work.'

'And how long was it before you left?'

'Forty minutes, maybe.'

'So just after eight am on Wednesday?'

'I guess so.' She swallows. 'Sorry. I don't remember, but it wouldn't have been much later than that.'

'That's okay. I know this is difficult. You're doing really well.' I give her an encouraging smile, then the same to Kristen whose brows are tucked low and drawn so tight it looks painful. Our job here is to test our timeline. We gather the minutes of Debbie's life given to us by her daughters and then we push every second down with our toes and wait to feel it give.

'You work at a hotel in Greystones, right?' I ask Margot.

'Yes. I started there six months ago.'

'How do you get there?'

'Lately, my boyfriend collects me.'

'Lately?'

She blushes. 'For the past couple of months.'

'That's David Sutton, correct?'

'Yes.'

'And you normally finish work at what time?'

'Four. I finished at four that day too but I met up with David afterwards. We went to the pub. Then I stayed at his that night, went straight to work from there the next morning.'

'Your mum didn't message you? You didn't talk on the phone?'

She chews down on her lip. 'No.'

62

'You didn't send her a text to let her know you'd be staying out?'

'She doesn't own a mobile.'

It's an unusual decision in today's world, and makes things bloody difficult. Investigations can turn on the sending of a text. It allows us to place our victims to some degree. Gives us a better insight into their last movements, even their final words, thoughts, mood.

'There's a landline in the house. Did you phone her, in case she'd be worried?'

'No.'

I find myself waiting for the rest of her answer, *I wish I had. Maybe if I'd called, she'd be . . . Do you think that would have helped, Detective?* But there's nothing. Her gaze remains steady, expectant, waiting for the next question.

'How's your relationship with your mum? Are you close?' I ask.

'Very,' Margot replies. At this, Kristen reaches across and takes her sister's hand.

'The next morning then and the day after, you didn't see or hear from your mum?' I press on.

'No.'

'And yesterday. You expected her to be home? Is that right?'

Her body, which had softened a little at the touch of Kristen's hand, pulls back a fraction.

She clears her throat. 'Yes. I was with David again on Thursday night. I came home briefly yesterday morning to get a change of clothes then went on to work. When I got home afterwards, Mum had gone out again. I thought. Then this morning, we went

63

to the airport to collect Kristen.' The small muscles around her eyes twitch. She swallows.

'Was the car in the drive yesterday morning when you came back?'

She pauses, eyebrows coming down. 'Yes. It was. Although, she often takes the bus to Dublin. I imagine wherever she went on Wednesday morning, it was a small errand and then she took the bus to Dublin.'

'But you're not sure.'

'No.'

'I just have a few more questions,' I say and she fixes her eyes on some point on the carpet. 'Do you know if anyone would want to hurt your mum?'

'No,' Margot says.

'Boyfriends?'

'She never mentioned one,' Kristen answers.

Margot straightens. 'There was something,' her voice a hoarse whisper. Her tongue touches her lips. 'A few things,' she says. 'Someone threw a rock through the window a while back.'

I picture a broken window. The burst of glass in a gleaming halo over beige carpet where somehow the aesthetics of the invasion make it all the more brutal. More of a violation. The safety of a home shattered with it and the words *Justice is a bitch* etched in my mind. And it's not an invention constructed on the back of Margot's statement but a memory. *My* memory of the threat that came through the window of my sister-in-law's house over half a year ago.

Whether Baz guesses where my mind has gone or curiosity makes him impatient, he jumps in: 'A rock?' he asks.

Margot looks to him, cups her palm, holds it out as if testing the weight of the rock. 'Yes.'

'You were in when it happened?' he asks.

I remind myself that what once came for me is not here. But the residue of that fear remains bitter on my tongue and I feel a savage kind of conviction push against the walls of my chest. It's another family. But I won't be making the same mistake again. I pull back from Margot. Watch her movements as she answers Baz's questions.

She's shaking her head. 'I came home from work and Mum told me what'd happened.'

'Did they find out who did it?'

'They?'

'The guards?'

'No.'

Baz pauses for a moment then: 'Was it reported?'

'I don't think so,' she replies slowly.

I look to Baz and he gives Margot a brief smile then leaves the room to have Mrs Ross check for callouts to the Nugent residence. There are some people – stalkers, abusers, murderers – who like to gain control over their victims by creating a false boogie-man. We call it the hero syndrome. Dark acts of minor terror designed to close off a victim's world or put them in danger. And guess who comes to the rescue?

'When was this?' I ask.

She searches her memory. 'I'm not sure. A month ago. Maybe more. I remember I was supposed to go out the following night with David but she said I shouldn't, that it mightn't be safe.'

'Not safe for you?'

65

Margot gives Kristen a careful look and I can't quite read it. 'I don't know,' she says, suddenly unsure of what she's saying.

Baz re-enters the room and gives me a shake of his head. No callout to the Nugent house reported.

'Why wouldn't your mum report something like that?' I ask.

'Mum doesn't like to cause trouble,' she whispers.

'We found keys to your mum's car in your coat pocket? Have you been using her car?'

'No.'

'Why did you have her keys?'

She bites down on her lip. Thinks. 'I don't know. I lost my front door keys. I could've taken them by mistake. Mum keeps hers on the same ring as the car's.'

'You didn't think your mum might need her house key? Or car keys?'

'She has a spare set. It's what I had been using.'

I pause for a moment then, 'I believe we found your house keys. They were in a box in the shed with a few other items.' I take out my phone, bring up the image of the shoebox I found in the shed. 'Do you recognize any of these other items?'

She takes my phone, looks into the screen. Her eyes widen. 'My purse. My keys,' she says. 'My old phone.' She shakes her head. 'I thought I lost them,' she studies the image further, expands it with her fingers. 'My necklace!'

'You didn't put them there?'

'No!'

I catch Baz's eye. 'I think we could do with a cup of tea or some refreshment.' I turn to the sisters. 'Have you eaten?'

They shake their heads in unison.

Baz straightens, puts away his notebook. 'Why don't we grab a coffee or a tea? It's like a sauna in here.' He pulls at his collar to emphasize his point, casts his smile down at both of them. They return it, Margot getting up quickly, wiping the heat from her brow.

Kristen goes to stand. 'Sorry, Kristen. If you wouldn't mind, I've a few more questions,' I say.

She sits. 'Sure.'

Baz guides Margot out of the room. I wait for the door to close then take out my notebook. 'This won't take long,' I say to her.

'Okay.'

'You arrived this morning. From France? Is that correct?'

'Correct.'

'Was it a planned visit?'

'Not really. I booked the ticket a few days ago. That's not unusual for me. I can find myself at a loose end and decide to come home for a bit. See Mum, you know. She never minds if I come home last minute. She likes us all under the one roof.'

And I hear a tinge of something in her voice. Bitterness maybe, or it could be grief turning a happy thought sour. 'So, nothing prompted it? There wasn't a particular reason you came back?'

I see the narrow columns of muscles in her throat tighten. 'My husband was away so I thought I'd come home for a while.'

I'm having a hard time believing Kristen just happened to arrive home and into her mother's potential murder scene. 'When was the last time you spoke to your mum?'

Her eyes shutter closed for a moment. When she opens them again she answers straight. 'A couple of weeks ago, I think. I called her.'

67

No contact for two weeks prior. At least we will have phone records to verify that. And already I'm beginning to suspect they'll show us many calls from Kristen's line in France to the Nugent household.

'And she sounded alright? Nothing unusual stood out?'

'She sounded fine.'

'What did you talk about?'

'Normal stuff. Her work, Margot's work.' She sniffs. Apologizes. 'It's hard not to think that something awful has happened to her.'

There's no hope in her voice when she speaks. And that's fair enough. The crime scene would spell out to anyone that her mother is likely dead but for relatives of victims, normally, they don't believe it, not this soon, not until they're staring down at the truth of it, looking on the corpse of their loved one. But it's like Kristen's already given up and I ask myself why that would be when we've only just started.

'Talk me through from when you arrived in Dublin airport,' I ask her.

She rests an open palm on her leg as if she's about to count off the steps that've led to her sitting in front of me. 'David and Margot were in the arrivals hall when I came through. I had carry-on only so I got through pretty quickly. They'd parked in the multi-storey—'

'Did you find it unusual that your mum wasn't there to greet you?' I temper the question with a smile.

'No. I thought she'd be working. Margot text to say they'd collect me so I wasn't expecting Mum.'

I nod, ask her to continue, make notes as she speaks, not so much for myself but it's a good display of faith for Kristen. Witnesses, suspects alike are comforted when they see you writing down their words. To them, it means you believe their tale enough that you're writing it down. And I see Kristen watching the movement of my hand, nodding to herself, drawing confidence from this fact.

'We got to the car,' she says, finding her place again. 'The traffic wasn't great. It never is getting out of the airport, but we were home shortly after eight this morning. We had some tea and it was soon after that we discovered the . . . the room.'

I hold up a hand. 'The living room?'

'Yes.'

I put down my pen. 'I got the impression the living room isn't used much?'

Kristen allows herself a ghost of a smile. 'Mum really only opens it for visitors or after dinner on Christmas day.' She shakes her head. 'It was ingrained in us very early on that we weren't to be making a mess in there.'

'What made you go in this morning?'

Her expression goes from soft, sad remembrance to confusion. 'We were looking for her.'

I tilt my head. Wait for her to see the conflict in her statements. In their statements. That they were searching for Debbie even though Margot thought she was in Dublin and Kristen's just told me she wasn't expecting her to be there. *I assumed she was at work.*

She coughs into her hand. Pushes her thick hair behind her ear. I see the muscles in her throat working. There are some people who are brought up with a lie fast on their tongue.

69

Could persuade you you'd only one leg and you'd go home hopping because they were so convincing. Lies as clean and honest as the truth roll from their tongues. Kristen is not one of these people. And I almost feel bad for her because of it. She looks fit to vomit, her discomfort painted in red patches over her neck and face, her fingers curled in painfully on her palm. I take the pressure off, needing more information, needing to get her back to the point where she believes I believe her. But I've loosened the first hand from the edge of the cliff and it's a long drop to the bottom and she, I know, feels the vacuum beneath her, for sure.

I take up my pen again. 'It looked like your mum was expecting someone. She'd made them tea. I know it was a couple of weeks since you spoke but she didn't mention any special visitors to you? Someone that she might take into the good room, perhaps?'

She straightens and I find myself impressed with her recovery. A few slow, steadying breaths and she answers: 'She never mentioned anyone to me but I know there was some trouble with the heating in the house. She has a gas fire in that room. I can only think that she was in there because it would be warm.'

She lowers her shoulders, senses that my questioning is coming to an end, feels the intensity of our search begin to point in another direction. To some other faceless person, far away from this room. And I'm okay with her thinking that right now, but there is nothing from this interview that makes me want to take either of the Nugents out of the suspect box.

'How about friends, in general?'

'Most of her friends work with her. Two that she mentions

70

often, Eileen and someone else.' She brings her fingertips to her lips. 'I'm sorry I can't remember the name.'

'No one else? In all the time she's lived here?'

'Mum doesn't seem to need many friends. She doesn't invite people into her life easily.' Again, that small tinge of bitterness in her voice. 'She's good at spending time alone. I guess it was a side effect of growing up an only child. She never gets lonely.'

And all I hear is a description of a woman who is not so much comfortable in her own skin as someone who put some deliberate walls up. I know enough about small towns to know it's not easy to come away with only a couple of people pushing themselves into your life.

'How about your grandparents? Your mum's parents?'

'They're dead. When I was very little. I don't remember them much. There are photos, somewhere. They lived out west, very remote. Farmers, I think.'

'And your dad?'

She shakes her head slowly. 'I'm afraid I don't remember him, either. Only that he left us. It was one of the reasons Mum moved here. She wanted to start over, I guess. She doesn't talk about him. We gave up asking her about him years ago. I think it still hurts.'

'Do you know where he lives?'

'I don't.'

'Have you ever tried to look for him?' I ask, then add quickly. 'It would be natural. Normal to want to find him.'

The corner of her mouth lifts into a cynical smile. It doesn't suit her face. 'No.'

'Photos?'

71

'No,' voice firm. She takes a breath. 'Don't take this the wrong way but he's not my dad. Not a father. I've no idea where he is, dead or alive. I don't care.'

'I'm sorry.'

She shrugs my apology away as if she was shaking a fly from her shoulder but her indifference doesn't quite reach her face where pain and rejection darken her eyes. 'It's okay,' she answers.

'He never tried to get in touch?'

She sighs. 'Not that I knew of. It was the three of us. Mum, Margot and me and that was it. He was never a part of our lives. In conversation or otherwise.' She looks up then, eyebrows raised. 'Do you think it could have been him?'

I leave her question there. 'Do you know his name?'

She looks down, turns one of her bangles around her wrist. 'I felt that to mention him or ask her about him was painful. When I was a teenager, I did wonder – wonder why we never knew him or saw pictures of us together and I might have been afraid to ask. I didn't want to upset what we had. But that curiosity passed.' She pushes the bracelets up her arm, brings her hands together, intertwines her fingers. 'Mum is a brilliant mother. A friend. And what we had was warm and safe and protected—' she pauses, sighs. 'You ever get the feeling that even though you're happy, I mean really happy, that it rests on something so fragile that the wrong word or question might cause it all to shatter?'

I shift in my seat, try to ignore how much her question unnerves me. 'Go on?'

'I had that feeling. I had it often. And it felt like my mum's past was the root of it. And why would I ever want to ruin our happiness?'

72

'I understand,' I say. 'One more question. What year did your mum move here? Do you know?'

'Nineteen ninety-three. I remember because I'd missed the start of term at school and it was difficult to make friends.'

'Where did you live before?'

'Dublin. I can't remember the exact address. I was only just seven when we moved.'

Another research quest for Helen.

I stand. 'Thank you, Kristen.' I take a card from my pocket, write my mobile number along the bottom and hand it to her. 'We've sent out alerts to all the hospitals in this area and in Dublin. There is always the chance that your mum fell and hurt herself.' The crime scene flashes before my eyes, deep, wide blood marks pooled on the carpet, spatter over the walls, ceilings.

She turns the card over in her hands. 'And you're sure it's my mum's?'

She means the blood in the house. It's possible that Debbie Nugent found someone in her home and that she was the one to attack. But it's low down in the likely scenarios. There was no sign of forced entry, although that wouldn't be enough on its own to rule it out – she could have invited someone in then attacked. No, what makes me sure – even as we wait for Keith to confirm it – that this is Debbie Nugent's death scene, are the two mugs on their sides on the floor, their milky brown contents dried into the carpet, blood overlapping. An indication to me that she made tea for her attacker before inviting them to sit in the living room. Someone needed something from that room, or from the house, and didn't have time for an extensive search. But mostly, I'm sure that Debbie Nugent was the victim here because of the few strands of long dark hair Keith found trapped in congealed blood on the cracked window pane.

'We believe so,' I answer her question and she pales. Grief or fear. Or both. All I'm certain of, is that, for a family who insist all they've felt for one another is warmth, safety and protection, how odd it is that not one of them noticed Debbie was missing. A woman who, from what we've gathered on her so far, did not break from habit. Who greeted her daughter every morning. Ate the same breakfast every morning. Would not even invite the guards to her home when someone threw a rock through her window. A woman who kept her walls high and her family close. *She liked us all under the one roof.* And neither of her daughters noticed she'd disappeared. Not until the moment they opened that door.

I stand. 'If there's anything else you want to tell me, you can phone me, day or night.'

'Thanks,' she murmurs.

'Do you have friends or someone you can stay with for a while. Just while we conduct our investigations?'

'Yes.'

'Would you mind leaving those details with Mrs Ross? So we can get in touch if we need to.'

'Sure.' She drops her head in her hands, presses her palms against her eyes.

CHAPTER 7

My dad, before he left the force, before his head pushed him out, on the evenings and hours when he was home, he'd tell stories of his day, always using words like baddies and goodies so we'd understand that he was the good side. A real hero and he was full of the cut and thrust of it; a sure confidence that he was walking the right path. He'd draw the picture of his day like the only thing that mattered was who took home the result of his work; a widow whose stolen wedding band he'd managed to locate, the shop up the road who'd had their Christmas takings stolen, the struggling farmer who was glad to see the return of that expensive piece of machinery my dad had managed to stop before it shipped at Dublin port.

And I could picture it clearly: my dad, his uniform immaculate, sharp creases down his trousers, the buttons on his blazer like new pennies, turning up at the victim's house, telling them that the world was right again, order had been restored and that they'd be okay. It was these stories that first made me want to work against crime. I wanted to be on that good side. But like all stories parents tell their children, the darker truths are left out. Dad never told me about the times he couldn't be that smiling man on someone's doorstep telling them it would all be okay. He didn't tell me about the murders, the mindless crimes, the stupid fucking mistakes people make that punch holes in their families' lives. And he didn't tell me that sometimes it's the goodies who make those mistakes.

Mrs Ross leads us through the station. The building is bigger than it seems from the front; stretching out well into the back. Kristen and Margot have found digs in a B&B outside town. Timmy retrieved Kristen's bags from the house. Margot didn't want anything from there. At the mention of collecting clothes for her, she blanched, visibly retreating from the thought, then assured us that she'd manage; go shopping and pick up some essentials.

We follow Mrs Ross down a narrow corridor, another leads directly off to the right where, she informs us, there's a holding cell. Never really held anything more than someone who needed to sleep off a night, she adds. She stops at a door at the end of the hallway, unlocks it.

'This is it. I thought in time they'd want to convert this one into another interrogation room but there didn't seem to be any point in wasting the money. All the good cases go to Wicklow.' By good cases, she means murder. 'For now we use it for storage,' she says with more than a small dose of disappointment in her voice. She pushes the door open. It's dark, and a welcome breath of cold air rushes out. She reaches into the blackness and switches on the light. The room flickers then settles into a white glare.

There are cork boards fixed at each end of the room, a shining whiteboard stretches the length of the facing wall; a set of marker pens rests on the thin silver shelf below. I walk around the perimeter of the room, find a connection for a phone line, a Cat V for computers, plenty of electrical sockets behind stacks of boxed files. A clothes rack, the stiff shoulders of three stab jackets, suspended and forgotten, hanging on the metal rail. It's quiet. The sounds of Dublin city, the hustle, constant burr of phones and the low persistent chatter of the Bureau office are a world away.

'I think we should set up here.' I smile at Mrs Ross. 'Don't worry, hopefully we won't be in your hair too long.'

Deirdre leans in a little, her voice lowering to a conspiratorial whisper. 'I knew there'd be a murder investigation, Detective. I'm just glad that we're all on the same page.'

'Thank you. Our tech specialist, Steve Garvin, is on his way out from Dublin to set up. He should be here in a couple of hours. If you could show him around—'

'Of course.' She waits inside the room but eventually she gets the message, nods, 'right,' and backs out. I close the door behind her.

Baz falls back against the wall of the room, relieved he's free of Mrs Ross. 'She makes me feel like I have to be on my best behaviour,' he says, pushing up the sleeves of his outdoor jacket. 'Had a quick chat with the Bureau. Paul says the phones have been hopping all morning. Soon as he puts one down, another line goes. Every media outlet in the fucking country wants news on Debbie Nugent.'

I remove my phone from my pocket, check for updates on the search. 'If there's a chance she's alive, it could work to our advantage.'

Baz crosses his ankles, hands in pockets. 'What are your thoughts?'

I pull out a chair, sit on the hard plastic. An update from Alex tells me that they've been through the garden but nothing yet on a weapon or a body. I look up at the narrow frosted windows that run along the top of the room. The day is already turning, the light dimming from the sky. It's too late to begin a wider search for Debbie. But we can work with the interest from the media, put out a press release, appeals on social media. The public can be hugely helpful in a case like this. Eyes and ears and all that.

'I'm not sure yet,' I reply.

'I didn't think it at first but after the chats we just had, my money's on the daughter,' he says.

'It's too soon to peg it yet,' I say, but if I'm honest, my thoughts are going the same way.

He peels himself away from the wall. 'Don't worry, I've not taken the cart down the road, only testing how it moves.'

I go to one of the file boxes, lift the lid. Reaching in, I push through the files, slide one free. The name of the offender, a Mr Patrick Rafferty, sixty-eight years. Charge: DUI. Arresting officer: Detective Sergeant Dennis Fitzsimons. The date of the offence is labelled for 1997, 24th of December, 2 am. I slide the file back into the box. Begin moving the boxes into a corner so that they're not in the way when Steve comes to set up. Baz sees what I'm at and helps.

I think about the possibility of putting Margot and Kristen

78

out there. Getting them to do a press conference. Pleading for their mother to return. Sometimes the voice lies but the body, a person's gestures and emotion, can give a lot away.

'Did Margot say anything else when you left the family room?' I ask him.

'No. Sat quietly in reception, scrolling through her phone.' He lifts another box onto the pile, dusts his hands off then straightens. 'There's something off about her.'

'People behave oddly when they're grieving.'

'That's it though. She doesn't seem to be grieving.' He crosses the room, studies the stack of boxed files. 'We've done so many interviews with families, siblings, parents, friends to try to piece together a victim's last movements. Almost all of them go around in circles, there's digression constantly. Always replaying the parts they know, questioning themselves, us about whether there was more they could do. What if they'd looked sooner? Phoned more? Asking whether this is really happening? Could there be another explanation? Some kind of mistake. There was none of that with Kristen and Margot.'

I stop, lean my palms against the boxes. A sudden craving gnaws in my gut. Cigarette. 'I noticed,' I say. 'I guess I'm trying to keep some balance. The lack of contact between them all makes me uneasy,' I answer. 'Both of the sisters say the family are close but neither of them phone Debbie? Neither of them try to get in touch when they haven't heard from her in days.'

'Well, they *say* they haven't tried to get in touch,' Baz says. He turns, heaves a box onto his knee, flicks open the cardboard lid, checks the contents before closing it over again and dumping it against the wall. 'Although, saying that, I've two

79

sisters. Both of them would proudly tell anyone who'd listen about how close we are. But I haven't phoned my folks in three weeks. It's all my head can stand, to be fair. But they live less than fifteen miles from me and I haven't seen them. Does that makes us less close?'

I think of my own family. The nights I've sat in the street outside my parents' house, watching, making sure they're okay. Not trusting them to live their lives safely enough; even though I know that if anyone is bringing darkness to their door, it's me. Justin, my brother, and I talk on the phone a lot. We're close. Sometimes I think he can gauge how happy I am by the way I stand. My family, we've our problems, our secrets but maybe that's what binds us. The close bond of conspiracy, rarely spoken out loud because we don't need to, we lived it. We live it still. And I wonder if there's something similar in Debbie's past.

'Perhaps not calling is normal for them,' I say. 'As you say, it's not that strange to go a few days without being in touch. And factor in that Debbie has no mobile. If she was away—'

'According to Margot.'

'Yes, according to Margot, agreed. But if they're the type of family who don't ask each other details when a rock comes through the back window, then forgoing the odd phone call suddenly doesn't seem too bad, right?'

'Why wouldn't Debbie call someone after that? The guards?'

I drag the clothes rail across the room and position it next to the door. 'I don't know. It does seem strange. But then, when the brick came through Tanya's window, it was my mother who had to phone it in. I'm sure Tanya would rather have pretended none of it was happening.'

80

'Denial?'

'Oh yeah. By the bucketload. Sometimes it's not the question people are afraid of but the answer.'

Baz dusts down the front of his trousers, gives his feet a little shuffle while gripping the front crease at the knees. 'Right, so, who else comes into the frame? A stranger? Some randomer?'

'I think we've to go with it being someone she knew. She let them in willingly. Made them feel welcome.' I push through the stab vests on the rails, checking the sizes, the pockets. They're good spec. A glance back at Baz. 'Don't forget Daddy could have come home.'

He plants his hands on his hips. 'And wha? She makes him a cup of tea after twenty fucking years?' He pulls a face. 'Fucking cup of weedkiller more like.'

'Okay then,' trying to keep the tightness out of my voice, 'whoever it was, I'd say they were known to Debbie but not close, not a friend who might have been in and out of the house before. A man friend possibly, new on the scene. Someone that warranted the good-room treatment. She wasn't dragged into that room, she went in voluntarily. But she was dragged out.'

'Well, you say they were getting the good-room treatment but it could also have been the case, like Kristen said, that the heating was shitty in the rest of the house. The living room had a gas fire, that'd be excuse enough for her and Margot to open the room up, right?'

I think that over. 'Yes.'

He takes a quick breath, captivated by the idea now. 'And did you see Margot's reaction when you asked about yesterday evening?'

'I'm asking the questions for a reason, you know.'

He's not listening. 'She noticed Debbie wasn't in, for sure. Then Kristen returns from France, not a word of it to her mum? Again, no phone call?'

'Still explainable though,' I say.

'Absolutely. But her reply was that she assumed her mum was working. And so why the sudden search of the house when they arrived home?' He lifts his chin, eyes looking at the far wall. 'They knew. They knew something was wrong.'

'It certainly looks like she suspected something. She comes home. Wants to see her mum, searches the house and discovers what looks like a murder scene.'

The door handle pushes downwards and Deirdre Ross enters the room again, rear end first, her hands busy with two mugs of tea.

'There you are now. Warm your hands on that.' She passes a mug to me then holds out the other to Baz.

He puts down the box and takes it with a smile. 'Thanks, Mrs Ross,' he says, as if he was thanking a friend's mammy.

'Sure it's no bother at all.' She pulls herself up. 'Right, I won't disturb you again.'

I take a mouthful of tea, strong enough to replace a meal. 'Have you lived here long, Mrs Ross?'

She pauses at the door. 'Please, call me Deirdre. Lived here since I was given my badge, must be forty odd years ago now. I know every nook and cranny of these mountains and all those that hide in them.' She shakes her head. 'That's what's so upsetting about this whole Nugent business. Never known anything like it.'

'Then you know the family well?'

82

Her face draws in. 'Well, they're funny ones. Oh Debbie would stop here and there to have a chat and sure I'd be often up at the garden centre for a couple of things this time of year but there was a wall there. Definitely. Always got the sense that they were an impenetrable unit and not one would get between them,' she says, her lips twisting together as if familial closeness was some kind of disease. She sniffs, pulls back, looks out into the hall, lowers her voice further. 'Perhaps, lately you'd see the younger one about. On her way to work and the odd time in town with David.' She pouts, throws her chin up briefly. 'Well, I'll leave you to it. Enjoy your tea.'

She goes to leave but Baz, hastily swallowing a mouthful of the tea, calls her back. 'You spoke to the garden centre, right? About Debbie's hours?'

'Yes,' she replies.

'What dates did you ask them about?'

She lifts her chin, expecting a challenge. 'For this week. They said she'd been ill on the Friday – that's Friday week past and then she'd a week's holiday booked.' She purses her lips briefly. 'And I checked that too, Detective, before you ask. Debbie put it in the diary herself, months ago.'

'And before that?'

She gives out a long, loud sigh, blinks slowly, gathering her patience. 'Before what, Detective?'

'Before the Friday,' Baz goes on, and I wonder if he's got a death wish.

Deirdre's face stiffens. 'She's only been missing a few days.'

'Yes. That's right,' he says, as if only remembering the details of the case. 'Sorry. Thank you.'

83

'Don't worry about it,' she says then looks to me, 'honestly don't know what they'd do without us. Heads like sieves, the lot of them.'

I smile at her and she disappears out of the room, closing the door softly.

Baz glances up at the clock on the wall, picks up his phone. 'I think they'll still be open. Let's nail this timeline down.'

'You can't be thinking she's been missing for longer?'

He looks up from the phone, his finger poised mid-scroll. 'As you're constantly reminding me, let's rule it out. At the moment, we've no other witnesses that report seeing Debbie this week. None other than her daughter, Margot. If Debbie drove to Dublin on Wednesday and even if she didn't return until Friday, we've not been able to get an image of her car, despite having a time frame to work from. And if she took the bus, there's a camera pointing right at the bus stop in Ballyalann and at no point did she get on the bus to Dublin on Wednesday.'

'She could have gotten the bus from any of the other nearby villages Rathdrum?'

He raises his eyebrow at that. 'Point is, if we're having doubts about the veracity of Kristen's and Margot's statements then we should corroborate them as much as possible, right?'

Relief settles over me, grateful that our thoughts are going in the same direction: that Debbie's daughters might be hiding something. That it's possible they may not want to find their mother. May not have wanted to protect her. Acid on the back of my tongue. It's all a bit too close. For the opposite reasons. If I had my chance again, I would have broken bones to keep my

84

family safe. And it wouldn't have mattered whose they were. I look to Baz as he paces up and down the room, phone pressed to his ear, his other hand making impatient circles on the back of his head; the chance of this giving us a lead brightening his eyes, the small muscle along his jaw ticking. And I think for a second that maybe I've lost something, that perhaps whatever internal compass sends me after one particular lead over another has broken.

I sip my tea. Baz stops pacing, nods at me and puts the phone on speaker.

'Quilla Garden Centre? Catriona speaking.'

'Oh hello. This is Detective Barry Harwood. I'm investigating the disappearance of Debbie Nugent and need to verify her time sheets, please.'

'Think we already spoke to youse.'

'We have a problem with Debbie's last sighting and we wondered if you could tell us when she last presented to work?'

The woman draws in a breath. 'Are you a journalist? Because we've no interest in talking—'

'I promise you, I'm not, but if you feel more comfortable you could come down to the station once you've finished your shift and give the information then?' He throws a smile over at me, knowing that there's no way Catriona will want to be giving up her Saturday evening to sit in a garda station.

Silence comes down the line and then there's the rustle of paper.

'Hold on,' Catriona says. There's a mumble of conversation in the background. 'Go down the second aisle there, where the acers are and you'll find all the planters we've got in stock.'

More mumbling. 'Yeah, yeah. Terracotta, stone, plastic, the lot. Have a look. Alright. No problem.'

Then she's back again. 'Sorry about that.'

'Debbie?'

'She's been on holiday, hasn't been in.'

'From what dates?'

'This past week.'

'Someone said she was ill the Friday before. The twenty-second. Is that right?'

Pause, then, 'Possibly. I only work the weekends.'

'If it isn't too much trouble, could you check? And if there's any way to know whether Debbie phoned in sick or someone did so on her behalf, that would be great.'

Another breath; hard to tell if it's an exhalation of impatience or not. 'Hold on, I've got the message book here. There's a good few who don't record the calls, which is very vexing.'

Baz puts his hand on his hip. His mouth tight.

'Right, here we are. She sniffs and I hear the turning of pages come down the line. 'Sorry, it doesn't say. Typical. Only that she's still ill.'

Baz gives me a meaningful look.

'Still ill?'

A sigh. 'Hang on. I'll look through the roster.' There's a banging sound on the other side of the line. Drawers opening, closing. 'Nothing here but Debbie was in last on Wednesday, the twentieth of March. Does that help?'

'Thank you for your time, Catriona,' Baz hangs up. 'Well? You want to talk to Margot again?'

I make a mental note to check in with Keith on the sample he took up from the carpet. 'Let's keep it to ourselves for the moment,' I say, hoping the test results from the analysis won't take too long. 'I've a feeling Kristen and Margot will stick to their stories unless we give them something they can't explain away. First thing's first, we need the phone records between the house landline and Margot's mobile to the centre on those dates. And Kristen's for that matter.' I button up my coat. 'You fit for gathering a few statements? Door-to-door are thin on the ground. Plus we've yet to speak to David Sutton.'

He sighs. 'It's late.'

I smile. 'It means everyone will be in.'

Before we can get out the door of the station, Mrs Ross appears from the office behind the reception, another mug of tea in her hand, a chocolate Hobnob in the other. She waves the tea in our direction, an expression of urgency on her face telling us she's news.

'Detectives, I know youse were planning on chatting to David this evening but he's just phoned to say his mother was rushed to hospital this afternoon and he's there with her now. She's in a critical condition.'

Baz zips up his jacket in preparation for going outside. 'That's convenient,' he says, a little on the insensitive side but I understand his cynicism. There's never a person more unlucky than the guilty about to face their truth. Any manner of ailments and tragedies can strike in those moments and we've heard them all. Trees falling across doorways so they're trapped inside. A beloved aunt who's had a heart attack, lives alone, in Spain, and needs you to leave immediately, 'Talk when I'm back'. Or 'I've severe laryngitis, dude. Been told by my doc that I've to keep the pipes rested for the foreseeable.'

'David has a lot on his plate. It wouldn't be right to trouble him,' Deirdre replies, throwing the statement at Baz as firmly as a smack on the backside. She takes a swig of her tea with a slightly defiant air.

'We'll talk to David first thing tomorrow,' I say.

She turns to me, her eyes softening. Good favour won as easily as lost in this place, it seems.

'Hospital or no,' Baz adds.

Deirdre takes a long, dramatic breath in, her heavy chest rising with it. 'I've confirmed the flight details regarding Kristen's arrival this morning. It's all as she said it was. I could request CCTV of the arrivals hall?'

'Thank you. Did Sergeant Gordon advise you to get the airport footage?'

She shakes her head. 'No. I thought it'd be helpful. You know, see how their mood was and that.'

'Good idea,' I say.

I'm impressed at Deirdre's thoroughness to request the CCTV footage. That she would think of looking at the Nugents in this way. What's worrying is that she got there before we did, thought to look at the Nugents' behaviour at the airport. It suggests that she, too, is not fully persuaded by Kristen's and Margot's statements.

CHAPTER 8

Baz sits in the passenger seat, finger tapping on his knee in agitation, still smarting at the desk clerk's stinging tone in regards to David Sutton. 'Surely we can't be waiting for him to get home before we question him?'

It's coming up on seven pm. Shadows have already sprung over the mountains in the distance. 'David Sutton isn't going anywhere. We'll have more from the crime scene tomorrow. If he's got something to hide, it'll be worth it to wait. We'll be able to challenge what he tells us with crime-scene evidence, right?'

We spend the evening working alongside door-to-door. The Nugents' nearest neighbours – the Reillys, an old couple in a small pink bungalow – live a quarter mile away from the house and offered us tea and a slice of Victoria sponge big and tough enough to hold open a door. The cream had begun to turn, leaving an unpleasant tang at the back of my throat, the crumb crisp and stale.

Mrs Reilly displayed a temperament that matched her baking skills. Her face, more accustomed to settling in sour lines than a smile, wore a relaxed scowl, as if someone had ran a thread through the centre of her face and pulled it tight. Small, intense blue eyes looked out from the folds, and when she spoke, it was through one side of her mouth, as if she could not risk any movement that would cause her to break free of her preferred expression. Mr Reilly, a small man, white-haired and loose-skinned, sat in a limp, life-weary pose on an armchair, thin and frail as a snowdrop.

'We had her over for tea when she first moved here,' Sheila Reilly began. 'She came over one arm as long as the other. Not that I'd expect anything, but not so much as a biscuit to go with a cup of tea. The two little ones never let go of her skirts the entire time,' she said, before upping her voice to a hair-raising level and bellowing at the armchair. 'Isn't that right, John?'

John's head lifted a fraction at the sound, long white eyebrows down over his milky eyes. 'What?'

Sheila turned back to us as if he hadn't spoken. 'That was the only time, mind. Not so much as an invite back in return. I'd see her the odd time at the centre if I went in for a few bulbs for the garden.'

During her speech, Baz was dissecting the sponge cake, picking out pieces of the stale mix and scraping the yellow cream from his fork onto the edge of the plate.

'Last week, did you see anything? A car on the road perhaps?' I braced myself for the answer, knowing the next question was pointless before I asked it. 'Did you hear anything at all, Mrs Reilly?'

'Sure, how would we hear anything from that distance? Amn't I after telling ye that we never hear anything from them?'

She pointed her face at her husband then, seeking backup, and he roused himself enough to say, 'Aye.'

With the garden centre closed, we chanced a call in to Debbie's work colleague who Kristen had mentioned at the station. Eileen Carty. She lives a few kilometres from the centre, in a semi-detached red-brick, with her partner, Abby – a woman with soft, sallow skin and a gentle face, who stood behind Eileen the entire time, hands on her shoulders as if she was holding her up.

Eileen was upset. 'Maybe I should have called in. I meant to,' she said, hooking her long silver hair behind her ear.

Abby gave her shoulders a squeeze of comfort. 'We were on holidays, love,' she murmured. 'We've been in Spain for the past fortnight. We only got back yesterday evening,' she added.

'Kristen, Debbie's daughter, said you're friends. Is that right?' The skin around Eileen's eyes tightened briefly then. A wince of guilt, pain or regret.

'Yes. I guess I'm as close a friend as any to Debbie. She can be difficult to get to know.' She looked round at Abby, who nodded encouragement and Eileen shook her head at me, her eyes filling with tears. 'I'm sorry. I feel so terrible that something could've happened to her. She looked after the garden here while we were away. It was my birthday and she planted some border trees at the front for me. She'd taken the trouble to order them in through the centre. Flamingo Willow. That would be Debbie, quietly surprising.' She nodded out through the front window where I saw a row of six small trees, covered in white flowers with a gentle pink hue. 'I've a thing for flamingoes. I didn't think she'd remember that.' Eileen smiled.

91

'Did she ever tell you or suggest that she could be in danger? Someone who might hurt her? Or somewhere she might go if she was in danger?'

'No,' she said, breathing out the word as if she could blow the thought away. 'I can't imagine who would want to hurt Debbie. She's such a good soul. Always happy, smiling. Gets on with things, you know.'

'Did she have a boyfriend? A lover?'

Eileen shook her head. 'As far as I know it's just her and the girls. Her parents died many years ago. She never seems interested in anyone in that way. I did wonder, you know: she's attractive and fun once you get to know her. A great sense of humour. It took a long time before I really struck up any friendship with her. I get the impression she's been hurt in the past.'

Everyone we speak to, all the feedback from other officers is the same: Debbie was a nice person, although, as Baz remarked, people do seem to become awful nice about others once they believe they're pushing up daisies.

Now, wanting to verify everything Margot and Kristen have told us, I ask: 'Did she have a mobile?'

'A phone?'

'Yes.'

'No. I tease her about it sometimes. She's very old-fashioned in some ways.' She looks up to Abby again. 'Isn't she?'

'She is.'

'You knew her too, Abby?'

'Not well but she has that air. Prefers solid ground beneath her feet and things that she can see, feel and hear in front of her.'

'Yeah,' Eileen joins in. 'We've a Facebook group for the town and at work. For notices and the odd bit of news. She isn't on social media at all. I can't imagine she'd even know what to do with a computer.'

Baz takes notes, or pretends to, on Debbie's blanket ban on all things digital. In a world where everyone wants to be found, Debbie seems to be the only one who likes to be hidden.

'How about her daughters? Did she talk about them much?'

'Oh she loves them rotten. She's a great mum. Talked about them constantly. She worries about them from time to time, though.'

Baz moves forward on the sofa at this. 'Why?'

Eileen frowns. 'It's what mothers do, isn't it?'

Neither of us bother to hide our dejection at the meagre scraps our evening has given us. Stomachs and energy levels on empty, the sour aftertaste of Mrs Reilly's cake still on the back of my tongue with every swallow. On our way to the hotel, we swing by the station to collect the rest of the door-to-door reports and statements, copies of the crime-scene photos and anything else we think might point us in Debbie's direction. Deirdre Ross has clocked off for the night and the younger guard Joe has taken up the late shift.

Baz dumps the box of papers in the boot of the car then gets into the driver's seat, while I settle into the passenger side, check that the heating in the car is dialled up to the max then search the glove compartment for snacks. Beneath a stack of opened bills and a pair of socks, which I quickly flick out onto the floor while giving Baz a disgusted look, I find a flattened flapjack bar. I hold it to my nose, sniff the cellophane wrapping, and feel hunger clench in my stomach. I tear it open, wait for Baz to pull out on the road then pass him half.

'Man, I've a bloody thirst on me,' he says, between chews.

The oats have the reverse effect on my hunger levels, stirring them up rather than sating them. I look at my watch, it's nearing eleven. I had imagined this case would be difficult; even as I read the initial summary in the office this morning, I knew it wouldn't be simple. There's little doubt that we're dealing with murder and that when we begin our search tomorrow we'll be looking for a body. But I thought, once we were here, we'd get more of a feel for what's happened. Given the crime scene we should have the thread of the investigation in our grasp, some particle of information that we can hold up and think, okay, yes, we can follow this, we can work back from here. But if this evening is anything to go by, unless we find Debbie's body soon, we're in for one of those cases where we're scratching around for weeks, desperate for any morsel of evidence or combing through transcripts for some throwaway comment from a bystander that has sudden relevance, a lip in the rockface that we can push off.

'The hotel's not far,' I say.

I scroll through the updates on my phone. A message from Deirdre to tell us that David is happy to talk to us tomorrow. His mother, out of the woods and stable, is hoping to be sent home in the morning. A short text from Keith: *Sent carpet sample to spectrometry. Results tomorrow. K.*

'Bloodstain results will hopefully come in tomorrow,' I tell Baz.

He lifts a hand from the wheel, rubs it over his face, stretches out his jaw. 'Good.'

I look up from my phone. 'And we missed Steve. He arrived when we were out. Says he should be almost finished set-up by the morning.'

'Is he staying in Dublin or out here with us?'

'I don't know,' I answer and continue to look through my phone. The rest of my messages are from the Bureau. Helen and Paul sending through the press on the case; a series of articles on Debbie's disappearance, headline-heavy and content-light. I put away my mobile and watch the black night move by. The mountains hidden, a pitch of darkness not seen in the city. The cut of the car's lights guiding us over the road and blackness moving in again behind us.

'You know Steve?' I ask.

Baz shoots me a quick look. 'What? Yeah.'

'Where's his family from?'

Another look, a frown deepening on his forehead, his eyes assessing me, concerned. 'You alright?' he asks, as if I've lost it.

'Just answer. Do you know?'

He thinks for a bit then says, 'Dublin.'

'I know, Dublin. But where?'

He gears down for a sharp bend, slows the car to rumble around it, then speeds up again on the straight that follows. 'The Southside somewhere? He seems like he might have had it alright growing up.' He gives me another look. 'Why the sudden interest?' he asks, the side of his mouth lifting. 'You got the hots for our Stevo? You need to know his creds?'

'I'm going to ignore that.'

'Well, I know something went down between you and our man sergeant here, so who knows what you're into now.' He grins.

'I don't know what you're talking about.'

'Oh come on,' he says, eyes on the golden strip of road ahead, a dry laugh shaking in his chest.

'My point is, that we don't really know who we work with, do we?'

He blows out a short breath. 'No, we really don't,' he says, raising an eyebrow at me. And I ignore that too.

'Steve has worked with us for years, right?' I say. 'I've always thought him a bit of a loner; he shies away from work drinks—'

'He's in a band,' Baz announces, extending a finger from the steering wheel to indicate a score.

'Right so, what does he play?'

The finger drops. 'I want to say bass.'

'That's what I'm saying. I'm thinking that Debbie's work mates might not be the best judge of her family situation, that's all. I mean Debbie's not going to be spending the day whingeing to her colleagues about how shitty her daughters are, is she?'

'I don't think my mother would hold back.'

'Well, in your case, I'm sure there are reasons.'

'Hey!' he says, but with a smile. 'So you're coming round to my way of thinking?'

'Just trying to get a feel for the family dynamic. The box of Margot's possessions in the shed. What is that about?'

'She might have left them there herself.'

'Why would she do that?'

His fingers drum on the top of the steering wheel. 'Or they got stowed away by accident. Or she was hiding them from Mum. The jewellery, maybe Debbie didn't approve of our 'good lad' David. Maybe David's a bit of a prick.'

'No, the phone and jewellery maybe, especially if Debbie was funny about mobiles. But the purse? She'd need that. Not to mention her house keys? Anyway, if Margot was going to hide those things from her mum then she wouldn't put them in the shed where the only other person who uses it could find them. Can't imagine Margot is the sort to go mowing the lawns on an evening,' I say. 'But if it was Debbie hiding them, then the shed would be the perfect place.'

Baz frowns across the car at me. 'Why the fuck would Debbie hide her daughter's things?'

I stare out at the blackness, my reflection wavering on the glass. I think about Margot's story about the rock coming through the window. That even though the damage had already been repaired, the drama was enough to stop Margot going out. I think of the clothes piled up along the walls of Margot's room, the stacks of dishes in the sink and the empty refrigerator.

'I'm not sure,' I say, eventually. 'Only we know that Debbie liked to keep her family close. Wanted to keep the circle of their lives tight. What happens when her youngest daughter, the only one left to her, wants to step free of it?' Baz is quiet and I continue: 'What happens when that circle gets tighter?'

He keeps his eyes on the empty road ahead when he answers: 'I'd tell you what would happen. A person would get awful resentful under that kind of pressure.'

I hold the door open with my hip and Baz pushes by me, his hands full with the box of door-to-door reports, crime notes and maps on the various routes around the mountains. A bottle of wine balances on top and he's stowed a wine glass in each

97

jacket pocket. The hotel kitchens are closed, the local takeaway doesn't deliver and so dinner tonight is a packet of crisps each. We debated returning to town but neither of us could summon the motivation, dulled as we were by near starvation.

My hotel room is large, double bed, twin lockers either side. The walls a soft terracotta. Near the single window that over-looks the back of the hotel, a two-seater and a round coffee table.

Baz crosses the room, puts the box on the table and removes the glasses. 'Bigger than the wardrobe they've given me,' he says, 'There are inmates on death row with more space than my room.'

'Don't look at me. I didn't book the rooms.'

'Who did?'

I shrug. 'Helen probably. Someone at the Bureau.'

Baz frowns. 'Ryan. Put bloody money on it.' He looks at the top of the wine bottle. 'Fuck it,' he whines loudly, as if someone had shit on the last good thing in his life. 'Forgot the corkscrew.' He turns around, a desperate fever in his eye. 'There must be one here somewhere.'

It's after midnight and the strain of the day pushes at the back of my eyes, waiting for a moment for me to sit, relax. 'It's probably best to hold off for now. One sip and I think I'll slip into a coma.'

He gives me a pleading look. 'We're off the clock. Technically speaking.'

'You know there's no such thing.'

'Some of us are human, Sheehan. All work and no play—'

'—gets the job done,' I finish with a smile.

He puts down the wine and rips open a bag of crisps, throws

the other packet across the room to me. I catch it and split it open, taking a couple before turning to our case. I remove the files from the box. Among the transcripts, I find a yellow envelope with CCTV/AIRPORT written on the front. Mrs Ross hasn't wasted any time in ticking off her to-do list.

Baz takes up a notebook and begins tearing out blank pages. I open a folder that I know contains the crime-scene photos, lay them out in a line on the floor. Baz writes yesterday's date on a page and the words 'crime scene discovered' in large letters. Beneath that he places another sheet of the notepaper with the proposed date the crime occurred, the 27th of March, then crosses that out and replaces it with 'last seen alive'.

We are attempting to construct a timeline. A timeline of Debbie's movements. Every encounter reported in the moments leading up to her disappearance is here in the small snippets of information provided to us by the residents of Ballyalann, her colleagues and her family. We work steadily. Both of us silent. It takes us just under an hour. When we've finished, the box of paper is empty, and almost every inch of cheap hotel carpet is covered with Debbie Nugent's last movements. Or what we have of them.

Baz sits down on the corner of the bed, hooks his feet on the base so as not to disturb the layout of the timeline. I relent to the pull of wine, find a corkscrew in one of the locker drawers, open the bottle and pour two glasses.

He takes one from my hand. 'Thanks,' he murmurs. His eyes trail the sequence of events before him, searching for the answer to the question that teases us all when we hear of murder: what happened?

I sit down on the floor before the spread of paper. Open my notebook, begin to make notes around Debbie's victimology. Victim analysis is possibly one of the core skills to have followed me from the beginnings of my training, studying forensic science and profiling, my initial years as a detective through every case I've worked on in my career. It's the keystone in any investigation. Rhythms and patterns in victim behaviour can throw a spotlight on areas that warrant a second look. *She never drove to work, she liked to walk, no matter the weather.* When you hold these tidbits against a suspect's narrative: '*when she left that morning, she was grand, got into her car and drove to work and I haven't seen her since*', you can often see where their story doesn't fit with a victim's normal routine.

Debbie was reserved. People seemed to like her. She was active, fit, enjoyed hiking at the weekend, sometimes for up to three hours. She didn't drink much, a glass of white wine occasionally. She was never late for work and was at Quilla Garden Centre most weekday mornings by eight. Family holidays when the girls were young were always in Ireland, never abroad. As far as our searches conclude and as much as her daughters are aware, she doesn't own a passport. Her laugh was deep and dirty.

And that's as thin as it gets. No one, including her own children, seems to have much understanding of Debbie's past. She has no social-media trail to follow. Her daughters say she hated photographs. She has no surviving parents and, even if she was liked by those we spoke to, she didn't have many very close friends.

I look down at the photos we've laid out across the floor. We work on the belief that a perp will always bring something to a

100

crime scene and leave with something from it. My eyes fix on the picture of the living room. Again, I cast my gaze over the lamp in the corner, then the light splash of tea soaked into the carpet alongside the darker stain of blood, then the sofa, still plump, waiting for Debbie to sit. I look over the other photos, the exterior of the house, the car, Margot's room, the hallway. Over and back I go, searching, like those spot-the-difference games I played as a kid, searching for the item that stands out, searching for a constant that's missing.

Baz is quiet, one foot on his knee, a second bag of crisps open to his side, hand going absently from packet to mouth.

Eventually, he licks the salt from his lips and waves a hand over our collection of images. 'So she gets home from Dublin, according to Margot, on the Friday. Of course, we don't know where she stayed in Dublin for those two nights, if she stayed. Helen can't find a record. There's no receipts. No evidence of a booking. No contact number.' He tips his head – raises his eyebrow acknowledging the looseness of the thread – but he stays focused on the timeline we've been given. 'She gets in, we don't know what time, makes something to eat maybe, chills out then someone comes around, if we go with the theory that it's someone on the outside.' He looks back at the photos and takes a mouthful of wine. 'She lets whoever this is in. She goes to make tea.' He stands, puts down his glass on one of the lockers. This is the part we know won't change regardless of which timeline we follow – Margot's or one that extends longer. Ten days ago.

'She's holding both mugs?' Baz says.

'It looks like it, from the way they've fallen.'

'She suggests they go into the living room, to talk, relax,

whatever. So, both hands full, she leans down on the door handle, pushes the door open.' He role-plays out the action, balancing the invisible mugs in his hands, pushing through the air with his elbow and nudging his shoulder against an imagined living-room door. 'We assume the killer is following behind, right?'

'Right.'

He shuffles forward a little, hands still out in front of him. 'She goes to move across the room towards the sofa but takes what – two steps?'

'Not much,' I add.

'Her killer strikes her head from behind?' He dips his head forward. Opens his hands. 'The tea falls.'

'The curtains,' he says, pointing a foot at the relevant photo. 'The hit on the window pane says they were open before the attack and closed afterwards.'

'Yes.'

'I think if the strike came from behind and it looks that way. The killer will have been the one to turn on the lamp. Otherwise, she would've had to put the tea down.' He nods, pleased with that deduction, then continues: 'So, if we're looking outside Margot, sometime that evening Debbie is – let's go with the likely scenario here – killed. Her killer pulls the curtains, turns on the lamp, searches the living room, goes upstairs, probably searches Debbie's room, wipes that room, comes downstairs, takes Debbie's body out, likely to a vehicle, possibly even the victim's, then comes back in and cleans blood from the hall floor and front door, but doesn't bother with the living room. Why?'

I stare down into my wine glass, feeling the weight of exhaustion and alcohol through my limbs, my eyes. I swallow the last of the wine without tasting.

'Time? It could be that Debbie's killer thought someone might be coming to the house? Or returning to the house?'

'That someone being Margot?'

'Perhaps.'

'I don't know,' he says. 'There's something around the daughter. The boyfriend maybe. I'm still not convinced about him.'

'His alibi checks.'

He snorts. 'I'm thinking she cleaned the hall area because she didn't want to look at it or because if she did have visitors, or had to open the door even if it was only to the bleedin' postman, she knew she wouldn't be able to explain away that drag mark across the hallway. And maybe David too. If he wasn't involved and he collected her or called in, that'd be reason to clean up the stains in the reception area, to keep it from him, but no need in the living room as no one goes in there.'

'I hear you, but to play devil's advocate, why wouldn't she clean the living room? If David did come round for a romantic evening, couldn't he have suggested they use the room with heating? It's freezing out there. Besides, she had the time. Or thought she did. She lived there. She had all the time in the world to clean that room.'

'Too messy,' Baz counters. 'She doesn't know where to start.'

'A new rug over the bloodstain. Bleach the rest from the mantelpiece, wash the walls or paint. A few hours' work.'

He swears. 'Fuckin' hell, I hope to God we find Debbie sooner rather than later. No motive, no body, no weapon and a murky timeline.'

103

'There's still a sliver of a chance that she's alive. Beaten, abducted, captive,' I say.

He gives me a pained look. Baz and I've always had something of a see-saw synchronicity when working a case. When one's down the other comes up and, despite the late-hour sulking from him, and my own crippling tiredness, I hear myself reaching to buoy him up.

'Let's see what Mrs Ross has got for us.' I get up, go to my bag and take out my laptop. I open it, wait for it to wake, then tip out the contents of the envelope containing the airport CCTV. There's a note from Deirdre, listing the name of the airport-security officer she got it from and the time frame we should be looking at. I push the USB stick into the side of the computer and motion Baz to my side.

The footage plays and I skip forward to 6.12 am. Straight away I can pick out Margot's red hair as she waits at arrivals. David is next to her: dark jeans, a hand loosely around her lower back. Every now and then, Margot's hand goes to her face, her shoulders high. A couple next to her, an older man, bald, stooped, and a woman, white-haired and dressed in a pale pink cardigan, lean towards her, say something. Their heads bob as they speak; cajoling, smiling. She nods back, moves her body closer to David's. Passengers trundle through, some backpackers still wearing the shorts and sandals of sunnier climates. Occa-sionally, a child is given a nudge by a mother's hand to run under the barrier and into the waiting arms of relatives.

Finally, I see Kristen. She moves with fast, determined strides, her long skirt rippling out behind her and I see Margot shrink against her boyfriend's side.

'Interesting,' Baz remarks.

But when Kristen comes free of the barrier, she pulls her sister to her and gives her a hard hug. The embrace lasts moments, Kristen's hand cups the back of her sister's head. David stands back. Gives them room. When they pull apart, Margot looks to David, says something, then the three walk quickly out of the arrivals hall.

'They're certainly not wasting time,' I murmur.

'That's for sure.' He picks up the empty wine bottle, gives it a hopeful shake. 'You hear of those cases don't you, where someone's lived with their deceased wife or husband for days. There was one I read where a woman had lived with her dead husband for four years. Just didn't want to let go. They found him in a bedroom upstairs when a relative who'd not seen him in a half a decade decided to call by unannounced and got suspicious when repeated attempts to see him were met with increasingly lame excuses by the missus. He was on the floor, where he'd apparently fallen after a heart attack, half-skeletonized, his glasses still on his face.' He makes small circles around his eyes with his fingers and thumbs.

'I do like these little stories you tell me,' I say. 'Those cases are usually natural causes though. Not murder. They're people who can't deal with idea of death.' Margot's face appears in my head. I remember the way she pressed up against Kristen during our interview earlier, checked her sister's reaction when she said something. She never asked how Debbie was or if we'd found her. It was Kristen who asked that question. 'Whoever killed Debbie very much dealt with it. They dragged her out of there.'

'Money,' Baz says.

105

'Money?'

'Sometimes, if there's a pension or a social benefit, the relative doesn't report the death because then the payments would stop. What's a bit of death between family. Still gotta eat, right?'

'That could explain why if she saw the scene in the living room, she didn't report it. But wouldn't she be afraid that if her mother was murdered that someone could come for her too?'

'Maybe she is afraid of that,' Baz counters. 'But I'm thinking, they had a fight, Debbie thought it was over, Margot didn't. Killed her in rage of frustration, over . . . something, then scattered a few books around half-heartedly to make it look like a burglary, then thought better of it, dumped the body and closed the door on the crime scene.'

'Look into the money thing. We'll need Debbie's bank details anyway and if she had any benefits, pensions that were activated already that may stop after her death.'

'I'll check in with the Bureau tomorrow. I suspect Helen already has encyclopaedic knowledge of all of Debbie's financial transactions going back at least five years.' He gets up, leaves the bottle on the side and goes to the door. 'What's the start time tomorrow?'

'I'll meet you in the lobby at five forty-five, for a six am start at the station.'

He groans. 'Alright.' He lifts a hand in a tired wave goodnight. 'See you then.'

He closes the door and I lift my foot onto the edge of the bed and stretch out the scar tissue that has tightened at the back of my leg. Whether it's the wine or the room, it feels too warm. I change into a T-shirt and go to the window, open the heavy,

106

floor-length curtains a few inches and search for the window latch. I push the window up and a blast of icy air sweeps over my skin. Below, there is an empty car park, the bays picked out in clear white paint. Beyond that, I know there are trees, then a slow climb on both sides upwards. The night is a canvas of deepest black. It's so dark I might imagine I'm falling into it, falling into nothing.

CHAPTER 9

I wake to the case already active in my head, twisted with the jagged, fractured images of my dreams; Margot's face half-turned, a secret smile on her lips, a bloody streak down her smooth cheek, flashes of Debbie, walking, the mountains behind her, her feet pushing up a soft pine trail. She turns, red-faced and breathless to admire the lavender views of the Wicklow valleys. Her breath is still in my ear as I sit up.

A message from Clancy late last night to say he's arrived at the hotel and will be up for debrief at the station this morning. There's no sign of him in the lobby when I get downstairs so I send him a message to meet me in Ballyalann. There's no sign of Baz either. A member of the hotel's staff is shoving around a vacuum cleaner, the clink of cutlery comes from the restaurant and the waft of bacon, sweet pastries and fresh bread almost knocks me flat. I walk towards them, have my hand out for a croissant when a man appears from the kitchen. 'Breakfast is not until seven.'

I smile. 'Thanks,' I say, wait for his back to turn then grab the croissant in a fit of rebellion and tuck it into my bag. When he turns again, he looks at me, the pastries, my bag then to me again, his eyebrows pinched in a frown. I stare back at him. Finally, he lifts a stack of empty silver trays from a nearby table and returns to the kitchen, his spine so rigid it would snap in a breeze. I feel a minor jolt of victory, try not to think of the flakes of pastry that are shedding over my notes.

I use the time to text Justin. *Might be a few days here. Can you look in on the flat? Water the bonsai?*

After a few seconds, he replies: *Thanks for the wake-up call!!! What's in it for me?*

The satisfaction of helping your sister out.

No.

A pint?

Ok.

I smile. Pocket my phone but it goes again. Baz. *Go on without me, I'm only up and awake.*

I throw my eyes heavenward. 'Fuck's sake.'

The team file into our new incident room at Ballyalann station, the early-morning start still swollen around their eyes, calling them to the large catering-size tea flasks that Deirdre has laid out on one of the tables. Fifteen officers, men and women. More promised tomorrow. A Sunday never being the best time to recruit gardaí to work. It's hard to believe that it's been less than twenty-four hours since we were called out. An investigation like this has a danger of slipping into cold-case territory, the pursuit so quickly sliding from excitement to frustration and then despondency. Keeping hope and motivation up is vital. It might

109

be early but results from our investigation have begun to come through. Blood results and the report from Debbie's car. At least these will give us something solid for debrief this morning. Any illumination, any confirmation of our theories is a good thing and what we've got so far tells us we're on the right track even if we're only a couple of steps into this race.

I spot Timmy Morris, the officer from yesterday, among the crew, although he's hard to miss. He backs slowly into the corner, to allow the other officers room to move, holding his cup of tea protectively against his chest. He catches me watching and tips a large hand to his forehead, his face breaking into a smile. I smile back then turn my attention to the dismal collection of officers.

I try not to despair at the numbers: we've almost twenty volunteers out at the Nugent house to fatten up the search party, all waiting for their team leaders to propel them into action. The whiteboard is not much more satisfying. Deirdre has blown up the picture we found in the family album. Debbie's grey eyes peer out at the room, the revelries of Christmas celebrations high on her face, an orange paper crown collapsing over the frizz of her hair.

A hand touches my back and I turn to find Alex.

'Morning,' he says. He passes me a takeaway coffee. 'I remember you're more of a coffee person. Deirdre takes it personally if we attempt to drink anything other than tea in the station, hence only tea for the troops.' He nods at the tea station. 'She sees coffee as a deviant,' he raises his eyebrows at 'deviant' so that I know the word is hers rather than his.

He's wearing a navy Gore-tex jacket, open to the waist, over a

110

thick sweater. A pair of heavy-duty waterproof gloves are stuffed in his top pocket. Jeans and a pair of hiking boots. I take the coffee and a hot waft of the rich, bitter aroma hits my nose.

I lift the cup in cheers and say thanks. 'Fair play to you for finding a café open this early.' It's barely past six and the place was quiet as a ghost town when I drove through it to get here. Newspaper bundles still strapped and stacked outside the newsagent's, waiting to be pulled inside. Shutters down on the supermarket, empty pint glasses sitting on the pub windows.

'You just need to know who to ask,' he says smiling and I don't know if it's the outdoor get-up, the fresh scent of him or the way his eyes don't leave mine when he smiles, but there's a little lift of something in my stomach, like the sudden, short, swooping sensation you feel on the descent of a slide.

Baz appears in the open doorway. His expression troubled. He turns towards the wall immediately upon entering, phone pressed to his ear, the other hand raised and in front of him. Every now and then he waves it through the air as if to drive home a point or plead with whoever is on the other end of the line. He's dropped his voice but I can make out the urgent, quick tone beneath the up and down rumble of chatter from the officers around me. It's Clancy who rouses him from the call. He walks in, head down, both hands in his coat pocket, driving the long wings of his trench out to the sides as he moves. He spots Baz, gives him a firm clatter on the shoulder; the sound clapping through the room, so the rest of the team, sensing authority in their midst, fall silent.

Baz looks up and around. Holds up a finger then returns to the call, 'I gotta go. I'll call you later okay.' Whatever reply comes back is cut off abruptly. He looks like he's had his arse handed to him.

Clancy pushes through the uniforms towards me, removes a hand from his pocket and holds it out to Alex. 'Hear you're the man?' And I wonder if he recalls that it was Alex who helped me bundle him into a cab on Friday night.

Alex shoots me a bemused look but puts his hand in Jack's.

Jack gives it a firm shake. 'I knew your old boss from way back,' he says, answering my thoughts; no recollection at all.

'Dennis?'

'That's right,' he says, then to me: 'I'm thinking I'll give him a bell, Frankie, see if I can get a fix on Debbie Nugent's past. If she moved here, out of the blue, a single mother with two kids, twenty years ago, he'll have the scandal that surely went with it.'

'Anything we can get would be helpful,' I say, then groan internally as I see Clancy's eyes light on Alex's coffee.

'That fresh?' he asks.

'Erm, yes,' Alex replies.

'Grand, so. Very generous of ye,' Jack says, scooping the cup from Alex's hand. He gives me a quick nod. 'Frankie, we right?' And he walks to the other side of the whiteboard.

I give Alex an apologetic smile. 'You get used to it.'

I move away and stand next to Clancy and the room turns to face us, waits for instruction. Cups are left down on nearby tables, as notebooks and pens are taken up, ready to jot down pertinent details.

'As the press have beaten us to it,' I begin, 'you'll know that we arrived at a house five kilometres out of town yesterday afternoon following a call from a local resident to alert us to a possible crime scene. The caller, David Sutton, is the boyfriend of Margot Nugent and the scene is at the Nugent family home on Ragborne Road.

'When we arrived we could confirm a very bloody scene and we believe there is a strong possibility that this is a murder scene. From among the main area of blood spatter, our crime-scene investigators recovered hair and bone fragments, as well as blood smears and drag marks leading out of the room into the hallway suggesting that a body had been removed. These marks had been cleaned but showed up with luminol testing. We've had blood analysis back from our labs and can say with some certainty that the blood matches that of missing person, Debbie Nugent.'

I pause, give the team a chance to digest the information. One of them takes the opportunity to ask a question and I feel Clancy tense beside me at the interruption.

'Sorry, Garda Murray here,' a man says. 'So is it still a missing-persons investigation?'

'If you bleedin' listen for a couple of minutes, your Chief Super will tell ye,' Jack says, and the guard shrinks a little into his shoes.

I find the guard's gaze. He's maybe late fifties, soft-faced and soft-cheeked, greying at the temples. The signs of an easy life on his face, but he's alert and attentive and I recognize the look of someone who went into his occupation not because it was a job but because it felt like a vocation. The earnestness in his expression catches me full in the throat, casts me right back to that room with my dad, his hope and faith in goodness still lifting his chest.

I swallow and meet the guard's eyes and answer patiently. 'We've launched a murder investigation. From initial scene analysis it would appear very unlikely that Debbie survived this attack.'

Garda Murray nods, bends his head over his notebook, his hand moving over the paper.

Turning to the case board, I point to the image of Debbie and continue: 'Debbie Nugent is fifty-five years old, a mother of two grown daughters and works in the garden centre north of the town. She was last seen by her youngest daughter, Margot, on the twenty-seventh of March, four days ago.

'According to our lead crime-scene investigator it's very unlikely she survived whatever happened in that room,' I repeat. 'Failing to locate her in any hospitals, there being no emergency calls made from the landline at her house, we believe that she is dead and yes, we've consequently opened a murder investigation. We are now wanting to locate her remains, the murder weapon and any other evidence that might have been disposed of with her body.

'This morning we've received preliminary results from tests carried out on the victim's vehicle, a light blue Ford Focus, registration 110 D 364801.' I point to a picture of the car on the case board. 'An eight-centimetre patch of blood was discovered in the boot. So we can assume that her killer used the victim's own car to transport and dispose of her body. Initially, we had trouble locating the car keys but eventually they were found in a coat pocket. That coat belonged to Margot Nugent – the victim's daughter.' A murmur spreads through the room at this, a collective scribbling of notes, and I raise my voice a little, push on: 'Margot thinks she took the keys because she had misplaced her door key and Debbie had a spare set on the same key ring as her car keys. 'There was also blood found on the key fob matching that of Debbie Nugent's profile. Given the nature of the crime and imagined time constraints imposed on her killer, we believe Debbie's remains won't have been dumped far from her home.'

I turn to Alex. 'Sergeant Gordon, who some of you know, will issue you with teams of five to six volunteers, whom you will lead through a search beginning at three miles out from the Nugent home, closing inwards gradually.

'I'm afraid we don't know what Debbie was wearing at the time of her death, however, her preference was for durable outdoor clothes of the sort she wore to work, usually green or navy hard-wearing trousers or blue jeans and a woollen sweater, again usually dark navy or sometimes grey. She wore small, gold hoop earrings and a thin watch, black leather strap, gold face. According to her daughters, she never took them off, even in bed. We can't locate them in the house so look out for them on the search, it could be they broke off and may indicate whether we're close or not.'

A few of the officers make a note of these details.

I pause, look out at the room. 'Any questions?'

A woman at the front raises her hand. 'Do we have any idea of what the murder weapon was?'

'No, but from the structure of the bony fragments we discovered on the carpet and other evidence at the crime scene, we believe we're looking for a blunt object.' I point to a photograph of in the living room at the Nugent house and a few of the officers come closer to take a look. A couple stare up at an ordnance survey map of the area, eyes fixed on the red pin in the centre of the map that represents the Nugent house. The atmosphere in the room has dipped. They know they're out for

115

a day of traipsing through ditches and unforgiving terrain in shitty conditions all with the likelihood of no return. No body.

I clear my throat, wait until there's a lull in the grumble of muttering that's slowly spreading through the team. 'I know we're on the back foot here but our investigation has only begun. Our golden hours since the crime may have passed, but the trail has not gone cold. We have forensics working on stain analysis, a canine team on route to help with the search and we have our detectives looking through CCTV footage to see if we can pick up Debbie's last movements. We've interviewed Debbie's daughters and colleagues to build up a profile and it's clear that Debbie was a person of routine but also a reclusive individual. Private. So we have to ask, who might want her dead? And from the layout of the scene, this was no heated argument that got out of hand. Someone came up behind Debbie Nugent and knocked her out cold. Someone she trusted enough to invite into her house. Who would want to do that? If we find her remains, we get a huge head start in answering that question. We will be better able to narrow down a time of death, pull back some of those golden hours, and with that, opportunity and possibly motive.'

And it's all they need. A reminder that if we find the key, Debbie's body, we already have a tiny pool of people who would have the opportunity and the motive to want her dead. And I see the hunger now on the team's face. Each one wanting to be the officer that brings that home.

I wait for more questions, but the team are already descending into chatter, zipping up coats and pulling on woollen hats, preparing to go out. I move away from the board.

Steve is working quietly on the periphery, ducking beneath tables and pushing cables into the backs of hard drives. He's already connected phones, organized the desks, pushed to the sides of the room, a large printer in one corner, leaving the floor open so that there's plenty of room in front of the case board. He crawls beneath one of the desks, comes up on his knees in front of the keyboard, rolls his hand over the mouse to check the connection.

I go to walk towards him but Alex stops me. 'You coming out?'

'Do you feel confident to handle it on your own?'

He laughs at that. 'I'm not saying I'd know every inch of these mountains, but I'd make a good go of it. I've lived here long enough.'

I make a note of David Sutton's address from the case board. 'Oh, sorry. I feel like I should know that.'

'In Glenmurragh. It's—' he waves a hand over his head, 'higher up.'

We move away from the board, go to one of the tables and take up a copy of the map. The areas that the teams are covering this morning are marked out in blue. Locating the Sutton house, I circle it on the map. Check the distance key at the bottom. Thirteen kilometres. 'Sounds remote,' I say. 'I would have thought Wicklow town would be easier?'

'I'm not a town person. I like my own company too much. It has a nice pub,' he says, an invitation in his voice.

'Sounds like all essential amenities are covered,' I reply. I take out my phone, try to get the GPS up for David's house.

'You're interviewing Sutton this morning?' Alex asks.

'Yes.'

'How was Margot yesterday?'

'I'm still unclear on how things played out.'

'You and me both.' He pushes his hair back.

I nod, then tell him about our conversation with Debbie's work yesterday. That Debbie hasn't been seen at work for ten days, which leaves us with only Margot's testimony of Debbie's last movements. 'So we're having some difficulty verifying the timeline Margot has given us,' I say.

He shakes his head as if he can't quite believe it. 'I guess with murder like this, we look to family first, right?' He catches my look of surprise, gives a modest laugh. 'Oh, don't get me wrong, I've never worked a case like this in my career. I have a few murder cases under my belt, like four maybe, but all of them non-complicated drug, money or grudge-related deaths.'

I look up at the picture of Margot on the case board. 'Yes. We look at family first.'

'We best get moving,' he says, then turns to call the team to attention.

The guards deposit empty tea cups on the table as they file out. A couple hold up their notes, point to some morsel of information their imagination has snagged over. A few are silent and I catch sight of Murray leaving – his face solemn, eyes down, mouth flat. He jogs his shoulders as he goes through the door, puffs out a breath as if he was composing himself for the beginning of a race.

'I'll see you later, okay,' Alex says. 'Phone you with anything that comes up?'

'Yes.'

He presses his lips into a kind of a smile then follows the search team leaders out.

Baz is back on the phone, a finger pressed to one ear, voice low and urgent again. Clancy has taken a seat in the corner. He removes a packet of biscuits from his jacket pocket, pushes his thumb up the plastic and slides one free. He leans back and looks up at the case board, the dimple in his right cheek dipping and lengthening as he chews.

'Shouldn't take too long, Chief,' Steve says at my side, wiping dust and sweat from his forehead. 'You want me to link to the Bureau's server? Might be more secure.'

'It would be good if the Bureau has access, yes.'

Steve winds a length of cable around his elbow and up over the open palm of his hand. 'Any chance she's alive?'

Baz takes his call outside, his face flushed. Trouble in paradise.

I shake my head. 'I don't think so.'

Steve winds a plastic tie around the spare cable, sets it in a box by the door. 'I couldn't get hold of anyone to get those phone records you requested last night. The calls to the garden centre, was it?' He pulls a chair out, drags the keyboard from one of the computers towards him. Clicks the mouse then a short burst of tapping and he's up again and onto the next one.

'I'd be surprised if you had,' I say, giving him a half-smile. 'I'm not sure comms companies are required to keep the same hours as we do.'

'I'll get on it again as soon as I'm done here.' The ginger crown of his head disappears behind the VDU and I hear the screen hum to life. His fingers tip across the keys before he gets up again. 'One down,' he says and goes to get the next hard drive. 'Is the daughter a suspect? Margot?'

'She's certainly a person of interest.'

119

'Always a motive where family are concerned.'

I sip my coffee. 'So everyone says. You sound like you're speaking from experience, Steve?'

His head appears around the side of a computer screen. 'I'm a middle child of eight children,' he says drily.

I allow myself a short laugh at that. Add it to the things I know about him.

Baz finishes on the phone, not that he looks any better for it, and we leave Clancy to his biscuits and the case board and head out to the car to go talk to David Sutton.

Baz pulls the seatbelt across his chest. He fishes his phone from his breast pocket, swipes at the screen, sighs then puts it away. 'So we're sure he'll be in?'

'That's what Deirdre said. You okay?'

'Yeah,' he says, pushing his mouth into a smile. 'I'm grand.'

I pull out my phone, dial Keith's number. 'Howya,' Keith says, loudly down the line. 'Sorry, Frankie, hang on 'til I get a bit of shelter. I'm beyond in Blessington at the lake, working with the scuba team and there's a fierce fucking wind. Rip the nipples off ye.'

'Scuba team?'

'Never lets up. Got the boys from Harcourt Street here. We've pulled a body from the lake, woman, shot right through the head. Organized crime is alive and well in Ireland. Good to know the economy is thriving somewhere, even if we're still stuck cleaning up the mess. Let me get to the van for a bit so I can hear ye.' His breath huffs down the line as he speaks, and I imagine him strutting away to his van, white-suited, the landscape around him wild and bare. A door slams and his voice booms down the phone. 'There we are now.'

'Body?' The hope it could be Debbie is a small one. It would've been straight out of Keith's mouth if that was the case but I can't help asking him anyway.

'No. This one's blonde. Younger,' he sighs. 'Although can't be sure about that last part, she's pretty bloated.'

Two bodies. I think of the distance between Blessington and here. A good hour's drive.

'No ID then?

'Not yet.'

'Time of death?'

'Christ. Let us get her out of the water first,' he replies. 'I'll let you know as soon as.'

'Any word from your specialist in Dublin on how old those bloodstains were at the Nugents'?'

'Not yet.'

'We're on the way out to David Sutton now, so if anything comes in, it'd be good to know before we talk to him.'

'I'll give your one a bell now,' he says, then his voice rises. 'Fuck's sake, be careful with that bloody stuff, it doesn't come out of a bleedin' tap.' He's back. 'Sorry, they're good lads but you wouldn't fucking know it by the best of times. Look, I have to go. Talk to ye,' and he hangs up.

CHAPTER 10

David Sutton lives out towards the village of Avoca. The road pointing south, well travelled by tourists who want to see the oldest, active woollen mills in Ireland.

Deirdre, Mrs Ross, has given us a description of the house: *a big white yoke, you can't miss it, bit of an eyesore really*, she added. She's not wrong. A white giant, round pillars at the porch, two floors, the top floor is a box of glass that reflects the grey shades of the sky. I see the signs of the recession on the property. No boundary walls, the gate flagged by traffic cones, the drive scattered with potholes and loose gravel.

I turn in, navigate over the rough terrain and pull up at the side of the house. The edges of the property are marked out with rusted thin spokes, small scraps of white plastic flutter from the top of the poles. Grass rises out of a mound of sand at the side of the entrance where a cement mixer sits rusting. David's silver Skoda is parked at the other side of the house.

'Well they used to have money,' Baz says, squinting out at the house. 'At one time, anyways. Do we know what the father does?'

'Well, according to Deirdre, who, let's face it, seems a bit on the judgemental side, he does,' I make air quotes, '"a shedload of fuck all". He works in sales, scratch cards, she thinks.'

'We're being watched,' Baz says. He flicks his eyes to the top window, where there's a silhouette of a woman. But just as I think I can make her out, the figure slips away. 'Let's go.' Baz puts his hand to the door.

Collecting my notebook from the seat, I pause for a moment before moving to get out. I consider the possibility that we could be walking into a place that houses a killer. Because really, even though we are still developing our understanding of who Debbie Nugent was, there are only three individuals orbiting this case. And David Sutton is one of them.

'What's wrong?' Baz asks.

I look out at the house. 'Nothing.'

He follows my line of sight. 'Not the best of vibes off this place, is there?' he says.

I reach into the glove compartment, remove a bottle of water, take a mouthful then get out of the car.

The doorbell sticks when I press it. Trills through the house like a banshee. I hear steps running towards me from inside. The sound stops and the thick walnut door is pulled inwards.

In front of us is a tall, thin man. Mid-twenties. Clear, pale skin with thick dark hair cut short and shaped into a peak at the top of his head. Heavy eyebrows, and eyelashes the same deep black, mark out his features. A flattering spray of freckles crosses his nose and cheeks. He wears a blue shirt that could've been colour-matched to his eyes, the light fabric rolled up to above his elbows.

123

'David Sutton?'

'Yes,' he says, 'come in, Detectives.' He widens the door, stands aside to give us room to enter.

'Thank you,' I say.

Inside, the house doesn't feel as spacious as you'd expect. The hallway opens out into a circle but then tightens like the neck of a bottle, rooms hidden behind closed doors; the light dim, grey and cold. There is a strong citrus smell, synthetic, overly sweet on my tongue, the tang of antiseptic and beneath that a dense note of something more human; sweat and urine. It catches at the back of my throat at the end of every inhalation. Death is not coming to this house, it's already here. I can feel it in every square foot of this place, waiting to strike.

David takes us into a kitchen area. One end of the room stark and clear of furniture, the other end, a cooker – an eight-ring hob buried in a cool grey worktop. An island, around which there are four stools. There are no photographs, no pictures, no tokens of past family adventures, ornaments. The only evidence that a family lives here is an array of medication spread out along the worktop. A box of latex gloves, a few wrinkled fingers collapsed over the top as if a hand has just shed its skin. On the island a spread of papers, menus, electricity bills and a notebook with a pen, which David tidies into a stack before indicating that we should sit down.

He reaches for the kettle. 'Would you like tea?'

I sit on one of the stools, Baz remains standing on the other side of the island. 'Thanks, Mr Sutton,' I say. 'But that's okay.' Then add, as we haven't yet introduced ourselves, 'My name is Detective Frankie Sheehan and this is my colleague, Barry Harwood.'

He nods, looks down at the kettle, contemplating whether he should make tea anyway, but eventually decides not to and turns from it, drags out one of the stools and sits. 'I'm sorry I couldn't stay around yesterday. My mum is very sick and I had to cover a couple of hours at work and then we had to get her to hospital.'

'We heard. I'm sorry about your mum.'

He straightens. 'It is what it is. She's sick and won't be getting better.'

'I'm sorry,' I say again. 'Would you mind answering a few questions?'

'Sure.'

'How long have you been with Margot?'

'Eighteen months.'

I weigh up whether that's long enough to form the sort of bond you'd lie for. Kill for. The financial point that Baz raised yesterday is lingering in my mind. How are the Suttons managing? The mortgage; his mother's treatment and utility bills must be significant. It would be impossible to cover it all on David's wage at the hotel. His mother's care alone must be crippling.

'You seem to know Kristen well, too?'

'She came back at Christmas. I had dinner with them. Mum was in hospital so they invited me over and yeah . . . ' he trails off.

'And Debbie?'

He plucks at the roll of his sleeve, freeing some speck of dirt or piece of fluff. He rubs the tips of his fingers together, lets whatever it was float to the floor. 'Yes, she's always been nice to me.'

'On Saturday, you collected Kristen from the airport with Margot, right?'

'Yes.'

125

'When did you decide to do that?'

'I don't know. Friday evening maybe. I wasn't supposed to be working yesterday, so I was available. It was only after I got called in to work.'

'How did she seem to you?'

'Margot?'

'Kristen.'

'Fine.'

'She wasn't upset?'

'No.'

'What did you talk about on the way home from the airport?'

He shakes his head. 'I'm not sure. How Kristen was doing in France. She's been struggling with the language but I think she's coming along great. She can be hard on herself.' He thinks on. 'The flight. How excited Debbie would be to see her. The usual kind of thing.' He swallows. 'My mum, how she's doing, but we didn't talk about that much.'

'It must be really difficult at the moment,' I say.

There's a small silence which he doesn't try to fill.

I go on: 'Is your dad here to help?'

'No.'

'But he helps financially, yes?'

He frowns. 'I'm not sure what that has to do with Debbie?'

I give his question a moment, consider the note of defensiveness in his voice. 'Probably nothing,' I answer slowly. 'I know it might seem intrusive but we like to have a clear picture of everyone who might have interacted with Debbie lately. That includes Margot and Kristen, and because of your relationship with Margot, it also includes you.'

126

David rests his elbows on the island, sniffs, his right hand rolling over the corner of one of the bills. 'No. He doesn't. Not enough anyway. Dad hasn't stayed longer than five minutes in this house for the past six months. Because of Mum,' he says bitterly. 'He pushed for this house.' He looks to the ceiling and then out to the wild lawn beyond the windows. 'Snapped up one of those shitty mortgages, you know those ones where you voluntarily slip a rope around your neck then ask for the economy to kick the stool out from beneath your feet. One of those.' He pauses, breathes out. 'Sorry. I'm angry. At it all. We can't sell because we're in negative equity.'

'Who looks after your mum when you're at work?'

'A nurse comes in to be with her if I'm out or working. I'm on my own. We have insurance. Medical. Mum took it out years ago. Before she had an inkling she would need it. When we thought we had money.'

'Right,' I say, feeling relief sweep through me at the mention of insurance. The more I talk to David Sutton, the more I can see how absolutely beaten he is by the life he's found himself living. 'Would you mind giving us the name of the nurse?'

He gets up, pushes open a drawer below the worktop. 'Here,' he says. 'It's an agency. There are different nurses that come, depending on the rota.'

I take the card, read: NIGHTINGALE HOME HELP. *Specialist palliative nursing care at your home.* 'Thanks. Margot said she stayed with you on Wednesday night?'

'She did.'

'Is there anyone who can verify that? The nurse perhaps? Your mum?'

'No. The nurse wasn't here and my mum has been in and out of it for the past week.'

'Okay. You met Margot for a drink after her work on Thursday evening and then she stayed over again? Was the nurse covering then?'

'Yes.'

'Okay,' I pass the card to Baz, who, phone ready, walks out of the kitchen into the hallway.

'And the nurse was here yesterday while you were working?'

'Yes,' he looks out over my shoulder. 'If you're going to make a call, would you mind going into the backyard?' he shouts to Baz, 'I don't want Mum disturbed.' He points to the back door.

Baz returns from the hall, phone at his ear, opens the door and steps out into the garden.

'Sorry, yes, the nurse was here yesterday,' David continues, 'until I got the call to go to the hospital.' He watches Baz through the kitchen window as he answers.

'What time did you get back to the Nugents' from the airport?'

'Early. Eightish. I remember because we all said how hungry we were. It felt like lunchtime.'

I frown, flip through my notebook. 'And what time did you discover the crime scene?'

He spreads his hands. 'Thirty minutes after, or so. After we got in. Kristen went upstairs. Asked where Debbie was.'

'She expected Debbie to be in?'

'It seemed so.'

I put this against what Kristen has told us. We keep shaking the pan and hope, with time, we'll be left with some nugget of truth. 'That makes sense.'

He frowns. 'I suppose. Margot said Debbie might be in Dublin, still.'

'But you weren't sure?'

He swallows. 'I can't say why but something felt off. The house was too quiet. Debbie's coat was there. Things we didn't notice first but then all of a sudden did. Her trainers, the ones she usually wears, were still at the front door.'

'What did you do then?'

'Kristen began to panic. She really got het up, quite quickly. She went outside, called out for her mum, checked through the garden, even though it was pelting down outside. We knew she wouldn't be out there. Then she started going through the rooms, downstairs toilet. So both myself and Margot started looking too. Stupid places, you know, like under the sofa, in cupboards. To be honest, it was clear she wasn't in the house. Then Kristen opened the living-room door.'

He stops. His lips paling. 'Myself and Margot were coming downstairs after looking through the bedrooms. And Kristen was in the doorway to the living room. Frozen to the spot.'

'What did you see in the living room?'

'The curtains were pulled,' He watches his hands, turns one palm slowly over and back on the other, his thumb occasionally massaging the flesh. 'There was a smell. Something off. Blood on the carpet. Dried, but we knew what it was. Looked like one of those scenes on TV, a crime scene. Only this was real.'

'What time would you make that?'

He doesn't lift his head when he looks at me, eyes looking out beneath dark brows. 'Shortly before I phoned the guards.'

'Are you sure?'

'Yes. I phoned straight away. It seemed obvious that Debbie had been hurt badly.'

'You didn't think to try the local hospitals? Her work?'

'No.'

'Did you phone them afterwards?'

'No. We assumed the guards would take it from there.'

'Take it from there?'

Annoyed. 'You know, check all that. To be honest, the whole thing looked like she'd been killed, not injured. I didn't say as much to Margot and Kristen, of course not, but it's what I thought.' He meets my eyes and there is a rise of something in the pitch of his voice. 'Do you think she could be alive?'

'Like you, I don't think so.'

Baz opens the door, steps back inside, his face and hands reddened from the cold. He stamps his feet on the doormat then gives me a small nod to let me know that yes, a nurse stayed on Thursday evening, but that still doesn't help us confirm whether Margot was with him Wednesday night. Regardless, it fits the timeline David has given us for his whereabouts and it's enough to satisfy me. For the moment.

I smile at him. 'We're almost finished. Could you tell me what you did after you phoned the guards?'

He thinks for a moment. 'We waited. The guards came. Sergeant Gordon, Garda Morris and another fella. After a few questions Timmy took Margot and Kristen to the station and asked if I could go too. I said I couldn't, had a call to work. I can't afford to pass up any new shifts going.'

'That's understandable. Just going back a bit here, did Debbie go away often? To Dublin or other places?'

130

He frowns. 'She's gone to Dublin a bit more over the last couple of months but she's a homebird. Doesn't go out often at all.'

'Okay. That does sound like her,' I say. 'Can you remember if Margot mentioned whether Debbie was visiting someone?'

'No. I mean, we messed around with the idea that she might've a boyfriend. I guess both of us would like to have seen her meet someone.'

Maybe she did meet someone. Let down her guard. Let the wrong person into her life. But it goes against what we know of Debbie. She kept people out. It wasn't easy to get close to her, however, no matter her isolation now, at one stage in her life, she did have a partner. A past.

'Does Margot ever talk about her dad?'

'I asked her once, early on, shortly after we started going out, whether she wanted to find her dad and she replied, "What dad?" That was enough. The way she said it, it was clear she didn't want to discuss it further. I've never heard them mention him. Haven't seen a photograph or know his name.'

'Perhaps there are some people who don't deserve to be part of the story, right?'

He meets my eye. 'I'd agree with that.'

I stand up. 'Thank you, Mr Sutton. We do need an official statement from you. If you could make it down to the station this evening or first thing tomorrow, Mrs Ross will take one.'

He gets up, slides his thin hands into the front pockets of his jeans. 'Will do.'

In the car, Baz hands me the card. 'The nurse confirmed it, even said she's seen Margot come and go at the house over the

131

last week, so at least we know David's telling the truth about that. But I did get another call when I was out there. From Keith. Said he'd tried your phone but it went to voicemail.'

'The bloodstain?' I ask, extracting my phone from my pocket. Two missed calls are displayed on the screen.

'According to Keith's colleague, the bloodstain could be as old as two weeks.'

'Two weeks!'

Baz looks at me, nods. 'Fits the timeline we got from the garden centre. The twentieth of March being the last day, bar what Margot told us, anyone saw Debbie Nugent.'

The 20th of March. That's ten days from the last sighting of Debbie Nugent to the discovery of her murder scene. I feel numb. Part of me sensed that something wasn't right. But there's no satisfaction with this new discovery, only more questions. Namely, why would Margot Nugent not tell anyone that her mother has been missing for well over a week? How could a daughter live with her mother's murder scene for all that time? And that question gently rounds on another: why would Margot Nugent kill her mother?

'It might be why they were all so tense at the airport,' Baz says. 'And why Kristen searched the house when she got back, even though she said she expected her mother to be at work. And it explains why Kristen came home unexpectedly. She must have known something was up.'

I dial through to Steve, who answers after the first ring. 'The call about the mother being ill wasn't from Debbie or Margot,' he says. Just when a solid lead is appearing before us, it's in danger of disappearing. 'Neither of them called in, the centre called out. On the twenty-first and again on Friday where it was answered by Margot.'

I take the phone from my ear, put the call on speaker so that Baz can hear. 'I need you to look at the calls from the Nugent landline, incoming and outgoing. Look for a French number, or calls to and from France.'

'Already done,' Steve says. 'Kristen, or at least her number, called at six pm on the twentieth of March. No answer. Again the following day. No answer. Every day thereafter twice. No answer until the twenty-eighth of March, the Thursday, where the call was picked up and there was a three-minute conversation.' Two days before Kristen came home.

'Can we get a time or booking reference for Kristen's flight?'

'Sure.'

'Thank you, Steve.'

'You want me to bring Margot in?' Steve asks, pre-empting our next move.

It can be a great temptation to bring a suspect in as soon as you feel you have something on them. But all of this could still be explained away. A good lawyer could easily say that yes, Debbie was ill, yes, Margot did answer those calls. That yes, she was confused and in grief when she talked to us. We need more. We need solid evidence that Margot was directly involved in her mother's disappearance. We need something that will nail this case in court. We need a body.

'We'll need to talk to her again. But let's wait.'

'I thought you might say that,' Steve says. 'I'll keep digging.'

'Do we have a unit we could put on her?'

'I'll see if Helen can rustle up a pair of plainclothes.'

133

'Thanks.' I hang up.

I look out at David Sutton's house. Door closed, the windows empty, as if no one is living inside at all.

'If he knew, they would've had plenty of time to get their stories straight,' Baz says.

'Yes. I just didn't get the feeling that he was lying.'

'For what it's worth, I agree with you. I think David Sutton has so much going on at the moment, the world could be disintegrating around him and he'd still plough on to work every day, still sit in his kitchen and work out his bills then meet his girlfriend for a drink, all to keep the machine of normality turning.'

'The same excuse can't cover for Margot though. She's been living with that scene for almost two weeks without telling a soul,' I say.

Baz clips on his seatbelt. 'The question isn't only why she'd lie about that, it's why Margot wouldn't want to raise the alarm for her missing mother.'

'We know what the most likely answer to that is,' I say quietly.

All at once, all other possibilities drift away. Whatever avenue my brain throws up – Debbie attacked by someone else in her home; Debbie, injured and disorientated, heading out into the mountains by herself – none of it explains Margot not reporting her missing or calling the guards once she found that scene.

CHAPTER 11

The evening has closed down, night blossoming on the horizon. The road ahead disappears into the shadows, black walls of fir on either side of me. I slow down as we approach the lane, the crime-scene lights signalling the presence of the Nugent house.

Ahead, I see Morris' huge frame. He's decked out in a high-vis jacket, a hat perched high on his head. He's addressing an exhausted search team. The small group that has survived the long day. A good turnout when all is said and done. I hate the thought of quitting the search for the night. Although the chances of finding Debbie alive are negligible, the idea that her remains could be out there for another night makes me squirm.

I park up, turn off the ignition and get out. The K-9 unit have been called. Handlers leading the dogs back into their crates for a well-earned rest in preparation for an early start tomorrow.

Baz gets out of the car, comes around to my side. 'Clancy is waiting in the house. He wants a walkthrough of the scene.'

'Tell him I'll be in shortly,' I say.

I go to walk towards Morris but Alex catches my eye and waves me over.

'Hey, anything?' I begin, although I know the answer.

He shakes his head. Face pale, shadows under his eyes. 'We've covered grids three and two,' he says, looking out beyond the tree line. 'Just couldn't get the last one in before the light went.' He drags in a shaky breath.

'You did well.'

'She could be anywhere. Normally, you'd want hundreds covering a search like this. We're barely hitting fifty. And then there are the old quarries . . . ' he breaks away, lifts a hand reddened with cold and pushes it through his hair.

'I'll see if we can draft in more people for tomorrow. Otherwise, keep to procedure. To what we know. This was a crime of impulse. Whoever it was, will have wanted to dispose of her body quickly.'

'Any more leads?' he asks.

'We've had bloodstain analysis through and it's showing the scene as up to two weeks old. We can narrow that down to ten days, given the last sighting from the garden centre.'

'Jesus.'

'It might help with the search. It makes me more certain that we're looking somewhere close by. Near a track or a road. She won't have had the strength to drag a body further in.'

'She?'

I don't have the heart to reply.

'So Margot lived with that all this time?' He looks towards the house.

'Yes.'

He shakes his head. 'I spoke to Georgina Waters who runs the fuel station out the road. She was asking about the search and said that she'd thought it odd that Debbie hadn't been in for her regular weekly refill. Said she'd usually be in on a Wednesday and fill the tank, regardless of how much juice she had, as a matter of habit. Never knew her not to stop by unless she was away.'

'Did she give you a date on when she was last in?'

'Yes.' He removes a notebook from his pocket, flicks through the pages. 'Here we are. Wednesday the twentieth. That fits, right? Given the new timeline we're working with?'

I look down on the information. Make a mental note of the details. 'It does, yeah.'

He takes another shaky breath. Pinches the bridge of his nose. 'Man, I'm tired.'

'She'd do that on her way in or out of work?' I ask. 'Fill with fuel?'

'On her way home, I think she said.' He stifles a yawn with his hand. 'We could run the fuel in the car maybe? I know the chances are slim but if Margot disposed of the body using Debbie's car, we might be able to calculate how far she went out.'

'I'll let auto know,' I say. 'Go home. We can finish up here.'

'Thanks,' he says, his voice dropping a little. 'I suppose there's no point in asking you for a drink?'

'I can't. There's still a lot to do here.'

'Thought so.' He gives me a final thin smile then says, 'Well, see you tomorrow, then.' He turns towards his car but I call him back.

'Yes?'

'Thanks,' I say.

137

'No bother,' he says then moves off again, head bent, blowing warm air onto his hands.

I walk up the drive to the Nugent house. The damp air has lifted, a stiff breeze sharp as blades on my skin. I squint against the crime-scene lights, pick out the shadow of the rockery, the dips in the lawn. A few of the uniforms are still prodding over the soil, looking for fresh graves in the flowerbeds. Or hopeful that the murder weapon might have been thrown over the boundary of the property and into the long grasses beyond.

Inside the house, it's as cold as the outdoors and I smack my hands together to get them warm. Baz is at the kitchen table standing next to Jack Clancy. Both of them looking over a newspaper. The dishes that were along the counters and piled high in the sink have been cleared away, the bin emptied. Crime scene having gotten everything they need.

Jack looks up when he hears me approach. 'Frankie. You need to see this,' he says and points to the open paper. 'Look at the neck on that!'

I do as directed and peer down on the double spread. The headline traverses both pages: DAUGHTER DRESSED TO IMPRESS PARTIES WHILE MOTHER STILL MISSING, PRESUMED DEAD. Embedded in the text are two large images of Margot. One a selfie taken with a female friend. The friend is blonde, her hairline low and sweeping upwards in a high curve with what my mother would call a cowlick. She's pretty, in the way that youth makes everyone look better. Margot's chin is hooked on the girl's shoulder, her grey eyes twinkling at the camera, lips curved in a soft smile, a sheen of sweat over her forehead. Behind them, white, pink and blue neon lights illuminate the dark interior of a nightclub.

138

While Baz and I were sitting over the grisly photographs and statements surrounding her mother's murder, barely a few hours after we had interviewed her, Margot Nugent was busy throwing shots of vodka down her throat and posing for selfies. Jack looks back at me for my reaction and I don't think my expression disappoints.

'Tell me,' he says, 'who goes out and gets half-cut with friends when their mother's murder scene has just been found in their house?'

I feel like I've been caught out. I've grossly underestimated Margot Nugent. I have an urgent want to drive straight out to the B&B she's staying in, slap steel around her wrists and question her until she tells the truth. I breathe out. Keep my emotions in check. Try to keep a clear head.

I meet Jack's eyes. 'Who's the other woman?'

'Priscilla Bryant.' He dips his hands in his pocket and produces a piece of paper. 'Think it might be good to have the chats with her. Margot may not be on social media, but Ms Bryant loves nothing better than a good ol' selfie and has put up a rake of photos of Margot. Turns out Margot's been having a bit of a time of it lately.'

I tell him about the scene, how long Margot's been living with it and he straightens, thick eyebrows up. 'No remorse, no grief. That says psychopath to me.'

Looking at the images on this newspaper, I'm thinking he's right.

'Where is she now?' he asks.

'In a B&B on the Wicklow Road. With her sister, Kristen. I've sent a unit out this afternoon to keep tabs on her, they're due to check in soon.'

'Well, don't be fucking messing about. We could be weeks searching these hills for Debbie Nugent. Mark my words,' he jabs the paper with his finger. 'That one knows exactly where her mammy is and we need to make her talk.' He reaches into his pocket, removes a slip with an address on it and passes it to me. 'Get out to that Priscilla one before she starts spinning stories to the press – although I'd say we're a good day too late for that – and get the low-down on exactly what Margot thought of her mother. From someone other than Margot. If we get enough morsels of the truth, Margot might save us the job of this search and tell us where the body is.'

I nod. Although, it's never that easy. Without a body, without something more, something that puts Margot Nugent in that room, weapon raised and with motive to kill, I suspect she'll explain all this away with a tear in her eye and a wave of her hand.

'Okay,' I say, fingering the slip of paper with Priscilla's address. Looking over at the living-room door, I try to picture Margot calmly pulling her mother's body out of the room and loading it in the car. 'How does a woman in her twenties bludgeon her mother to death, then load her into a car on her own?'

Clancy straightens, his stomach straining against his waistband. Hand pushing back his long coat and finding his pocket. 'She'd have had all the time in the world,' echoing my words from earlier. 'Sure lookit where are we? Who'd have seen her?'

I can see the eagerness in Clancy's eyes to tie this up quickly. To call Margot back into that station, sit her down and question her until she breaks. It's a tricky juncture switching from casual interview to interrogation and I always prefer to have something irrefutable up my sleeve before going in for the arrest.

It's difficult to create a feeling of trust with a suspect, if you're bringing them in every second day to ask them the same questions, with nothing else to push them into giving different answers. You want evidence that can't be shaken or explained away. Or as close to it as you can. At the least, in a murder investigation, you want a body.

'Did you get anything from your friend?' I ask Clancy.

'Fitz? Dennis?'

I nod.

'Nothing. Says Debbie was a quiet one. Wouldn't have known her well, only to see and that in all the years he'd worked these parts she never had so much as a speeding ticket.'

'But then,' Baz frowns, still stuck on Margot's image in the newspaper, 'as you said before, Frankie, why not clean the living room too, if she'd all that time? Now we know she'd even longer. Ten days.'

Clancy huffs in a way that says, does it fucking matter. He closes the paper, folds it and stuffs it lengthways into his coat pocket. 'Lookit, someone here knows something. Will've seen something,' he says, then raises his voice with a shot of optimism. 'Keep this easy on the budget. Talk to people and we'll find out what happened soon enough,' he says and sweeps out, grumbling about the fucking cold and how we won't be seeing the sun's arse again this year.

I think of Deirdre Ross at the station, her commentary on Debbie, her sympathy for David and her need to taint every morsel of information with more than a slant of gossip. I'm not sure Clancy's tactic will give us a clearer picture. Everyone does know everyone here. That's the problem. Loyalties and betrayals are dished out with equal weight and both of them have the potential to muddy our waters.

Priscilla Bryant ushers us into the front room of her parents' house. She sits on the edge of the sofa, tugs the thick towelling of her dressing gown closed over her equally thick pyjamas. Her hair is pulled back off her face in a messy bun, full face of make-up, dark sweeps of bronzing powder beneath her narrow cheekbones, a fierce pair of eyebrows drawn in wide, thick angles over her blue eyes.

She waits, watching us as we sit down. A nervous smile on her lips. Baz has settled his notebook on a table. He barely has time to remove his pen before she speaks.

'Sorry about the cut of me, I was getting ready for bed when yis called. Wasn't the sharpest today,' she starts.

'We appreciate you taking the time to speak with us, Priscilla. I know it's late,' I say.

'Prissy, please,' she says, then adds in a coy sort of way. 'Everyone calls me it and it's grown on me.' She pauses. 'Is this about last night? I never meant for those pictures to be used in that way. I'm really upset about it, actually.' She lifts a hand to the neck of her dressing gown, draws it closed in her fist. 'It's a violation. I never had anything like that happen before. I've taken them all down now. Started getting calls this morning. Mammy was hopping. Said that Margot was a bad influence on me; what kind of girl goes out when her mother's lying dead in a ditch somewhere?' She lowers her voice, flicks her eyes at the door as if Mrs Bryant was due to appear at any moment, even though she knows she's out. 'I've had to shut my account down. The abuse, I've been getting all day.'

142

'Have you known Margot long?'

She frowns, shocked that we aren't here to talk about her Insta account. 'Since we were kids. At school. I know it probably looks like I'm always putting up photos of myself but it's just a bit of fun. I'm not one of *those* people. Only I never had many friends at school, and so it feels good when people like things that I put up.' She glances at me then adds. 'Margot was my only friend really back then. What people are saying about her can't be true. She loved her mother. And Debbie doted on her,' and off she goes again. 'I slag her off about it all the time. You know she didn't even have to get a real job until she started working at the hotel, and that was only because David persuaded Debbie it'd be good for her. Used to make me so jealous that she could be at home all day, doing what she liked.' She snatches a quick breath before she passes out. 'I work at the local radio station. Do the traffic. But occasionally I assist on producing. Gather interview research,' she says, giving herself a nod in recognition of this achievement. She keeps her eyes on Baz's notebook on the table, watching what he puts down. Her face brightens then the sharp corners of her drawn-on eyebrows come up, high five in the centre of her forehead, and she waves at the pen, prompting Baz to write this down. 'We've been doing a lot of shouting out for Debbie on the radio. I made it my business to get it mentioned. For people to keep an eye out. Every newsround and travel slot.'

'That's good. Thank you,' I draw breath to ask her another question but she beats me to it.

'Debbie did all the cooking, drove Margot wherever she wanted. The papers have it all wrong. Why would Margot want to hurt her?'

143

'Did Margot talk about Debbie last night? Mention anything to you about how long she'd been missing?'

'No.' She frowns. 'We went out to let our hair down. I text her for a few drinks, thought it might take her mind off it. We hadn't really planned on going clubbing but . . . ' she shrugs. ' . . . that's how it goes. But no, neither of us mentioned it. We're very in tune like that. I knew she wouldn't want to talk about it.'

'How about Kristen? David?'

'They're so angry with her. I called her, Margot, this morning, to see how she was feeling after I saw the papers. Kristen had banned her from leaving that crumby B&B they're staying in. Margot says David wants a break. That he can't deal with all this with his mother dying. Which, and I said this to Margot, is fair enough, to be honest.'

I hear Baz scratching away at the notebook, unsure what he's getting from this but hoping there's something.

'Is she really dead?' Priscilla asks suddenly.

'It looks that way.'

Her hand covers her mouth. 'Oh,' she says. 'Oh, that's terrible. Poor Margot.' Then her eyes widen. 'Is that why you're here? *You* think that Margot did something to Debbie?'

'Margot didn't happen to mention that Debbie had not been home in over a week, did she?'

Her eyes drop to her lap, a tear tracks down her face, washing a pale line through her make-up. She shakes her head. 'No.'

'Have you seen each other over the last couple of weeks?'

'Well, yes. We went out Paddy's Day, and again the next day,' she pauses, bites her lip. 'Then she phoned again on the Thursday for drinks out.'

144

The day after Debbie was last seen. Thursday the twenty-first. 'Yes?' I prompt her.

'I did think it unusual. To be out so much in one week. She doesn't like to go out often, despite the fact she's beating off fellas with a stick when she comes out.'

'Oh?'

'Oh yes. I mean, Margot's shy and she has David and all but she likes a good old flirt.' She gives Baz a meaningful look, purses her lips briefly. 'Who doesn't?' She sighs, arranging the edges of her dressing gown over her knees. 'But Debbie worries and Margot doesn't like to worry her.'

'Did they argue?'

'Never. I've never even known Margot to fight with anyone, let alone do something like this.' She sniffs, rubs her sleeve under her nose. 'To be honest, she's a bit hopeless, or Debbie lets her be.' She looks up, her eyes red, swollen. 'She'll be lost without her,' she sighs.

But Margot doesn't seem lost. In fact, if her night out is anything to go by, Margot Nugent seems absolutely fine.

It's quiz night at the hotel; great, if it wasn't ten o'clock on a Monday night. The quizmaster's voice comes up through the floor. Loud enough to stop my train of thought but not loud enough so I can hear the questions. I'm not sure which is more grating.

Another whole day searching for Debbie's body gone. I put in a request for help from the armed forces, along with a hopeful suggestion that a search-and-rescue helicopter wouldn't go amiss, but I know we'll get neither, especially now we know

145

Debbie has been missing for ten days. Pennies and resources get somewhat sparse when dealing with an ageing crime scene. I joined the team today, expanded the search out, walked slowly across ragged terrain over and again, pushing brush and branches aside with a stick; the ground, hard from a late frost, sending cold creeping up through my legs until my muscles were stiff and aching. But apart from a crushed plastic sandwich box and a sodden woolen glove, we found nothing.

I straighten the pillows under my head, pull at the covers which appear to have been stapled to the corners of the bed. Kicking them free, I wrap them around my feet. It's cold. Or I'm cold, tiredness taking hold. The warmth of my laptop spreads through my abdomen. I open the file, stretching out a hand to the tea-tray on the locker, fingers feeling blindly for another of the hotel's oaty, raisin, harvest bickies, then play the latest CCTV Helen's managed to unearth.

Debbie's face turns full to the camera, almost like she knows I'm watching her. And, although it's impossible to make out, I imagine I recognize the look in her eyes. A pleading glance to whoever is watching. But I know it can't be the case. The time stamp in the corner says 12th of March, a Tuesday. The location: Store Street, Dublin. Eight days before she was last seen. She goes on. A brisk walk and then another look over her shoulder as if there might be someone following her. I slow the footage, study the few pedestrians that move around her, by her. Two men sit in a car parked up on the other side of the road. Despite the rain, the window is down. The driver puts a cigarette between thin lips and lights it. There's a guard, pushing a bike along the pavement behind her. The guard does not look up, can't know the fate in store for the middle-aged woman speeding up the street ahead of her.

I watch the footage two more times, slowing it down, trying to learn something, anything new from it, although I know it won't answer any of my questions. The only thing I'm left with is a nagging sense that Debbie's not happy in this footage. She looks tense. She looks like she's being pursued.

CHAPTER 12

We move where a case takes us but sometimes there isn't a clear path. At the moment, the bottle has been spun, its mouth pointing to Margot Nugent. All she needs to do is reach out, re-spin that bottle and tell us why she failed to report her mother missing. How she could live with such a murderous scene and not tell anyone.

I think on the many complications of this investigation. There's still no sign of Debbie's remains. It will be difficult to prosecute a no-body case. I've only known one to get through the courts in Dublin. But Keith has given me the final findings on the Nugent house: a dilute droplet of blood on the pillow in Margot's room, matching Debbie's profile, and another smudge on the underside of the bannisters where someone's hand left its mark while ascending the stairs. Between these findings, the car and the crime scene we might have enough. But still I'm hesitant about an arrest. If I'm honest, I can see that these are my own issues. Part of me wants to hold out for Margot's innocence because I don't want to face the fact that a daughter could harm her mother; to see a family break apart through murder. But this family is already broken, and no matter how tragic it all is, and it is fucking tragic – for everyone involved – I have to remind myself that I'm not here to protect Margot. I'm here to get justice for Debbie.

I sit with this turning in my head while I wait for Margot Nugent to appear. Kristen set up a Facebook page in an effort to find her mother, but shut it down within a few hours when a barrage of abuse filled up the comments, photographs and videos appearing of Margot out in the local pub, drunk, hair loose, a drink clutched in her hand, eyes closed as she moved to music. These photographs were dated, Thursday twenty-first of March. And then more photographs of her out with Prissy. David appears in some too, in images from after the discovery of the crime scene. Hand over his face as he walks towards the entrance of the hotel he works at. Questions surrounding motive. Whether he could be involved. Sources saying that his money troubles might have persuaded him to look for another stream of income: Debbie's home, which would be set to go to her daughters on her death. The same photos are now on the front of every newspaper in the country. When I went through the press coverage this morning it was with the very clear mental image of the commissioner's face slowly tightening in anger as she read the headlines.

The search team are becoming disheartened. Some of the volunteers have called in at the station, hats literally in hands, shaking their heads, voices low, regretful, ashamed, asking quietly to take their name off the list. That they don't have the time to help out any more. The initial anger at what's happened, the panic that a killer could still be among them fading fast. Maybe Debbie had injured herself, maybe she has simply left town. She was always something of an outsider. But mostly it's the idea of Margot as killer that has put them off. An unnatural killing. Even if it's to find the victim's body, they want to steer clear.

Margot has pushed us into moving before we're ready. The media pressure is what speaks. The public cry for a head. Donna Hegarty says, give them one. And so we're bringing her in.

I stir a sugar into my coffee then stretch my legs out beneath the table, massage the scar down my thigh. I peer out the café window on the gentle bustle of the town. On the surface, the town moves and creaks along in its various cogs, the same mechanical patterns every day, every night, the only changing faces the tourists that pull up to take in the views or navigate the numerous walkways over the hills and mountains. But as much as the town appears to be consistent, it changes in an instant; a quick slant of sunshine from between parted clouds or the purpling of the mountains under a sudden roll of rain can switch the atmosphere from sunny and quaint to dark and claustrophobic in seconds.

When I was little, we once holidayed in the Wicklow mountains. I can't remember which part exactly, only if I were to come across it again, I'd recognize the toy-box cottage we stayed in – one of six that sat on the lip of a lake. I remember the magnificence of the mountains around us, the lake pooled in the centre, as if a giant hand had scooped out a chunk of land from the middle of the earth.

The cottages were occupied by other holidaymakers, hikers, newlyweds, an elderly couple wanting some 'air'. We cycled, read, played games, walked, picnicked, but at some point in the week I fell ill, some virus in my stomach leaving me clutching my middle with pain, sweat rising on my skin. I was in bed for two days and, on one of those evenings, too hot to stay under the covers, I lay on top of the bedclothes, listening to the low mumble of my parents as they enjoyed the evening sun at the front of the house. Wanting so much to join them, I got out of bed and pushed the curtains back, opening the window a fraction so I could feel and hear their company. I climbed back into bed and focused on their voices, still low, but I could make out the occasional word, a shot of warm laughter from my dad, and it made me feel better.

I must have drifted off that night because I woke to a dull thud on the window. I sat up, not sure if I'd dreamed the sound. Beyond the pane the sun was beginning to bleed over the high crests of the mountains, the sky turning burnt orange and casting the hills in a shimmering pink hue. I got out of bed, went to the window and found on the glass a thin streak of blood, narrowing to a tail at the end like a comet.

I left the room, the house, walked around to the window. Below it, head down, a lustrous iridescent mix of black, emerald and white feathers, was a magpie. It sat there, no movement. I couldn't tell whether it was dead or stunned. But as I reached it, it moved; a round black eye turning towards me. Then, with a flap, it lifted away and I watched it disappear into the trees in the distance. I went to return to the house but some black thing caught my eye. Another bird, smaller, neck turned, its legs drawn up, claws curled, tiny wings folded over its back, broken and dead; a fledgling starling. And I understood what

151

my eyes had not. I felt fooled that I had given even a moment of compassion to that magpie and stared down at the true victim. The young starling, driven against my window while trying to escape a predator.

It's her red hair that catches my eye. She steps out of a grocery store, her shopping stuffed into brown paper bags, at least two newspapers rolled in a fat wedge beneath her arm. She doesn't see the customers come to the door after she leaves, doesn't see them gathering, staring after her. A teenager has his phone out already, snapping the back of Margot's head as she moves down the street.

As much as I'd wanted to hold off bringing Margot in until we had more, I find myself eager to question her now. Steve has retrieved messages from her old phone. The one we found in the shed. The last message, dated almost a year ago. The phone must have been sitting out there for a long time. The sim was somewhat degraded but the memory chip brought up a sequence of messages between Kristen and Margot.

Margot: *I think you were right.*

Kristen: *About what?*

Margot: *The necklace David gave me for my birthday is missing. Can't find your mood ring. I know I left them in my jewellery box. I was careful.*

Kristen: *Did you ask her?*

Margot: *No.*

Margot: *Maybe I lost them. Sounds like me.*

Kristen: *Sounds like Mum's up to her old tricks again.*

Margot: *Don't.*

Suddenly, the quirks of the family's relationship do not look like quirks at all but something more sinister. I have some sympathy for Margot. She'll not have an easy time of it. Already the media are delighting in her story. Or rather the image of her story. And the public will not hear a bad word against Debbie, a woman who, it would seem to me now, also had her dark side.

I finish up my coffee, leave payment on the table. Clancy's car is across the street, Baz in the passenger seat next to him. I imagine I can see the blustering rage on Clancy's face even from here. The morning papers have not been kind to Margot Nugent but this time we're dragged in there too. No body. No Debbie. What are we doing? The stages of our investigation summarized: locals interviewed, embellishing or playing down the questions we asked. All out there in print to salivate over. Although, out of the entire hideous mix, I think it was the shot of Clancy mid-swing at the local golf course that did it; his old-time mate, Sergeant Dennis Fitzsimons standing behind him, leaning on the handle of his driver, white golf shoes crossed at the ankles.

Garda assistant commissioner plays golf while Debbie Nugent remains missing.

The heat from the media had Donna Hegarty on the phone to me this morning and she was hearing none of my arguments. A gentle reminder from me that a no-body homicide was very difficult to take to court caused Hegarty's voice to rise to such a pitch I had to hold the phone away from my ear. *Bring her in, Sheehan*, she hissed. *Put the pressure on and get a bloody confession.*

I check my phone once more, picturing Alex exhausted and grainy-eyed, but pushing on through the slicing cold with the search. Factoring in her return from the petrol station that Wednesday, the remaining fuel in Debbie's car when we seized it

153

suggests just under four kilometres travelled. I swallow down my concerns. Wherever Debbie is, she'll have taken crucial evidence with her. But in these conditions, and with time sifting away, the likelihood of us discovering her remains diminishes by the hour.

The wind lifts the hair back from my face as I step out onto the street. Clancy and Baz exit the car at the same time and we begin after Margot. Whatever groceries she has in her bags right now won't be seeing the inside of a cupboard any time soon.

CHAPTER 13

We settle ourselves into the interview room. It could almost put the Bureau to shame with its feeling of newness: ivory walls so clean and unmarked you'd tell yourself you could still smell the paint fumes in the air. It's a simple layout though. There's no two-way window, no video feed, a standard black cassette recorder sits on the table. Against the far wall, a magazine table on which sits a stack of plastic cups and a jug of water. I welcome the sight of three deep-padded chairs around the table, a definite upgrade on the hard blue plastic ones in our makeshift incident room.

Steve is standing on a stool in the far corner, black trainers off and set neatly to the side, his feet splayed out for balance, toes gripping the edges of the seat. His thin arms are over his head, body stretched towards the ceiling where he's fitting a camera so we can record the interview. Body language, gestures and discomfort not always easy to pick up when replaying the audio of an interrogation. If a picture paints a thousand words, a moving one can tell the whole story.

Steve runs the wires up the corner wall; around his wrist a roll of duct tape that he brings to his teeth every now and then, ripping off a chunk and using it to secure the wires to the corner walls, a slice of pale pink flesh, tight as the skin of a drum appearing from beneath his black T-shirt every time he reaches up. Eventually, he steps down, bends and runs the wire along the floor until he feeds the end into a connection on the wall.

'I'll secure it properly later,' he says to me, dusting off his palms, his long fingers snapping against each other. 'This will have to do for now. It's wireless, so we'll be able to pick it up in the incident room.'

'Good work, Steve. Thanks. Keep watch and feed back with anything from the search.'

Steve gives me a nod of his narrow chin, then leaves the room.

Baz pulls out one of the chairs, sits himself into it and pats the armrests with satisfaction. 'These will do the job,' he says, then he springs out of the chair again and goes to the jug of water, pours two cups.

I open my notes, look over the new information we have on Debbie Nugent and our newly arrested suspect, her daughter Margot. Helen has enclosed a copy of Debbie's marriage certificate. Finally, we have something on her background. Debbie Tyne married on the 17th of December 1985 to Rory Nugent at Dublin's registry office on Grand Canal Street Lower. The name of Kristen's school, St Mary's Primary School in Clondalkin, has given us an idea of her previous address. A chink of light on Debbie's past. Baz has conducted his own inquiries on Debbie's financial situation. Mortgage payments met and still going out but up to date. Savings of twenty grand in the Credit Union.

156

He places a cup of water in front of me, reclaims his seat.

'Thanks,' I say.

The sound of footsteps comes down the hall and I close the file.

Margot appears in the doorway, Joe at her back. She's wearing a loose white shirt beneath a soft cardigan of rich, vibrant green. She turns towards Joe so he can remove the cuffs, and three tiny buttons in a neat line up the cuff of her sleeve wink gold as she lifts her hands towards him.

'Thanks, Joe,' she says, when he slips the cuffs free. He tips his head as if he were touching the brim of a trilby, waits for her to take a few steps inside then disappears out of the doorway, pulling the door closed softly on his way.

'Hi, Margot,' I say. 'Come in, take a seat.'

'Hello, Detectives,' she says, glancing at each of us in turn. She sounds relaxed but there is a stiffness to how she walks to the chair, her hands clasped at her front as if still bound by the cuffs. She sits down slowly, not fully back but on the edge, spine straight. She rests the bundle of her hands carefully on the table. I notice her nails are bitten down to small round-topped stubs, the skin dry and cracked around the nail beds.

'Margot, would you like a lawyer?'

A quick shake of her head. 'No, thanks.'

'DCS Frankie Sheehan and Detective Barry Harwood interviewing Margot Nugent, April third 2013. The time is ten-thirty.' I pause for a beat, look to Margot. 'You ready to start, Margot?'

She moistens her lips with the tip of her tongue. 'Yes.'

'Can you tell us what happened to your mum?' I ask.

Pale auburn lashes fall to her cheeks. 'I don't know. I'm sorry.'

157

'When was the last time you saw her?'

Pale grey eyes look up at me. 'Like I told you, Wednesday.'

'Wednesday the twenty-seventh of March?'

'Yes.' More confident.

There is always a moment of relief when you hear the first lie. The suspect sticking to their story which clashes with the truth as you know it. 'Okay. I know we've been through this before but we're having some trouble pinning the timeline down and it's vital that we get it right. Do you understand?'

'Yes.'

'Could you tell us, in your own words, what you did from waking on the Wednesday you last saw your mum to when she was reported missing?'

I challenge anyone to recall a day in detail without constant turnarounds, tangents, additions and false starts. For most of us, the days all meld into one. Unless something happened. Something significant. You murder your mother, you're going to remember every waking moment.

'Yes.' She takes a breath, readies herself. 'I had breakfast,' she starts, then thinks better of it, shakes her head. 'I got up.' She checks with me that she's got things in the right order and I give her a nod of encouragement.

'I got up with my alarm at seven-fifteen. I had a shower, got dressed for work and headed downstairs. It was cold, so I put on my coat, my scarf. There's no point in turning up the heating if you want a quick blast of heat in our house. It takes a millennium to get going, the system is so bloody ancient. Mum had intended to get it done,' she catches herself. 'Sorry.'

'Go on.'

158

'I put my coat on, my scarf,' she says again. 'I had a couple of slices of toast for breakfast. Went upstairs to do my hair, put my face on. When I came back down, Mum was at the kitchen table. She'd made a pot of coffee and was drinking a large mug of it, out of her favourite mug.' She looks up. 'It says World's Best Mum on it, I got it for her when I was little. She never drinks out of anything else.'

'Did you speak?'

'Not much. Said good morning, that kind of thing. And then I gathered up my bag as I could hear David pulling up outside. I gave her a kiss and said goodbye.' She retreats into herself now. Her gaze frozen on that final image. 'I can still see her sitting there, looking sleepy, in her PJs and dressing gown.'

Baz holds up his pen like a child in a classroom wanting the teacher's permission to speak. 'Oh sorry, hold on there,' he says, and Margot looks to him. He makes an exaggerated expression of confusion on his face. 'I'm not sure if I'm remembering right but I thought you said your mum left before you that morning.'

'Did I?'

He flicks back through his notes. 'Here we are. You said: "She went out, I think." Then stated that that was at seven-thirty,' he says, helpfully.

'No, I got that wrong. I left first,' she replies.

'You're sure about that?'

'Yes.'

Baz bobs his head, pulls back. 'Grand so.' He looks to me, 'Sorry, go on.'

'Anyway, David drove me to work. The traffic wasn't half bad

159

that morning and we were at the hotel well before eight am. I got out of the car and headed inside.'

'Did you and David talk about anything in the car?'

She frowns. 'Oh gosh, I really can't remember. I think we had the radio on again. The sports. It's usually what David listens to when he drives me to work.'

'But you can't be sure that day.'

She brightens. 'I think I fell asleep,' she says. 'Yes, it was so cold and when I got into the car, David had the heating turned right up and I think I drifted off.'

She pauses, takes another breath before she goes on. 'I get in, say hi to Emma on reception. Go to the kitchens. Get a chamomile tea. Leave my bag and coat in my locker. Oh no, hang on. I checked my phone, for messages, that it's on silent, that kind of thing.'

'Were there any?' Baz asks.

Her head snaps in his direction, looks at him as if she's surprised he's still there. 'Any what?'

'Messages?'

She frowns again. 'One from Kristen. Sending me her flight details for Saturday morning. I forwarded it on to David. I guess I was hoping he'd offer to do an airport pick-up with me. I didn't want to ask him outright. He's a lot on at the moment. With his mum.' When she mentions his mum, her voice drops to an almost whisper. A look of sadness widens in her eyes. It takes all my reserve not to scream at her that her own flesh and blood is likely dead.

'Did he answer?' Baz asks.

'Not then. He text me later, that afternoon, suggesting we collect her together as a surprise.'

'That's nice,' Baz says.

A smile softens the corners of her mouth. 'It was. Then I worked my shift and left just after four.'

'After work?' I move her along.

'I went to David's.'

'You stayed over and then went into work the following day?' I prompt.

'Yes. More of the same, I'm afraid.'

'But you went home that afternoon?'

'No. I stayed at David's again.'

'You didn't hear from your mum?'

'No.'

'The next morning? Friday?' I ask.

A flash of something, confusion, amusement, irritation flies across her face. Too quick for me to really get a sense of it. 'I went to work.'

'Tell us what you did after work. Did you go home on Friday evening? Did you see Debbie then?' Baz asks with impressive patience.

'No. I thought I'd missed her again.'

'Is that usual?' I ask. 'For her to go out without telling you or leaving a note. Dinner?'

She doesn't look at me, keeps her head bent low so that I'm looking only at the curved top of her head, fiery red hair glinting under the fluorescence. 'I did think it was strange, but we're both adults. I thought she'd just prolonged her stay in Dublin. I wasn't worried or anything.'

161

'Okay,' Baz says, nodding at me as if persuading me into Margot's version of events. 'You have to respect each other's space, right?'

'Yes,' Margot says, but her voice has lost its conviction.

'And so, it would have been, what? Three days overall, from when you alerted us to when you last saw her?' Baz continues.

'Three and a bit until we . . . until we found the room.' She picks at a flake of dry skin on the edge of her finger, pulls it free and lets it fall onto the table before sweeping it to the floor. 'Is Kristen here?'

'She's not, no,' Baz says.

'Could I call her?'

'We're almost finished here. Can you wait until after our questions?' He keeps his voice as light and bright as a summer's day, not wanting Margot to sink just yet; a call to her sister will only bring lawyers.

She examines the rest of her nails, finding another piece of loose skin and seizing it between her fingertips. 'Only, I'm supposed to be meeting David for lunch and I need to let him know if I can't make it.' She looks up, eyes hopeful. 'Or I could call him, if that was possible?'

Baz gives her a patient smile. 'I'll see what I can do about a phone call. Do you think you can answer a few more questions?'

She swallows. 'Sure.'

I straighten, draw her attention to me. 'Margot, why didn't you report your mum missing?'

She looks to Baz, a line of confusion deepening in her brow. 'I told you, I thought she was okay.'

'But you didn't,' I say. 'You knew she wasn't okay. You haven't

162

seen your mother for close to two weeks. Her work, the garden centre, said they called you and you told them she was ill on the twenty-second. Why did you do that?'

She stills. A pink flush builds over her skin. She drops her head down again in an attempt to hide it but I watch the flush creep, colour the pale strip of flesh that divides the fall of her deep, red hair. 'I can't remember. I think she was ill. She might have asked me to.'

'Your mum asked you to phone in sick?'

'Yes,' she mutters. 'She wanted a few days away and knew she wouldn't get the time off.'

'So she wasn't ill?'

She takes a quick breath, keeps her eyes down. 'No. She wanted some time off.'

'But she had holidays booked for the week after. That doesn't make sense. She was about to have an entire week off. You told us she left for Dublin last Wednesday, the twenty-seventh of March. But there's not a single person who recalls seeing your mother at Ballyalann bus station. I imagine you know how difficult it is not to be seen in your local town?'

'I don't know.'

'We have footage of the bus stop though. Footage of your mum waiting for a bus to Dublin.'

She looks up at this and the hope on her face makes me blink. 'Really?'

'It dates from the sixth of March, not the twenty-seventh as you told us. There is no evidence that your mother took a bus to Dublin last Wednesday. There is no evidence because she didn't take a bus to Dublin on that date. And I believe she didn't or couldn't take that bus, because she was dead.'

This time the colour drops from her face, recedes like water on sand. She looks up at me, a pleading expression wavering on her face. I feel a sudden and alarming jolt of sympathy that throws me for a second and I force myself to keep eye contact.

I open the file and remove the list of texts that Steve retrieved from Margot's old phone. I slide it across the table.

'Do you recognize the numbers here?'

Her tongue touches her bottom lip. 'Yes.'

'Whose are they?'

She rests a finger on the form. 'This is my old number,' then moves it down slightly. 'This is Kristen's.'

'Do you remember sending and receiving these text messages?'

She is quiet for a moment, her eyes pinned to the page in front of her then eventually she whispers: 'I think so.'

'What do they refer to?'

'I lost some of my things.' Her hands go to her throat. 'A necklace David gave me. The items you showed me, that you found.'

I reach over, point to the last line on the page. 'What did Kristen mean by this: "Sounds like Mum's up to her old tricks again?"'

'I don't know,' she murmurs, and she chances a look up at me, tries to assess how easily I might be thrown off this line of questioning.

'I think you do,' I say. 'Did your possessions go missing often, move about, or did you put them down only to find they were no longer there?'

164

'Yes.' Again, voice so low and quiet I worry that the tape won't pick it up.

'How about the rock through the window? Had that happened before?'

This time her teeth come out over her bottom lip, they press down and I see the skin beneath them blanch.

'Margot?'

'Yes?'

'Has it happened before?'

'Yes. The front window.'

'How long ago?'

She clears her throat. 'Before Kristen left for France.'

Taking the list of text messages, I slip them back into the file and her shoulders droop a little, relief that she's not being pushed on it further. But I don't need to. Slowly, a motive is forming. A mother who spent years controlling her daughters, using underhand manipulative tactics to get what she wanted. Kristen moved far away. Margot though was an easier target. More reliant, being the youngest. Softer in nature, perhaps. Or so Debbie thought. There's always a breaking point, and sometime two weeks ago, Margot broke.

A sharp knock at the door makes all three of us jump. Steve's head pokes around it. 'Chief,' he says and it's all he needs to say. I know he won't have interrupted our interrogation unless it was important.

I shoot Baz a quick glance and he gives a tiny nod in response. He gets up out of the chair. 'Would you like some water, Margot?'

She's watching me warily as I scoop up my notes. 'Yes,' she clears the stickiness from her throat. 'Thank you.'

165

'Not a bother at all,' I hear Baz reply as I shut the door.

Steve walks stiffly to the incident room ahead of me, his long legs not quite breaking into a run.

'They found her,' he says, as soon as I've closed the door. 'Just got the call in from the teams. In a ditch, off a by-road approximately three-quarters of a mile from the Nugent house.'

There's the sting of tears at the back of my eyes and I have to take a few short, sharp breaths to get my emotions under control. 'What state are the remains in?'

He goes to the computer. Taps the screen awake. 'Not terrible, but it looks like she's been there a while. The cold has limited the decomp a bit so luck, if that's what you'd call it, is on our side.'

I peer down into the computer. At first, you could mistake the image as showing nothing but spring greenery awakening over a bed of rotting leaves: a mulch of varying browns, yellows and reds, wet and sodden in dank ditch water. It's like looking at one of those optical illusions that pass around the Internet. Slowly my eyes adjust, pick out the shape of a corpse. The white, glistening curve of the top of Debbie Nugent's skull is the first thing that breaks the pattern for me. From there, the dark wad of hair stuck over the rest of her face. The remainder of her body is mostly hidden, wrapped in a blanket. I lean closer. I recognize it immediately as the one I saw in that picture on Margot's dressing-room mirror, the quilt gripped in her hand as she sat on the bed, her face pressed up close to David's, both of them smiling into the camera.

Steve goes on: 'The coroner's on her way out now. They've begun sealing off the area already and have blocked access from the by-road.'

166

'Any murder weapon?'

'None visible.'

I pull my gaze away from the screen. 'Let the sergeant know and I'll be out as soon as I can. We're almost done with the interrogation.'

He turns back to his desk, picks up the phone, his eyes settling on the computer where now the screen is showing Margot Nugent in the interview room, making the most of the quiet, her soft-cheeked face resting in the crook of her arm, her eyes drifting closed on the bright light of the interview room.

CHAPTER 14

The shape of Debbie's body flashes behind my eyes as I return to question Margot. I pause outside the door, scribble a note to pass to Baz when I step inside, fold it over, knock gently on the door and go inside. I sit down, give the note to Baz, who turns away to read it. After a moment, he slips it into his pocket, not a flicker of a reaction on his face.

Margot straightens, gathers her hair and twists it into a knot at the base of her neck. She waves a hand in front of her face, giving me a half-smile. 'That's better,' she says. 'It's hot in here.'

'Interview resumed at eleven-thirteen am. Third April 2013,' I say. 'Margot, when did you discover the scene in the living room?'

She tenses. 'When Kristen opened it on Saturday.'

'You hadn't been inside that room for ten days?'

Something crosses her face. 'We don't use that room often.'

'Did you kill your mother?'

The flush rises on her cheeks again and I see a small twitch along her bottom lip, a shine in her eyes. 'No,' she says, her chin dimpling with emotion.

'We found your mum,' I say.

'What?' Eyes widen, go to Baz then to me. 'Is she okay?'

I look down, summon my patience. 'No. No, she's not okay. She's dead.'

Her hand is at her throat. She pulls at the top of her shirt, her thin neck arching forward, the smooth wings of her collarbones standing out from her chest. She blinks a few times, tries to hold it back, but the first sob comes anyway. A squeaking cry which turns into a horrible, gasping sniffle. She brings her hands up, hides her face in them and the sounds magnify behind the cup of her palms.

We wait until she stops, watch her fight the shake of her shoulders. It takes a while but finally she drags in two long, juddering breaths. I know from experience this is the time to jump in, make the walls of the interview room bear down on our suspect. Baz's fingers thrum away on his thigh. Waiting for me to make my move. I open my mouth to speak but Margot gets there before me.

'I saw it,' she says, lowering her hands. Her grey eyes are red, swollen and watering. She rubs her nose. 'I did. And I searched for her. But when I opened that door . . . ' she trails off, drags in another shaking breath, it bubbles and coughs in her throat. '. . . I saw . . . There was so much blood. I don't know why I didn't tell anyone. Mum always handles everything. I . . . didn't know what to do, so I just closed the door.'

'When?'

She can't look at me. 'I don't know,' she whispers. 'The day before I spoke to the garden centre.'

'Thursday the twenty-first?'

169

She nods.

'Can you speak up for the tape, please?'

She raises her voice a little. 'Yes. I thought she wasn't in the evening before. The last time I saw her was breakfast time, that was true.'

'But breakfast on Wednesday the twentieth, not the twenty-seventh?'

'Yes.'

'Why didn't you call someone. The guards?'

She shakes her head. Over and back, over and back. 'I don't know. I don't know!' She grips the front of her shirt again. 'I wanted it to go away.' She descends into a heart-rending sob. Her narrow shoulders tremble, her hands so tightly wound together it looks like the small bones might snap. But somewhere through her sobbing she manages to get out: 'I want to talk to my sister,' she says. 'Please.'

It is four hours before Debbie Nugent's remains are removed from her shallow grave and the forensic team have collected what they can from the surroundings. The track off which she was dumped, rises high over one of the mountains, narrowing gradually to where the trees close in and only a snaking footpath continues. But it's used. Two thick grooves on either side of a grassy mound show that cars come up here. Hikers maybe wanting a head start on the mountain.

I imagine Margot taking her chances here on a dark evening or maybe with dusk approaching quietly through the valley below. I see her pulling over, opening the boot and heaving her mother out. Getting the body from the car would have been the hardest part. Once it hit the ground, she could have rolled Debbie into the ditch easily.

We drive out the road to where Kristen is staying. Rain pounds the car, the wipers not quite managing to clear my view. I slow, change down gears and peer through the grey swash. Kristen hasn't been informed yet of our discovery but has been spitting feathers since this morning over Margot's arrest and I'm not relishing the thought of adding to her troubles. But there are other reasons we need to speak to her. We need the truth. Baz's head is back on the passenger seat. Letting tiredness in. We're almost at a close. The autopsy tomorrow, then we charge.

Baz's mobile rings and he jumps to consciousness. He presses answer before looking at the screen, puts the phone to his ear and immediately slides an embarrassed look in my direction.

'I know, babe. We're nearly done,' he says, an edgy sound to his voice that makes me want to wince, but I keep my expression clear, look out at the road and pretend that he's somehow slipped into an alternate universe for this call and I can't hear him.

'I know I said a day. You can't really tell until you get here. Right.' He's half pressed out the door now, his body trying to sink into itself. Then he puts on a professional sounding voice that I've only heard him using when in meetings with the commissioner. 'Okay. Okay. Thank you. Thank you.' And hangs up.

There's silence for a moment.

'Everything okay?' I ask.

He blinks hard. Adjusts the position of his seatbelt. 'Oh yeah. Grand.'

Detective work is not easy on a relationship. Some would say you can't have both. The long hours and case obsessions,

171

not to mention the knowledge that the job is not the safest of occupations, the stress, the psychological trauma causes most relationships to sputter out before they've begun. How do you spend the day walking the murder scene of a six-year-old then sit with your family for dinner later and be normal? It's not something I've ever managed to figure out.

'That's good,' I say. I pull down a side street, the wheels of the car sending out an arc of water over the pavements. The B&B is the second on the left. I park up and get out, ducking back over the seat to grab my coat. I hook it over my head and hurry for the door. Kristen is waiting. Her face pinched and strained with worry; her arms, folded tightly, look as if they're the only things holding her upright.

She steps back quickly when we arrive to let us in from the wet.

'You can come into the morning room here. Mrs Thomas is in the kitchen.'

'Thanks,' I say and step into the warm hallway, stamp my feet on the doormat. I hang my coat on a stand inside the door and wait for Baz to do likewise, then we follow Kristen into the room.

We sit down. There's tea laid out already on a pretty floral tray. Fruit cake on a side plate. But none of us reaches for it. Kristen sits on the sofa and I sit down beside her.

'We found your mother,' I say quietly.

Her nod is barely there. Her lips go pale. 'Where?'

'A few kilometres from the house.'

'No. Where?' she insists.

Debbie's dark hair, half-fallen away. The smell of death. The stink of rotting leaves and rank ditch water.

'In—' the words fracture across my tongue.

'Among the trees, in a hollow. She was sheltered,' Baz says softly, syllables falling like pebbles into the silence.

Kristen is already shaking her head. Her hands twitch, fingers trembling like antennae over one another. I know she wants to reach for her ears. Cover them. A long breath, drawn in, a gasp from the surface of grief. She swallows it down. Outside the rain hounds down, turns the windows to walls of water, the wind combing long fingers across the panes. Beyond, the green world wobbles.

'Kristen, we still have a couple of unanswered questions.'

She looks up. Wipes a tissue under her nose. 'I can't believe she'd do this,' she whispers.

'Margot?' I ask.

'She loves Mum.' And I hear that hint of bitterness in her voice again.

'Did you know Debbie was missing? Is that why you came home?'

She shakes her head but doesn't answer. Baz gives me a look that tells me to go further. 'You made quite a few calls to the house over the last couple of weeks. You spoke to someone. Was that Margot?'

Again silence. Then quietly, 'Shouldn't you caution me or something before asking these questions?'

'You're not under arrest.'

She takes a shaky breath, tips her head back, rubs the wetness from her face. 'I knew for a week that something wasn't right. Margot had gone quiet. And then when I couldn't get hold of Mum, I just had this feeling.' She presses her hand to her stomach. 'I knew that something had happened.'

173

'Your mum? She was controlling?'

Her mouth opens to speak, a look of surprise registering on her face, then closes again. I wait for her to find the words.

'She had her ways. We loved her. We did.'

'I believe you,' I say, and reach out and rest my hand over hers. But she pulls it away, tucks it inside the other. 'We'll be releasing the house soon. If you'd rather not return, we can arrange for a packing company—'

'No. It's my home. Our home. I want to get back to it. It's what Mum would want.'

Back in the car, Baz wipes rain from his face, stares moodily at the black clouds ahead of us. 'Christ, that was desperate, altogether. You wanna go get shit-faced?'

I start the car, turn around, and head towards the hotel; the wipers slapping on top speed across the windscreen. 'I'll drop you at the hotel. Clean-up have been in and I want to look over the job before we return the keys to Kristen. It's the least I can do.'

'You're a glutton for punishment. You sure you don't need company?'

I give him a smile. 'Get some rest. I'll phone the station, let them know I'm there.'

The drive out to the Nugent house is slow-going. There's no let-up in the rain. It runs in waves across the windscreen and the wipers, on full throttle, are unable to keep the window clear. Eventually, I pull down the lane and park up in front of the house. I unclip my seatbelt and reach into the back for my mac and the large wide-beam torch I keep under the passenger seat.

174

Despite the rain, I make myself walk slowly over the drive. Check for scraps of garda ribbon, coloured markers left behind on the ground, anything that might say 'crime scene' for when Kristen returns. I get to the front door. A loud trundle of water is falling from the roof above the living-room window. Leaves or a crack in the gutter guiding water down in an angry stream. I retrieve the keys from my inside pocket, rainwater sliding down the sleeve of my coat. I open the door and step inside. Turn on the lights. Everything looks familiar but not. The kitchen is clean of debris. Too clean, I'd say. The soul of the house erased. I look over the coats, the shoe rack. But the smell has changed. Bleach and other chemicals stain the air. I walk into the living room. They've done the best they could. The carpet has been removed from the room. The concrete floor, exposed, naked.

As soon as I could, I asked Keith to bring in a specialist cleaning company. Whatever Kristen's desire to protect her sister, I couldn't bear the thought of her returning to the scene of her mother's murder and having to clean it herself. The books have been returned to shelves. The walls washed. But even from the doorway I can make out a dull pattern of blood on the cream surface. I go to the window. The crack still there but no trace of blood.

I move upstairs. The bedrooms too have been cleaned. Margot's laundry packed into black bin liners, labelled. The bed remade. Debbie's room too. I close the door, satisfied, and go back down the short hallway towards the stairs.

A cool breeze drifts over my face and I pause on the top step. Returning to the rooms, I search for open windows. The cleaners may have been trying to clear the stench of cleaning products

175

from the house and forgot to close one. Anyone hearing the house is now unmanned could do worse for their pocket by getting inside and taking a few photos. Every window closed upstairs, I check the ones downstairs. All closed.

I turn on my torch and head for the front door but pause in the porch. It's open. Beneath the damp of my jacket, I feel my skin prickle, my body stills, my hearing strains against the incessant lash of the rain against the house. I try to remember if I closed it or not. I look once more around the main room, push the living-room door open again. It's empty. I close the door over. Send a text to Deirdre Ross to let Kristen know she can pick up the keys in the morning. Turn out the lights and step outside. I pause for a minute in the doorway, scan the garden with my torch. The rain slices the black horizon with a million blades. A little way off, rainwater spills angrily from the gutter.

I move towards it. Direct the torch upwards. Twigs and small pieces of debris jut out from the edge of the gutter. I sigh, figuring I'm soaked through anyway, and, not wanting Kristen to have to deal with a blocked gutter when she gets back, I think about what to do. I hurry around to the shed. Move the paint tin and scan around in the darkness. The shelves are now empty. Things have a more ordered feel, like they've been removed and placed back with more care than they were put in there in the first place. Along the side, there's a stepladder and I pull the lawnmower out of the way and drag the ladder out, pushing the mower back in quickly before closing the shed again.

Working quickly, I position myself to the right of the blockage. Test my footing then climb up, the torch heavy in my other hand. Run-off from the gutter rushes cold down my front. I move some leaves away, icy water up my sleeves, down the inside of my jacket. I scoop out the twigs, more leaves and eventually the water runs free. Shunts down the gutter. My hand goes back in. And my fingers touch against something heavy. I grasp at it and lift it free. Eyes adjusting to the darkness, I don't need the torch to know what I'm holding. Even with my eyes closed I could guess from the balance of weight, from the handle perfectly fitted to my hand. A hammer.

The hotel restaurant is nice. Now that the case is moving, more than moving, almost done, I can appreciate it. It's modern with a touch of country. The reception floored in wide stone slabs, the walls a pleasing deep blue. Outside, the odd car slushes by, the gold trail of light flashing briefly on the dark windows before being swallowed again by the night.

I turn my spoon through the soup, bring it to my lips, but it's gone cold and I push it to the side; lift up my wine glass. Baz has retired to his room, no doubt to rescue the scraps of his relationship. Jack is out to dinner with his old friend, Fitz. I'm on the edge of exhaustion but too tense for sleep. I realize I wasn't expecting we'd ever find Debbie. Or maybe I hoped we wouldn't. That part of me not wanting to believe that Margot could be guilty, or maybe it's because I've a feeling we've missed something. Like we've put all the pieces of our puzzle together and we've one spare. I shake out my shoulders, swirl the red wine in the glass, take a long drink.

The restaurant is surprisingly full. Two waiters make slow circuits of the room, occasionally bending to refill a wine glass or see to a diner's requests. White linen towels neatly folded over their arms, notebooks tucked into the aprons at their fronts. By the window, a couple sit, hands curved around their plates towards one another. And I think about how natural it looks. Normal. The simple comfort of one hand in another. I put down my wine glass, drag my phone towards me, turn it on. I open my contacts and find his name. I pause for a moment, then before I can think on it too much, I send him a text. His response comes through quickly. *I'll be there soon. Alex.*

CHAPTER 15

DATE: 4th April 2013
TIME: 08.30
NAME: Debbie Nugent
SEX: Female
AGE: 55
ADDRESS: Rathborne Road, Ballyalann, Co. Wicklow

The stained patterned blanket still surrounds our victim's body. Abigail, the pathologist, pauses her dictation to cut through the thick wool. Her assistant, a slight man in his twenties, assists in shuffling the body free of its cocoon. He deposits the blanket quickly into a large clear bag, takes it off to the side, notes the contents. He leaves the blanket in a large plastic box near the door of the room where the rest of Debbie's clothing, once removed, will be left, ready for processing later.

Clothes clear, Debbie Nugent's body is photographed. The colours of decay and death. The assistant checks the video occasionally, ensures it's filming, capturing the right angle. CSI have placed bags around her hands to preserve any evidence that could be trapped beneath her fingernails. Abigail removes them and the assistant places them in an evidence bag too. Then Debbie's nails are cut, the clippings falling into another bag, scissors dropped in alongside it. Sealed. Labelled.

It takes a good half hour for Abigail to complete the external exam. As she works, she narrates the story of Debbie Nugent's death. Lividity down the left side of the victim's body, words like putrefaction, fluid, contusion rise up from the room. The victim's x-rays glow on a light box to the right of the autopsy table. Abigail glances at them every now and then. She cuts away the thick swathes of Debbie's hair. A dark bruise over the skin. I lift my eyes from the room below, look instead at the screen displaying the autopsy in front of me. The wound looks deceptively tidy, a deep impression in the gentle curve of Debbie's pale skull.

Abigail holds a ruler along the injury. 'On the anterior parietal region of the cranium, there is a four-millimetre-deep and twenty-five-millimetre wide depression of the cranium, radiological examination confirms a depression fracture. The subcutaneous tissue and dermis are moderately decomposed. The outer parameters of the injury display a curvilinear arc suggesting a disc-like impact.'

When Abigail finally pulls the plastic cover over the body, I stand, stretch out my shoulders then look over the numerous scrawls in my notebook. Abigail pulls her gloves from her hands, drops them into a yellow pedal bin in the corner of the room. I watch her for signs of fatigue, irritability. She peels out of her scrubs and leaves them in another bin, then reaches for a white lab coat that's hanging on the back of the door. Her assistant

180

leaves and I move out of the viewing area, down towards the examination room and knock on the glass partition of the door. It buzzes open and I step inside.

There's no natural light here but the room has that spaceship brightness. The overhead LEDs could fool a person into thinking they were standing outdoors. The gentle whir of air-con hums from the corners of the room. Abigail is sitting in the far corner, her head bent and moving between her computer and her notes. To her right a microscope, a selection of slides on a metal tray beside it. She reaches across, removes a slide then snaps it onto the mount. She looks into the eyepiece briefly, then she's back making notes.

'Hello, Detective. The forms are at the door,' she says with a nod of her head towards a clipboard that's slotted into a holder on the wall.

I move towards her. 'I wondered if I could ask you a few questions. On the exam.'

She looks up from her work, her expression still intense from concentration.

I see her check the time on the clock on the wall over my head. 'How is it not even midday?' she asks. 'I've another two autopsies to do today. Murder is fashionable at the moment. What do you need to know?'

'Has the decomp affected your examination much?' Abigail always appreciates a direct approach. She'll know what I'm after.

She purses her lips. 'It always does. Time of death is difficult, for one. It will be a few hours before I can tell you anything.'

'Can you give us what type of weapon it was from the injuries on the body?' My tone is not far off begging.

Generally, Abigail is quick to give us anything that might help, but with a case like this, where she might be called as a witness, where the press have their noses right up against the glass, she could be wary. But she pulls away from the computer and indicates towards the x-rays, still lit up on the light box. 'It's a depression fracture. There's enough tissue around the injury site to give me a good sense of the weapon type. Blunt force trauma that I suspect led to death. Two very hefty strikes. There are no scratches or marks on her hands or arms, so I would think there was an element of surprise involved.'

'That fits with the results of our investigation.'

'As for the weapon. I've seen it before. Many times on homicide victims. Any amateur pathologist could tell you what caused it. The impact with such a weapon makes a distinctive mark. Not definitive but highly likely.' I hold my breath. 'I feel certain that the wound was caused by a hammer.'

I could hug her with relief. Because of water and air exposure on the hammer I found at the Nugent house it's possible that any forensic evidence it possessed has been destroyed. This might be as close as we'll get to linking it to Debbie's murder. 'Thank you, Abigail,' I say.

'No problem.' She looks over at the body. 'The blows were significant. A lot of power in them. And the first landed midway up the parietal bone with a sharp downward stroke.' She turns to the fracture pattern on the x-rays. 'Your suspect, it's a woman, right?'

'Yes.'

'Tall, well-built?'

'I'd say the opposite.'

182

'Hmm. Okay. Her height?'

'Five foot five, roughly.'

She glances at the light box again. 'There is a distinctive downward trajectory to these injuries where if I was to look at them quickly, I'd say the offender was taller. But we can't always account for the victim's posture at the time. It's possible your victim was flexed, bending to leave something down.'

'She could have been,' I say, thinking of the tea.

'Okay,' she says.

'You're sure it was a hammer, though?'

'Yes,' she says. 'I'm sure.'

I imagine Margot waiting for Debbie to turn her back then, later standing over the body, chest heaving. She hadn't meant for things to escalate so quickly. Hadn't meant for her to die. Does she scream? Or is there someplace inside her that knows this was how it was going to be? Does she feel a kick of power? Does it disgust or thrill her? The mess. The blood. She feels a jolt of panic. Now, she can't undo it. Can't get her mother to go away quietly. There's so much blood. She walks the length of the room, stands at the window, gets as far away from her mother's body as possible; fists tight, knuckles shining white around the slick handle of the hammer. She'll have to move her.

And frustration wells up inside her, at her mother, at what she's done and, before she knows it, she's hit the window pane. The glass doesn't smash, instead it fans out in a burst of fractures, a dry crunch, not wet like her mother's head had been. A few deep breaths and the roar of adrenalin in her ears quiets. She pulls the curtains. Turns on the lamp.

★

Blue sky is reflected in the curved glass windows of the central criminal court. Already journalists have gathered. Media vans are parked along the street, their reporters perched on the steps of the building; their eyes searching every vehicle that slows on the street. A man and a woman sit on their mopeds, compare camera lenses, buddies for the moment until the hustle for the first shot of Margot Nugent comes into play. A few hacks are huddled in the corner, sharing a cigarette and morning coffee, planning out their best position for the ultimate picture. They know they have time.

I unclip my belt, ready myself to get out, but Clancy calls me back.

'You may wait a minute. It's another while before proceedings start.'

What he means is that Margot's defence won't get here until the last possible moment. I settle back into the seat and Clancy pushes the window down and lights up.

'Don't mind do you?' he asks, as the first plume of smoke shunts out the window.

I shake my head. 'No.'

'Do you miss it?' he asks.

'Not really,' I answer.

He looks at my hand, tight on the steering wheel. 'I can put it out if it bothers you.'

'It's grand.'

'Wonder will they go for the aspiring youth with all her life in front of her or the innocent girl look?' he says.

'I don't think we'll have to wait long to find out,' I answer.

A gleaming black Beemer sweeps to a stop in front of the

courthouse. The crowds step back, make way for the shot of whoever is about to exit the car. There is a flurry of camera action as the door opens. Clancy leans forward in the passenger seat and looks out beyond me towards the Beemer. A man gets out, tall, hair slicked back: the State's prosecution.

'Fintan McCarthy,' Clancy announces. 'Fucking show off.'

McCarthy embodies everything the public want to see in a lawyer. A veritable caricature of himself. Expensive navy suit that I know without the benefit of getting close to him will be pin-striped. His shoes – leather, patent – will give a satisfying click as he walks through the courthouse; possibly the waft of some expensive brand of male perfume trailing after him. I've sat in court with him before. Witnessed the effect of his performance on many juries. The guy hardly needs evidence to help him. He requires only a stage, and by the third act of this play Margot Nugent's conviction will be a certainty.

Clancy pulls on his cigarette, not minding this time to blow the air at the open window. It fills the space between us and the sweet smoke awakens a pang of longing.

'Jesus, does the guy have to be such a fucking slick bastard,' he says.

'I'm just glad he's on our side,' I say. I could barely believe my luck when I saw the State's representation. Tanya, my sister-in-law, a defence lawyer, would hate this, I think suddenly. One more way to point out that the law favours those with money and power. In my head, I tell her to wait. Who knows what the defence might be. It could be a fair race. Besides, Fintan has not been hired by money this time. It's the circus around Margot that's attracted him. A false show of integrity to turn up for

185

the victim, waive his fees, fight the good fight. His face will be on every front page and news channel in the next twenty-four hours. He must have been smelling his own farts all day when he heard he'd got this case. Bloody delighted with himself.

I watch as he takes the steps. Unhurried by the push of journalists around him, who, despite their eagerness to capture him on film, keep a respectful distance. He pauses at the entrance to the court, moves to the side where on a pale granite wall are the words: *The Criminal Courts Of Justice*. He waits for the cameras to follow. His experience showing, he positions himself so that when he's in shot, the word, Justice, is at his left side. McCarthy is all about how it looks and every movement, every posture is carefully thought out to present himself as pure and honest; the voice of reason.

He makes a short statement then holds up both palms, as if pleading with the paps not to bother him further. His delivery patient but friendly. A man asking a favour of friends. Someone who assures the public that he's coming at this case from the side of honour and goodness.

'This might not take too long,' I say.

Clancy points through the windscreen. 'You could say that again.'

I follow his gaze to a blue Zafira that's parked in front of us and I swallow. She's arrived. I wonder whether it's an indication of the defence's incompetence that her driver has pulled up across the street from the courthouse, leaving Margot Nugent to navigate a street-full of traffic and a waiting mob before she can reach the safety of the courthouse. A door opens and a young man appears. He's wearing a three-piece, his young face shaved clean, hair tight up the sides. He reaches into the passenger side of the vehicle and lifts a wad of files out, holds them protectively to his chest.

Clancy stares at him. 'Christ, he's only outta fucking nappies that fella.'

There's a shout from across the street and suddenly McCarthy is without his audience. The paps gather like a pack of dogs. Traffic slows to a stop. Not a horn goes as drivers strain to witness the commotion. Windows come down, arms reach out, phones ready for when our suspect exits the car.

'Who's the kid anyway?' Clancy asks.

'Hugh Devlin,' I say.

'Oh here we go.'

Margot's red hair appears first. A shout of colour on a bright morning. It's gathered into a smooth knot at the base of her narrow neck, showing off pale, peachy skin. She's wearing a light blouse, cream with a soft, feminine ruffle that gathers down the front. An A-line skirt in a rusty brown goes to below her knees, tidy black pumps on her feet. At first I thought it was her lawyer's inexperience showing that he didn't cover her face, throw a jacket over her head to protect her from the mad crush of cameras, but I notice him take a moment as if to let her acclimatize to the attention and I know that this is purposeful. The demure wardrobe accentuates Margot's youthful complexion, drives away the thought that she could be capable of this kind of murder.

The shouts of the paps come through the window. *Margot. Margot. This way.* She keeps her eyes low, the occasional solemn glance out at the sea of lenses in front of her. She's been coached well. *Margot. Margot. Give us a smile.* And that catches her out. I see her lawyer move forward, anticipating her response, but it's too late. She finds the right camera and the corner of her mouth lifts, her hand waves at her waist. Devlin steers her through the crowd. He doesn't stop walking until they reach the entrance, where he takes the time to ensure she's gone in ahead of him. Turns, nods at the paps then follows his client inside.

The journos check their images. The ruckus goes quiet. Slowly they disperse to nearby cafés or to sit in their vehicles for the short time it will take for the pre-trial to run.

'We right?'

'Yeah. Come on,' I say, and push out of the car. I stretch out my leg, wait for Clancy to join me, but as always he's gone already, halfway across the street. Fuck's sake, I mutter, then check the traffic and cross to the courthouse.

He waits in the foyer. Which is a gleam of polished stone tiles. White round tiers spiral up around us, broken up by dark wood pathways that curve upwards to the many floors above.

Clancy checks the listings. Signs us both in. 'Courtroom five.'

We make our way up, join the queue of people filtering inside. The courtroom, although slightly modernized, still holds the whiff of romanticism. Wooden benches that creak satisfyingly as witnesses and visitors shuffle along and take seats. Wooden galleries are suspended over the action. Wooden panelling covers the walls. The bench padded out with maroon leather, buttons embedded in the shining upholstery. And I have a sudden memory of my granny, her bent fingers drawing a needle through a cushion, my eyes following the round disc of the button as it's pulled deep into the soft padded fabric. *Tufting*, she tells me.

188

We mightn't have much, Frankie, but that shouldn't stop us adding a flourish or two to life when we can.

We sit close to the front, next to the wide aisle that leads to the bench. There's not many here. I recognize Eileen from the garden centre in the seat in front of us. Her partner, Abby, next to her. A few choice members of the national press. I catch the eye of one reporter. Sitting to the left of the bench. Shelley Griffiths. She gives me a hesitant look of surprise. Shelley is a friend of mine. I lift my hand to wave but she's already turned her attention to her notes.

Margot sits at the front, Hugh Devlin next to her; the back of his neatly combed hair just about visible from where we're sitting. Fintan McCarthy sits opposite. I look for Kristen but can't see her in the family area.

The judge, the Honourable Ms Justice Maeve Connor, strides in, sharply cut dark hair striped with light grey, a severe heavy fringe comes down to her eyebrows. Her black gown floats back from her shoulders as she takes the bench. She pushes it away from her hips with an impatient hand before she sits. The court is silent. Not a pin-drop heard, only the rustle of the judge's papers as she opens the folder and peruses the case before her.

After a few moments she looks out, finds Margot Nugent, gives a small nod to herself then focuses on the papers and speaks.

'Good morning, Ms Nugent.' She looks up, stares out at Margot.

'Good morning, Ma'am,' comes Margot's quiet reply.

'How are you?'

I see Margot's shoulders come up slightly, her head turns a

189

little to the rest of the court, her profile giving away a bemused look. 'I'm fine, thank you.'

'My name is Maeve Connor and I'm the district judge assigned to this case. Number,' she checks her papers, 'IR326. Case brought by the State against Margot Nugent under Section 4 of the Criminal Justice Act 1964.' She looks up at Margot again. 'You understand that you are here under a charge for murder?'

'Yes, Ma'am.' Quiet.

The judge directs her steady glare at Devlin. 'Counsel, we have no trial date set for this?'

'Not yet, Judge,' Devlin responds.

'This is the first hearing?'

'Yes, Judge.'

'Okay.' She turns over a paper on the bench. 'I see you've submitted via the Director of Public Prosecutions a request for a suppression order?'

'Yes, Judge,' Devlin replies. 'We would like to protect the anonymity of our client and limit prejudicial pretrial publicity.'

Justice Maeve Connor looks to Margot first then to Devlin. 'There has already been exposure in the press, no?'

Devlin clears his throat. 'Not detailing the particulars of the charges brought against our client.'

Maeve Connor's mouth presses into a line. Unconvinced. 'I shall not be granting your request, Mr Devlin.'

Devlin doesn't reply. His hands are clasped behind his back. His fingers tightening and loosening over and again.

The judge looks to the prosecution, her expression inviting McCarthy to speak.

He clears his throat, lifting his chin, and speaks out. 'Forensic results strongly imply that Debbie Nugent was killed in her home. Her body was then disposed of in the Wicklow mountains. She was killed with two blows to the head from a hammer. There is a ten-day gap between when she was last seen to when she was reported missing and the discovery of the crime scene.'

She sniffs. 'Where are we with witness statements? Have you conducted all your investigations otherwise?'

'We have completed as many as we can presently.'

'How many?'

'Fifty-six, Judge.'

'Mr Devlin, how many have you been through?'

'We're at thirty, Judge.'

She nods. Margot Nugent raises a hand to her face. Yawns into her palm.

'There's a request to deny bail, Mr McCarthy?'

'We believe the nature of the crime is serious enough to warrant that request, Judge. The defendant is a danger to others or could be to herself.'

A hardening of the lines around the judge's mouth. 'That is for a court to decide on, Mr McCarthy, is it not?'

'Of course, Judge,' McCarthy replies.

She turns to the side of the bench, sorts through some more paper. 'But I see your point. How would an October date suit? That will give you plenty of time, Mr McCarthy, to conclude whatever other tests you deem necessary, and for you to complete your analysis of all statements and affidavits, Mr Devlin? Is everyone available in October?'

'Yes, Judge,' McCarthy answers.

191

'October's fine for me,' from Devlin.

'Bail is denied. Trial date set for October fourteenth 2013. Any requests for alternative dates to be received by me no later than two weeks from today's date. Is that clear?'

'Yes, Judge,' both lawyers answer in unison.

'Okay. That's it. Thank you.' Judge Connor gathers up the files in front of her. Nods to the escorting guards, who shepherd her out of the room again.

Margot turns to Devlin, who gives her what should be a reassuring smile though it wavers on the corners of his small mouth. He indicates that she should exit in the direction of the guards, who wait at a side door. As she turns, she sees me, smiles. And I hear the click of a camera from behind me as one of the journalists captures the moment. Devlin, again, too late, puts his back between Margot and the cameras and escorts her to the waiting guards.

I try once more to catch Shelley's attention. I meet her from time to time. She works with the *Herald* in town but we took some of the same classes in university where her obsession with the ins and outs of the criminal world, it's fair to say, equaled mine. She was enthralled by the story, me the solution. She looks up and I make a gesture for a cup of coffee but she taps her notebook, makes a face that could be, *I need to get to work*, gets up quickly and walks through the court. She is one of the first to leave the room.

'What did you do to her?' Clancy asks.

I look after her, the door of the court sucking shut. 'I don't know.'

I hesitate for a moment then push out of the court after her. Out on the street, journalists have closed in but beyond the heave of cameras, Shelley is marching off down the street. I push through the crowds in her direction.

'Hey,' I say when I get close enough.

She stops.

'Shelley, how are you?'

Shelley was made too small for her skin, her energy trembling in every move. But she seems more twitchy than usual. Her eyes meet mine then flit over my shoulder and back again.

'Frankie,' she says. 'I'm sorry to run, I've a deadline.'

'You reporting on the Nugent case?'

'Yes,' she says. The deep hollows of her cheeks draw in. She's always been thin and it may be the fall of sunlight across her face but she looks more so than usual. I count back in my head to how long it's been since I've seen her. Four months. In a tapas bar off Grafton Street when we bitched about the system and drank too much.

She begins to move off again. 'Sorry, I really do have to go.'

'How about a coffee or drink soon?'

She pauses. Her eyes rest on my face, a long sigh, and I can see she's debating something. I have a jolt of fear that I'm about to lose a friend. Finally, she sighs, looks over my shoulder to the ruckus of reporters then walks back to me. 'I might have some information on the Nugent case. Might,' she reiterates, when she sees my reaction. 'Give me a few days, okay? I'll call you.'

I reach out to her. 'Shelley, if it affects the case—'

'I'll call you. I have to go.' And she speeds off down the street, almost at a run.

'Frankie!' Clancy shouts from somewhere behind me.

I turn, Clancy is at the car on the far side of the street. He waves a hand impatiently and points to the door. I find the keys, press the central locking then make my way towards him.

CHAPTER 16

Jack turns off the engine and pats the dash of his car, as if quietly praising it for getting us there.

'It's a grand little wagon, all the same,' he mutters.

We're celebrating. Or Jack is anyway, with an invite to dinner at his friend's house. Baz has managed to dodge it because he had to run back to the city to save his relationship with Gemma, which has been haemorrhaging in a very fatal way since we arrived in Wicklow. Margot Nugent had barely warmed her cell before he took off but prior to him leaving, he sent me a disclosure from her defence team along with a note saying: 'interesting but doesn't change much'. Debbie Nugent wasn't just a Tyne before she got married, she was one of The Tynes. A family known for their involvement in organized crime. Drugs mainly but wherever there's money Magnus Tyne is in it. Baz is right. At this stage, it doesn't add anything to the picture. Debbie had clearly removed herself from that life twenty years ago and she would've been on our radar if not. But it gives the defence a foothold.

When this gets out to the papers, which it will, Debbie's like-ability goes way down. In some ways it could be a good thing, take the media heat off the case. As much as it makes me grind my teeth, the press like a tragic victim. There's no allowance for a fuck-up in your life if you're a murder victim. And a victim with a hand in the criminal biscuit tin, in the eyes of the press, is barely a victim at all. But the revelations around Debbie's past might go another way, highlight what we've failed to bring to the table. Margot had the opportunity to kill and dispose of Debbie, a possible weapon was found on the property and she concealed her mother's death. All these things fit together but none of them says that Margot took that hammer and drove it against her mother's skull. That's what the defence will say, and Debbie's past adds another wrinkle of doubt to the fabric of this case. Hugh Devlin will play this hand well.

We walk up to the Fitzsimons' house. It's free of the mountains, they sit far behind us. Instead it's the sea air that fills my nose and runs fingers through my hair.

'It's a bit of alright here,' Jack remarks, looking out at the vista, the dark grey sea curling white horses along the coastline below. 'Don't know what pension scheme I'm on but it's clearly the wrong one.'

When I don't respond he looks over at me. 'What's wrong?'

I pull on my coat. 'What do you mean?'

'You've barely uttered one syllable to me in the drive here and as much as I'm grateful for the peace, because God knows it's not often coming from you—'

'Alright, no need to throw insults into the mix. You're not so chatty yourself.'

'I am!' he says.

'You're avoiding talking about the case.'

He closes his mouth, throws me the side eye. Then he lifts his chin. 'The case is done. Over.'

I get to the doorbell but wait before I push it. 'Do you think there's anything to this Tyne connection? An old foe, perhaps?'

'No.' He reaches over me, jabs a finger at the bell.

'What if Margot and Kristen's father was involved? What if he had dealings with the Tynes and he retaliated by—'

'By what? Killing a woman who hasn't spoken to or been involved with any of that family for two decades. No. People are allowed to have pasts, Frankie. Doesn't mean everything is linked to now though.'

I allow myself a brief sulk, but add: 'Baz and Helen are going through some of Tyne's old charges, in their own time, don't worry. I'll feel happier if we can look into it a bit more.'

'Magnus Tyne is still about. I'm sure he'll have a chat with ye, if you ask nicely.' He laughs at that and just about manages to get hold of himself before the door opens.

Fitz is dressed in a dark blue-and-white check shirt, his stomach straining over light tan trousers. His greying hair thick and swept back from his pink face. 'Detective Fitz, thanks so much for the invite,' I say and put my hand out.

He laughs. 'What are we here? Strangers at an interview.' He reaches around me and pulls me forward into a hug, patting me on the back. I stumble against him, shrinking from the close contact; mercifully it's brief and he lets me go and turns to Jack who he also pulls forward. They bump chests as if it were an

197

old habit. 'Well, well. Come in, come in,' he says, one hand on the door the other extended out into the hallway.

We move inside and the scent of cooking onions drifts around us. A woman appears in a doorway at the end of the hall, a tea towel in her hands moving over her palms.

'Hello,' she says. Her voice like the tinkle of bell, sweet and inoffensive. 'Jack it's so good to see you again.'

Jack walks towards her, takes up her hands and kisses both her cheeks. 'Winnie, great to see you.'

Winnie steps back, lays a hand on Jack's cheek. 'A few more lines but still as handsome as ever,' she smiles.

'Christ alive, you're only a moment in my house and already making the moves on my wife. Get in will ye,' Fitz says, ushering them inside and waving me forward.

The warmth of the house, the smell of home cooking wraps around me, makes me think of home. For a moment I feel out of place, as if I'm seeing something from the past, my hearing swims in and out, a brief hiss of tinnitus then it's gone. Winnie's hand is on my back, directing me into a long living room.

No TV. Twin bookshelves on either side of a window looking out on to the street. Deep sofas. A rich green, green curtains to match. Cream wallpaper of that oat-meal variety. Side lamps of cream and emerald stripe fringed with gold tassels give the room enough light to be inviting but not so much that it's glaring. The sofas look towards a set of double French doors that serve up breathtaking views of the Irish Sea. I let my eyes run along the grey horizon, catch on a shipping vessel in the distance. A pin-prick of an image. The same height as the waves falling against the shoreline, even though I know the vessel probably towers over this house, several times over. A reminder that sometimes the eyes lie. That we can't always trust what we see.

'Would you like a drink?' Winnie interrupts my thoughts. She holds out a silver tray. 'Gin and tonic to get the party started,' she smiles, teeth a bit too even; that over-white that suggests dentures, or more likely veneers. 'Or there's tonic water with a squeeze of lime.' I glance over to where Jack and Fitz are standing next to a book case. Fitz has one of the books in his hands. He's holding it out, his other hand on Jack's arm. Jack is laughing at something he's saying, nodding, a glass of red wine going to and from his lips. Looks like I'm driving.

I turn my attention to the drinks. 'Thanks,' I say and take up the tonic water. She looks a little disappointed that I've not chosen the alcohol, as if I've already ruined whatever atmosphere she was attempting to create. 'I'm driving,' I feel compelled to say.

Despite the homely cooking and the homely atmosphere Winnie's not the aproned-up type. Her clothing is yacht chic: light blue shirt, stiff collar upright along her neck, overlarge cuffs turned back over a pale pink sweater.

She takes the final drink for herself then puts the tray down on a side table. 'It's all very strict nowadays, isn't it?' She takes a sip of the drink, the ice clinks against the tip of the glass. When she brings the glass away, she smacks her lips and makes a small shivering movement of pleasure. 'That's good.'

'You must be pleased Dennis has retired?'

'Oh yes. I could never quite relax when he was working. It's such a dangerous job. Unfortunately for people like Dennis that's the appeal,' she says.

I think of all the times I've run into danger, sought it out, pushed against that line for a case. When I smile back at Winnie I can see she's watching me. I feel myself flush.

'When did he retire?' I ask.

'Oh, many years ago. He did a bit of private work for a while but it wasn't the same.' She shakes her head. 'Ah well, there's always plenty of golf, right? I think dinner will be ready soon. Excuse me.' She leaves for the kitchen and my gaze returns to the French doors. All space in this house is reserved for the view.

After dinner we remain at the round dining table. Fitz gets up, reaches beneath a sideboard and removes a bottle of whiskey and three glass tumblers.

He holds them up. 'Will you have one, Frankie?'

I think of the dark, narrow road back to the hotel. 'I'm fine,' I say and he gives me a loose smile.

He sits at the table, passes a glass to Jack. 'I don't know how you do it my friend. Where's the fun in being law enforcement if you can't bend a few rules, eh?'

The whiskey glugs into the glasses. Jack's face pulls into a wide smile, the long dimple down his right cheek deepens, his blue eyes glint.

'Well you see that's why I'm not plagued by cold cases,' he says. 'Some of us know how to do our job, Fitz.'

Fitz blows out a breath in mock offence. He looks at me. 'How do you put up with that fucking arrogance?'

Winnie groans, collects up the empty wine glasses and moves to the kitchen. I take a sip of my tonic water, which has gone flat and sticks at the back of my mouth.

200

Fitz laughs. 'One cold case. Think I may have cracked it though.'

Winnie re-enters the room, sets down a coffee pot, hands me a cup.

'A cold case?' I ask.

Fitz leans back in his seat. Happy with an audience. 'It's over thirty years old. Jo Phelan. A young mum in her mid-twenties goes out one day to get the basics, bread, milk, etcetera. It's two in the afternoon, May, and the street is busy. She walks there, gets her groceries but never makes it home. No body, no witnesses, nothing. She has a three-year-old in her home that she left in a playpen. A neighbour hears the baby crying a few hours later and goes to investigate. She finds the front door on the latch, the toddler is screaming the house down but there's no sign of Jo.'

As Fitz goes deeper into the mystery, I find my elbows creeping forward on to the table. I picture her. Jo. Light brown hair tied in a plait; clear, youthful skin, but beneath her eyes the telltale smudges of motherhood. Was the father still around? She walks down the street, throwing a cautious glance or two over her shoulder as she's left her baby unattended. But everyone does it these days. She didn't have the energy to get him wrapped up and loaded into the buggy for a dash to the shop for milk. She'll only be a couple of minutes.

'Was she wearing a coat?' I ask.

A brief look of surprise passes over Fitz's face at being pulled out of his story but he recovers, nods. 'We think so. She had a denim jacket she wore often. There was no sign of it in the house,' he says. 'Anyway, I got some new information yesterday on her brother. A witness came forward and said that Jo's brother had called round that morning and they believe it's possible he might have been in the house when she left for the groceries. Which would make sense, you know, her leaving the door on the latch like that. I mean, it was the eighties sure, but it's still bleeding Dublin.'

Jack slides him a teasing look. 'As a Dub I'm offended by that. Don't know what you mean.'

'Would take the fucking shoes off your feet as you're walking, the lot of them. Anyway, that part always made me uneasy.'

Winnie sighs. 'I really wish you wouldn't talk about this at the table, Dennis.'

'It's okay,' I say, not wanting him to stop. 'So the brother?'

'He passed away three years ago.'

I feel myself sag a little on his behalf. No DNA, no CCTV.

Jack laughs, gives his friend a consolatory smack on the shoulder. 'You'll have to do better than that. A witness coming through after three decades, no other evidence.'

'Well the neighbour who found the baby later said that she'd heard raised voices that morning, which she thought were coming from Jo's house.'

'Raised voices! Come on,' Jack grimaces. 'There's always "raised voices",' he says with a healthy dose of cynicism. 'You and I both know that auditory witnesses are almost impossible to persuade a court.'

Fitz takes a comforting sip of his whiskey. 'I know.' He reaches behind him, tugs open a drawer on the sideboard and removes a red folder. 'Don't panic, this is a copy,' he says. He hands it to me. 'Fresh eyes,' he says.

202

Winnie mutters something under her breath about the work never being done. 'He never stops, Frankie,' she says. 'Worked all the hours God sent when he was active.' I catch a look pass from Fitz to her at that and she silences, gets up, snatches a few items from the table and goes to the kitchen.

The file is fat, the folder not quite holding the contents; held together by a thick blue elastic band. I pull the band free of the thin cardboard and open the case.

'Don't mind that bit, they're my notes.' He reaches out and removes at least half of the papers, which I can see are indeed pages and pages of handwritten notes.

Jack shakes his head. 'Always the competitor,' he says. 'Never did share his copybook.'

'Well, it's not fair if she has a head start,' Fitz counters.

I look over the first page. There's a picture of the young woman pinned to the case summary. Young, light brown hair, in this one loose around her face. The date of birth says she was mid-twenties but she could easily pass for late teens. I tap the photo, 'This was recent when she went missing?'

'Oh yes, this was taken on the day of her son's third birthday.'

'Right.'

I can certainly see how she would have blended in, how she might have walked to the shop without many witnesses. Through her right eyebrow a thin strip of hair is missing. A scar perhaps, an old childhood injury. I continue through the file. Jack and Dennis move the conversation on to the Nugents. Clancy, even in his half-cut state, colours in the picture of our case. Gathering tidbits of information, different views, different angles on the family. And it makes me think that I'm

203

not the only one not ready to let go. It makes me think that we're not just here to socialize.

I turn another page of the old case file, half-listening for any valuable insights on the Tynes or Debbie Nugent, and come to the gardaí investigation of Jo's small three-room bungalow. In those days, the lead forensic specialist or the detective would walk the scene, talking into a recorder giving a verbal appraisal of what they can see. I'm always impressed by these recordings when I come about them. A good analyst could light up the scene in your head with the right words. I scan down the contents of the page. It continues on the overleaf. I look down through that too. If the latch was open on Jo's house, an intruder may have been waiting for her. Or perhaps she disturbed a burglar. But there's no evidence of violence or a struggle. All theories Fitz will have been through, but, as he says, fresh eyes on a case can often throw up a new angle.

A mobile rings and the chatter at the table stops. It takes me a minute to realize it's mine. I slip it out of my pocket with a quick apology. I'm about to turn it off when I see Baz's number.

'I'm sorry, I'm going to have to take this.' I move out through the front again, flipping the latch on the door and pulling it quietly behind me. The wind raises goosebumps on my arms and I stand huddled in the porch for shelter.

'Baz?'

I can hear the familiar ringtone of the Bureau phones in the background.

'Hey Frankie.'

'I thought you were out with Gemma.'

'Yeah well. Things didn't work out.'

'Oh, I'm sorry.'

'Thought I'd come in, join Helen on the night shift rather than suffer drinking on my own. Listen, I went through all the Tyne arrests over the last three decades, got the files through from Headquarters, the unit that deals with organized crime. What I can find is more or less what we know, that there are two families in regular conflict over territory as far back as the early eighties.'

'The Conahys and the Tynes.'

'Yes. But tensions between them both really began to ratchet up somewhere in the late nineties where it seemed that the Conahys were encroaching on Tyne territory, big time. There were a few ambushes by Vincent Conahy's brother, John-Joe, where they intercepted a drug delivery set for Tyne, and apparently one of Magnus Tyne's crew stabbed him outside his home. Although gardaí were never able to make the charges stick against Magnus Tyne. The Tynes haven't had a lot of luck over the last twenty years; at least two thirds of their deliveries are said to be going to the Conahys. The only reason we know of it is because every time it goes down, one of Tyne's men is left injured or dead.'

'Always more to fill empty shoes, right?'

'Like bloody whack-a-mole. Anyway, thinking on this, it seems to me that Tyne had a leak in his camp. Someone was feeding information to Conahy about Tyne's distribution, planned operations and whatever else he was up to.'

He gives me a moment to turn this over. 'Yeah, could've been the case.'

I hear him take a steadying breath. 'So Debbie's man, Rory Nugent, I'm thinking he was working for Tyne. It fits the timeline for Tyne's run of bad luck with Conahy. Married to Debbie, in or around the same period. And if he was part of Tyne's gang but feeding information to the competition, and Debbie, who knew or didn't know whatever, moved away to protect the kids.'

'Have we found Rory Nugent yet?'

'No. He's disappeared like a fart in the wind. Helen's tried everything to find him. I've never seen her this agitated. Think she might actually be beaten. We've searched prison records. Death records. Not a trace of him.'

I think on this for a moment. If Debbie wanted to disappear, maybe her husband did too. How easy it is to disappear. Easier still if you were never the person you said you were in the first place.

The door behind me opens and Jack appears, frowning at me for my rudeness. 'I got to go,' I say to Baz. 'Let's dig a little deeper. I'm not sure how or why it could be linked to Debbie's murder but we'll keep scratching away until we can rule it out.'

'And Margot?'

'It doesn't change anything.' I frown, not quite believing my own words then add, 'yet. Thanks, Baz.'

I hang up, go back inside.

'I'm sorry about that,' I say.

'Don't worry, we all know how it is,' Winnie says, although the tight line of Jack's mouth says he's not as ready to overlook my rudeness. He stands, turns to Winnie and spreads his hands. 'It's late. We should be getting going anyway.' Winnie allows him a quick hug. 'Thank you, Winnie. That was smashing. It really was.'

'So good to see you again, Jack.'

There's much hand-shaking, arm-gripping and back-smacking

206

between Jack and Fitz before we get to the front door. We're outside when I remember Fitz's cold case. I turn, my hand held up. 'There was milk in her fridge already,' I say.

Fitz frowns at Jack. 'Come again?' he asks me.

'The forensics team took an inventory of the house,' I say. 'There was a half loaf of bread in the bread bin and a full litre of milk in the fridge. Not sure how they missed it but easily overlooked, I suppose.'

He shakes his head. 'I don't get the relevance.'

'It was reported that she went out to get some.'

'We know she definitely got that milk. The shopkeeper was very clear on the time, knew her well.'

I think of her son, how young he was, the door on the latch. As Fitz says, it doesn't make sense that she'd leave it open.

'Maybe she was faking it.'

'I'm not following.'

'She leaves her purse behind, takes her coat and enough money in her pocket to get milk and bread. She knows she's not coming back. She leaves the door on the latch so her neighbour has access to her son. She feels wretched. She loves her son and can't bear the thought that he will grow up believing that she left him. She buys the milk so that it looks like she intended to return. But she knew she wouldn't be coming back.'

Fitz stands in the doorway as if stuck to the spot. His eyes have that far-off look, he's imagining the sequence of events. 'Well, fuck me,' he says. 'So not murdered or abducted.'

'Thanks again for dinner,' I say. 'And for letting me take a look at the case.'

'No, thank you,' he replies.

CHAPTER 17

The offices of the *Dublin Herald* are located above a newsagent's and curry house in Rathmines, Dublin. The only indication of their presence is a square of white cardboard sitting in one of the windows on which the newspaper's logo and name is emboldened in large green letters. Since seeing Shelley after Margot's pre-trial, I've left two messages on her phone but received no reply. I'd have given up but, this morning, four days after the pre-trial, and with the papers showing no let-up in their pursuit of information on Margot's personal life, Shelley phoned and asked if we could meet.

The day is mild, a hint at better weather to come, patches of cornflower blue breaking up the cloud, sun so sweet in the sky I might've been tempted to come out without a jacket. I stand outside the newsagent's and peruse the display of posters in the window as I wait. Margot Nugent's grey eyes look out through the pane.

In one of the photos, Margot's about to get into David's car. It must be from a few weeks ago. Back when Margot spent her days how she wanted. They've captured her in profile, half-turned, chin slightly angled down, her gaze up, looking at the camera, mid-blink so that her expression appears flirtatious. The femme fatale. An irresistible image for the public. IF LOOKS COULD KILL reads the headline.

Each spread shows various shots of a similar nature, pictures of Margot out partying, a timeline in a scathing tone runs beneath the pictures. *Two days after her mother went missing, Margot was out clubbing until 3 am.* Margot, her head back, a glass tipped at her lips. Margot dancing: short skirt, heels, low-cut top. Margot, laughing with friends, as they exit a pub. I recognize Prissy Bryant.

My phone beeps and I open a text from Shelley. *I'm on my way down x*

She appears out of the building through a door at the side of the shop, a denim jacket over her arm, soft tan leather beneath the collar and at the cuffs; the same one she wore at our graduation ceremony. The leather now shining and soft with time. She pats a hand over her short silver hair and peers up at the blue sky with a look of distrust.

'Christ, what a fucking shit morning,' she says, her voice soft and light. She leans in, wraps her arms around my shoulders and plants a firm kiss on my cheek. She smells of musky rose perfume and cigarettes and the scent immediately triggers an intense craving for a smoke.

'Thanks for returning my call,' I say to her. 'A busy few days for the paper, no doubt.'

She grabs my elbow, leads me away from the door of the office. 'If Harry catches me with you, he'll finally have an excuse to fire me,' she says. 'There's a coffee shop down the street.' Shelley rummages around in her handbag, finds her cigarettes and lights up with a quick draw. She sighs out the smoke as she walks. 'We're all over this case.' She throws an apologetic expression at me.

'You're doing your job.'

'You know I sold my soul when I signed up for this but a story is a story and this one's got a lot of legs. Do you think the trial will go on for long?' She's keeping the questions light but I can hear the test in her voice.

I laugh. 'You're not drawing me into that one.'

'I had to try.' She gives a short laugh.

She stops outside the coffee shop, takes a couple of hasty drags then flicks the fag into the street. It lands in the middle of the road, a burst of sparks. The café is a small boutique affair with trailing plastic violets and fairy lights looped over the walls. It looks like a child's bedroom. Ceramic unicorns share shelf space with dozens of tiny potted cacti. 'Harry wouldn't be caught dead in here, nor most of the other soulless creatures I work with. It's tack central but it does a good coffee.'

We order our drinks and sit down. Shelley sets her bag on a spare chair, rummages about inside it for a moment, then produces a box of caffeine tablets. She pops two free from the packet, along with a paracetamol and swallows them.

'Same old at the office, then?' I say. 'Harry still breathing down your neck?' I'm hoping the pressure for an angle isn't why she's asked to meet now. It wouldn't be the woman I know but a journo is a journo and Shelley has the bloodlust for a story as much as the next.

'It's not easy being the favourite,' she says, lifting the steaming mug to her face and taking a mouthful. 'You'd think by now, I'd have gotten my break. Be sitting in some cushy office, an assistant typing up my considered, world-changing segments and not sharing a cubicle with John-I-don't-like-to-bathe sweat-letch, inhaling the fumes of curry from the Indian next door and turning out the majority of the paper's copy.'

'You'd be bored stiff in a plush office. You like the scrum too much.'

She sighs again. 'Oh, I don't know. Jess is on at me to quit, says I leave human in the morning and return a demon.'

'How's Jess?'

'Saintly, as always.'

I straighten. 'You didn't stop for long at the courthouse.' I wince at the tone in my voice.

'Yes, sorry about that. I know it was weird but I wasn't sure about where I was going with this thing and it could be . . . look—' she rubs a hand over her short hair. 'I'm tired. I don't know what the deal is with Margot Nugent but I don't like the discourse. Maybe it gets the feminist in me riled up but we're deluged with information on her personal life. Honestly, what you see in the press is the tip of the iceberg. Past sexual partners, neighbours, brief contacts who haven't spoken to her in real life since she was a child. There's something about it all that makes me feel so fucking jaded, you know. Can we deal with the bloody facts, here?'

'Don't let Harry hear you say that. You're in the business of selling newspapers, not facts.'

'He sees my expression when he drops another word count on the table and tells me to write around the colour of her fucking hair. Yesterday, he asked me if I could write up a quick segment on five notorious killers who were redheads.' A brief scowl of anger. 'If she killed her mother, which to be fair is not looking like it could be any other way is it—' I shift in my seat, not sure if she's asking me. 'Oh don't look so bloody uptight. What I'm saying is: her appearance shouldn't fucking matter.'

'People can't help it. They want to see what monsters look like.'

Shelley tips her head with a sharp movement. 'And what do they look like?'

'You. Me. The person next door.'

She reaches out for a sugar packet, tears it open and dumps it into her coffee. 'They believe she's guilty because of the cut of her hair, the way she smiles.'

'But it's not what *we* look at.' I lift the cup to my face, take a hasty sip of coffee. 'We have a strong case. You know I wouldn't charge her if it was otherwise.'

But Shelley knows me too well. 'Christ, you'll break the handle off that, if you grip it any tighter.'

I put the cup down quickly. 'Sorry.'

She lowers her voice. 'Do you remember the guy in the park? Shot himself in front of everyone.'

My head snaps up. The Iveagh Gardens, witnesses, a troubled man and a gun. 'Yes.'

'It wasn't investigated.' She says this as a statement, not a question.

'It was suicide.' She makes a humphing sound and I can't help bristle in defence of my profession. 'We can't throw every

212

resource at every death that occurs. There were many witnesses. He killed himself.'

'But why?'

'Only he knows that.'

'I ran the story on him. Harry wanted me to move on but I couldn't let the story go. Initially, it was the spookiness of it all. To walk into a park like that, full of people, and blow your brains out. I hunted down one of the witnesses. She'd been only ten yards from him. Saw him walk in, said he was thin, fit-looking. But she said something that really got under my skin. That when he took out the gun, he stood for a moment, like he was waiting for people to notice him. To see him. I mean, she thought he was going to open up fire on the entire park but in hindsight she'd the feeling that he was about to say something. Like the way a speaker waits until the crowd quiets. Like he was about to make an announcement. Of course, we know he didn't, but I thought there was something there. If this was a message. Why and who was it to?'

I search for the man's name in my memory, matching it up against anyone who has touched the Nugent case and coming up short. But I find myself leaning in, a slight watering in my mouth, the pulse picking up in my throat, stomach tight. 'McGrane, wasn't it?'

'Rory McGrane,' she says and I feel a cold sensation creep over my skin. *Rory*. 'I dug around his background,' she continues. 'Worked as a civil servant, apparently, but I couldn't find out as what exactly. Got hold of his mother, Kim, in her eighties now with advanced dementia. She lives in a nursing home in Lucan and wouldn't speak to me. It was near impossible to get a feel for the man. About a week after, someone phoned in to the paper after seeing my article. Said Rory lived in an apartment building on Mount Street. Wealthy enough place. Anyway, this fella looked after the communal garden and Rory would often pop out for a smoke while he was there. Didn't speak much, only to comment on the weather and that. I went to the address and it was like something out of *The Godfather*, these blokes in suits, clearing the place out.'

'Police?'

'There was no crime-scene tape or forensics people out but they had that air. That arrogance.' She throws me a quick apologetic look, 'No offence—'

'None taken.'

She goes on. 'The look of them was enough to keep me well back. But I waited in the street, watched them go in and come out with boxes of stuff. Here,' she takes out her phone, flicks over the screen for a while then turns it towards me. 'I got a few photos of them as they were loading up their van.'

I take the phone. The back of the van is open and I see the shadow of a man inside, caught bent at the waist arranging the contents to make room for more. Both of the other two men are carrying brown cardboard boxes; one has their back to the camera, the other is in profile and I recognize the straight sweep of his nose, the low overhang of his forehead. The Chief of the Gardaí Surveillance Unit, Adrian Redmond.

'You know who they are?' she asks.

I shake my head. Mouth gone dry. The conversation Baz and I had yesterday pushes up against the bones of my skull. 'Sorry, no.'

214

'Anyway, I couldn't let it go. Went to an old friend, who got me Rory McGrane's autopsy report.' The clink of stainless steel comes from behind, the hiss of steam as the barista makes up another cappuccino. 'Took a couple of weeks but got it eventually. However, my source said, I wasn't the only one who requested a copy.'

'Family?'

'You tell me. You see, the person who requested it was Debbie Nugent.'

I feel myself drawing back from the conversation, my thoughts rearranging themselves, throwing up avenues of possibility. Debbie's extended family being one of them. The Tynes, gang crime, drugs. Cold sweeps over my skin. Where is Margot in all of this? When I add McGrane's death to the mix, it has the effect of pulling me back, yanks me out of that claustrophobic town buried in the Wicklow mountains and places me on the outside of something much wider, where the chess pieces I thought were in play now look like pawns rather than deadly big hitters.

Shelley reaches out, puts her hand over mine, stops the train that's speeding through my head. 'You know I shouldn't be here. I should be running with this story, but I'm lost. It feels big,' she emphasizes the word 'feels', presses the palm of her hand to her chest. 'To be honest. I'm scared. I don't think I can dig any further into this without being noticed. It seems every way I turn there are walls and I'm thinking those walls might be of the variety that it doesn't pay to cross. Not until someone else is in control anyway,' she says, meeting my eyes.

And I notice now that she does look tired. At first, I'd mistaken her hyper mood to be just Shelley's usual fractious energy, but now I see how her gaze moves, seeks mine, constantly reading, how her thin shoulders have curled inwards, as if bracing for some blow or side tackle. She pulls her hand away from mine, the tips of her fingers shaking, makes the effort of smiling but it doesn't quite work. She reaches for her bag again, removes an envelope. 'Here's the report,' she says. 'I don't know Frankie, but I'm not convinced Margot Nugent killed her mother. I think Debbie, for whatever reason, was getting close to something regarding Rory McGrane's death. But I can't for the life of me work out why.'

I don't tell her that Rory McGrane was likely Rory Nugent. If she's gotten this far, she probably knows already. Instead, I nod to the fags on the table. 'Do you mind if I bum a cigarette?'

The autopsy of Rory McGrane should have been short. Gunshot wound to the head. But now I see why Shelley is nervous. Numerous old wounds, fresh bruising around his lower ribs, no fractures, blows that don't read to me like they could have come from a fall. A sharp drive of curved knuckles to the base of the ribs, aimed upwards right into the kidneys. There were other marks around the shoulders, upper arms. The pathologist had listed bruising, yellowed and approximately a week old. But they hadn't remarked on a cause. But I can see it: one holds him while the other hits. Again and again into his side until he is aching and winded, his weight pulling through his shoulders, only held up by the other's tight grip. He was beaten in the days before his death.

Toxicity shows antidepressants. Fluoxetine. I experience a quick jolt to the past, and my dad's face flashes up in my memory accompanied by the usual haze of fear and sadness. I blink hard and force myself back to Rory McGrane, back to my phone conversation with Baz on the Conahys and the Tynes. That it looks like Rory was feeding information into the wrong hands. Add the head of our Surveillance Unit to the picture and Rory's position begins to make sense. He was undercover. No wonder his past has been scrubbed out so effectively. An agent embedded in one of the country's biggest criminal families. Married into the Tynes to harvest information for us; only, if Baz is right, we weren't the only ones getting tidbits from Rory. It appears he saved the cream for a bigger cat.

I wonder if Debbie knew of his double life. Was that the reason she left him? It doesn't seem likely if she only started investigating Rory after he died. Suddenly her visits to Dublin make sense. Had he contacted her before his death? Revealed his true self? I swallow. It must have been crushing to discover your marriage was a sham. That you'd had children with someone who only existed on paper. A ghost. A lie. The trauma of such a discovery, for Debbie. For her daughters. Every happy moment turned to a memory that needs to be scrutinized. How much of his love had been real or for the purpose of maintaining cover? Each family milestone an act of deceit, an act of abuse. If it was me, I would definitely want answers. I would want someone to pay. But the people that Debbie Nugent would have been up against would not want that getting out. There would be plenty of reasons to keep her quiet about it. Reason enough to kill.

217

CHAPTER 18

I sit in my office in the Bureau, the muffled sound of the phones ringing beyond my door, the scent of wood polish, the tang of printer's ink. The scents and sounds of coming home.

Helen sits across from me. 'Now we've his address,' she's saying, 'we've been able to search the CCTV in the area and we have him on camera on a number of occasions . . . '

I tune out, dark thoughts turn in my head. Rory resigned from the force in the early nineties, the same time he removed himself from Debbie's life. Had she known where he was all this time? Had the decision to stay away been a joint one? Obviously, whatever happened in the past, the months, weeks, days preceding Rory's death left him scared. Alone. With no one to trust but his own hand. Why did he not seek help? Maybe whatever past was coming for him, he believed would come for Debbie and possibly the girls too. My fingers curl in against my palm. We might never know. The image of him walking towards the Iveagh Gardens on that bright day plays in my head. I imagine him turning through the stone pillars of the park, sweat under his collar and a gun in his bag. Whatever led him to the centre of that lawn, left him feeling that there was no other way. I feel the thrum of a headache begin at the base of my skull.

'Magnus Tyne,' Helen's voice cuts through my thoughts.

I look up. 'Sorry?'

'Debbie's uncle. Debbie's murder could've been a revenge killing from a rival gang but it doesn't quite fit the picture, right? It's too messy, slow.' Her voice drops to a mumble, hands now empty of reports, the papers stacked on my desk in front of me. I hadn't even noticed her placing them there. 'I don't think they'd care much for dumping the body. It's usually: boom!' she makes a trigger action with her thumb and forefinger. 'And they leave them there.'

I raise an eyebrow. She takes a breath, lets it out slowly, nostrils flaring, and I see that this has really gotten under her skin. I'm not sure which aspect of it all is upsetting Helen most: the thought of Debbie Nugent caught up in someone else's criminal game or Rory's desperate attempt to cut them both loose and failing or simply her need to know every detail of this mystery.

She composes herself, waves a hand over the papers on my desk. 'It's all relevant but the best theory I can come up with is, Rory never resigned. He continued to work covertly and, whatever hot water he got himself into, he knew it might threaten Debbie. So he shot himself in that public way to make headlines, get word out quickly that he was out, taking whatever it was that had got him in the shit, down with him.'

I feel my mind opening again. Sense the movement of a solution on the horizon, hazy and unclear, more of a feeling but it's there. If Rory did continue to work all this time undercover,

219

there's one person who could give us answers. The only question is whether his niece's murder is enough to compel Magnus Tyne to talk to us.

'Do we have an address for Magnus Tyne?' I ask.

'Only the house in Ballsbridge. Don't think he's ever been seen there though.'

I push my fingers against my temples, hating cases like this more than ever – no one saying who they are, no one staying where they're supposed to be.

'But,' Helen goes on, 'it's his auntie Lyn's anniversary tomorrow. Of her death.' She smiles, she knows she's done well. Auntie Lyn is the woman who fostered and raised both Magnus and his sister Evette Tyne. A woman Magnus called Mother Lyn, and who he credits for putting him on 'the right path,' although I challenge anyone to say that about Magnus Tyne and keep a straight face.

'She's buried at Glasnvein cemetery,' she says. 'I'd get there early. Dawn or maybe just before.'

There are a few traits that come in handy if you're a detective. The ability to keep your emotions away from your face, the absolute belief that you can get the answers you seek – no matter how fucking impossible the odds – and, the most important one, knowing when to admit you've gone down the wrong path. You need to give yourself the freedom to grasp that wheel and turn your case around. And quickly.

And I tell myself that this is what I'm doing as I head south out of the city, back down the country roads towards Ballyalann, the Wicklow mountains rolling out ahead of me. There's a loose

220

thread left dangling after Debbie's murder even though our prime suspect is tucked safely behind bars. It will take some explaining to Donna Hegarty why I'm still 'wasting' time and resources on a case that should be closed. But I'm not ready to close this investigation, not when there's a chance there might be bigger players involved in Debbie's murder. And it's not the first time we've put people behind bars for a crime they didn't commit. Debbie invited this person into her home, made tea for them and I can't help feeling that she knew them.

Everything her victimology tells us says that she wasn't one for a wide circle of friends, she wasn't one for inviting people into her home. Now, of course, her self-imposed isolation makes sense; intimacy with others brings questions and Debbie didn't want to answer questions about her past. She guarded that part of her life from everyone, even her own children. She buried it.

Baz is still attempting to dig out the name of Rory's handler. He's managed to find his passing-out ceremony picture and, comparing it with an image used by the media after his death, we've confirmed a match. But the trail goes cold after 1983, enough for us to believe he was pulled for undercover work. And this is the difficulty. The Gardaí Surveillance Unit do not give up the names of their agents unless they are commanded to by a court. A necessary barrier but one, it could be said, allowing for a lack of accountability. I feel the acid churn in my stomach when I think they placed Rory in among the Tynes, allowed him to manipulate Debbie. Whether he loved her or not, their relationship was built on deceit and lies. And their children. I know if I'd been Debbie, I'd have wanted to know who sent down the orders, who clapped their hands or praised their agent for a job

221

well done when they managed not only to win the trust of one of Ireland's biggest organized criminal gangs but also secured their place through marriage. If I had been Debbie, I would have been out for blood.

It looks like, after he left Debbie, Rory continued to work with her uncle in the city. Residents in Clondalkin have confirmed his presence there up until a few months ago.

I find Clancy not on the golf course but in the clubhouse. He's sitting at the bar, among a row of other golfers, Fitz at his side, both deep in conversation. I look over the dining tables, full despite it being only three in the afternoon and a Wednesday. A selection box of men in their late sixties through eighties, a grander variety of chinos and soft cashmere sweaters you'd be hard put to find in a Ralph Lauren catalogue. Clancy clocks me glancing at the sherbet lemon shirt he's wearing and mumbles something about a dress code.

'I've just met Fitz here for a bit of lunch,' he says, nodding at Fitz, who moves his head along like a nodding dog. 'Thought a bit of a celebration was in order.'

'Hi Fitz,' I say, then to Jack. 'I wanted to talk to you about that.'

He meets Fitz's eyes and gives him a grin as good as thrusting his thumb in my direction and saying, *Will you listen to this one*. 'The case is closed, Frankie. That's it. Pre-trial over. Have a rest, will ye.'

'Something else has come to light,' I say.

'Don't mind me,' Fitz says. He makes a point of looking away, turns his body and pretends not to listen.

'Jack?'

222

He takes a longing look at his pint. 'It was good while it lasted.' He heaves off the stool and claps a hand on Fitz's shoulder. 'I'll be back.'

I walk ahead. Get into the car and wait for him to join me. He gets in and closes the door. 'Was getting bored of golf anyway,' he mutters. 'What is it?'

'I've had some information from a friend. They brought up that bloke who shot himself in the Iveagh Gardens a couple of months ago. Rory McGrane. It turns out he was Debbie Nugent's husband, the father of her kids at the least.'

He turns in the seat, lifts his weight on to one hip, supports himself on the dash with a hand. 'The father?'

'We're pretty sure.'

His hand drops from the dash. 'Christ.'

'Yeah. It seems to me that Debbie was on the hunt. My source tells me Debbie requested Rory's autopsy report. I think this is what she was doing in Dublin over the last few weeks. We know him as Rory McGrane,' I say, 'although Debbie would've known him as Rory Nugent. He worked undercover, it looks like he was tasked with infiltrating the Tyne family to feed back on their organization.'

'Covert work.'

'Yes. But the records show that McGrane left the force in 1983.'

'Let me guess, the year he went undercover.'

'I'm guessing so.'

'Well him being six foot under makes it difficult for him to be the one who killed her,' he says, then chews on that thought for a moment, his face growing increasingly intent, eyes troubled.

'So, if Debbie Nugent had information in the house about his undercover work, or perhaps some other nasties her husband had been dealing with, there'd be reason for someone to want that.' He shakes his head. 'Nope. Hang on. She knew them. Let them in,' he nods at this, liking his train of thought. 'She wasn't afraid of this person and sure, if she had information in a physical form then why would they kill her first then look for it. But if she knew what that information contained or possibly could have worked it out then she'd have to be disposed of.'

My heart picks up speed in my chest. Rory sent something to her. For leverage, protection. Something he would have told her to take to the right person. And maybe she did, or thought she did. I think of the mess of the living room, how it looked like someone had searched for something.

'If he'd sent her information, who'd want it? The Tynes? Would they have anything to do with her murder?'

'I doubt it,' his hand drums on his knee. 'I've been around the block with these kinds of criminals for most of my career. And one thing I know is that, estranged or no, family is everything to Magnus Tyne. I can't imagine he'd hurt his niece.'

'Baz has been looking at the Conahys. They've had a run of luck over the last couple of decades. We think Rory was either an informant for them, or perhaps his handler was.'

Jack is nodding. 'That's more like it. If he sent information to Debbie and someone found out about it, the wrong someone, we've got a bent handler, abusing a covert agent's information on one criminal organization and passing it to another, for money, security.'

'Did Rory know?'

224

'He might have. Then decided he wanted out. Word comes down that he'll keep his backside where he is or his wife and kids get it.'

'So he shoots himself.'

'Publicly. Hoping that it keeps Debbie and the girls safe. Sends her the whole set-up or some of it anyway, mentions names, so that if someone does come knocking she's got a bargaining chip.'

Jack sighs. Rubs a hand over his face, his palm rustling over the bristles along his jaw. 'There was no break-in. Debbie let this person in. If they had a badge, she would've done that.' He looks off towards the clubhouse.

And I see it now. A garda in the doorway of the Nugent home. Uniform smart. Blazer stiff across the shoulders, hat tucked respectfully under their elbow. A symbol of trust. Asking if Debbie would mind if they came in, that they'd had word about her husband.

'I'm sorry to tell you, Mrs Nugent,' he says, 'but your husband died a couple of weeks ago. We have a few questions.'

She invites him in. He asks her when they last spoke. She's confused, wary. Says she hasn't seen her husband in decades. But there's a part of her that wants to tell this person what she knows, she's angry, wants justice for the years of lies. Wants someone to pay for her husband's deceit. And this person seems trustworthy. They don't seem to know about Rory's undercover work. But she keeps silent until she's sure. That's what Rory told her to do. She makes tea. They ask her if she has any papers, personal details so that they can confirm his death.

She reminds them that he left her two decades ago. She has nothing. Maybe there's something in this person's expression, a

225

tightening around the eyes, a brief flash of anger that she won't give them what they want. But if there is, she misses it. They know she received information from Rory before he killed himself. Know that this could lead to them.

But they control their temper, offer her a sympathetic smile. 'Only, we believe he was in some trouble. That you could be in trouble. A friend of his told us he might have sent something here?'

And she gives herself away, doesn't deny the theory quickly enough. Curiosity is piqued about what this person might know. The kitchen is cold and she suggests they move to the living room where she can turn on the gas fire. She takes up the tea, leads the way.

'The Surveillance Unit were seen clearing out his gaff in town,' I say.

'Two-faced assholes,' Clancy mutters. 'I don't know how we're going to do this Frankie. It might be well left alone.'

'Margot,' I remind him.

'Look, we can't. Not yet anyways. The charge still stands up. She didn't report her mother missing for ten days. You're forgetting that Debbie's daughter might also have found this news upsetting. In her eyes, she won't have been deceived by one parent but two. Until we get more—'

He holds up a finger at the objection on my face. 'I promise you, as soon as we get anything that looks like we're on the right path, we'll pull that charge. I swear. We're not in for an easy ride here. The Surveillance Unit will give us less than fucking nothing. And they won't be compelled to, either. We could throw the truth at them all the live-long day and it will just slither off their greasy fucking backs and disappear into the rotting ground they stand on.' He sighs again, a blast of anger down his nose. 'Gimme a fucking cigarette.'

I fish out my new box of fags, pass him one and he pushes the end between his lips, lowers the window and lights up. 'These people, Frankie, they operate differently to us. They play by different rules. They have their assignment and anything that gets in the way of it is collateral damage. Money, property—' he points the cigarette in my direction, '—even a wife and kids don't matter. If we're going to go after them, we need something big, colossal, to take them down. Proof. In our hands. As real as you or I. We can't go in with this bullshit, they'd just applaud themselves on a job well done. And I don't think they'd be above coming after whoever decides to go kicking this hornet's nest.'

'But surely the Surveillance Unit wouldn't want this on record?'

'What fucking record?' he says, cigarette pinched between index and middle finger, pointing at the air between us. 'An operation like McGrane's, there might have been as few as three people running that. That's the whole fucking point,' he jabs the air with his hand as he speaks. 'It's *covert*. And there's no way Adrian fucking Redmond is going to go lifting his skirts and showing us his knickers. No, if we go after these lads, we go all the way,' he looks to me. 'And that means we play by the rules on the surface, but we're going to have to play a little dirty to get our answers. Do you hear?' I do. He meets my eyes. And I experience a stab of fear, then the surge of adrenalin comes. I've never heard Clancy speak this way. He's usually the one with a grip on the back of my shirt telling me to hold on, think twice and play by the rules. His thick greying eyebrows drop down over the bridge of his nose, his blue gaze strained and sad. 'Fuck it.'

He doesn't say anything for a moment, his hand on the dash, tapping a slow beat with his thoughts. 'Let's debrief the Bureau tomorrow. Keep a functional incident room at the station here, but this has to remain tight as a duck's arse until we know who we're dealing with.'

I nod. Tell him about my plans for the rest of the evening. If we want to know what Debbie discovered, then there's one man who could tell us. Jack's not happy but knows we're stuck without it. He doesn't return for the rest of his pint. Phoning Fitz to say he's to head back to the city, adding in a teasing tone that some of us have to work. And Jack does, I know he's already preparing our reports in his mind, before we've even begun, softening future blows that are sure to come down to us from the commissioner. Crash helmets ready.

CHAPTER 19

Magnus Tyne casts a narrow gaze over the spot where we found his niece, his van parked well down the thin track that leads to the site. He's not dressed for hiking up hills and his shoes, thin black loafers, are shining wet from the climb. He's smaller than he looks in the papers. Bald, hatless, a wedge of thin white hair over each ear, which he slides a hand over every time a breeze shifts past. On his coat, a carnation is pinned to the lapel.

He spits on to the ground next to the shallow grave. 'How long was she here, then?' His accent is strong, hard Dublin, with a guttural kick and punctuated with low, round vowels.

'Two weeks,' I say.

'Fucking cold place, alright. I'd told Nugent to stay away,' he says, meaning Rory. 'I didn't want Evette's bleedin' kid getting pulled inta this business, ye 'now. It was for the best.' He sniffs. 'Evette never wanted a part of it and I'd always felt guilty tha' she was killed because of me.' He checks that I follow. I know Evette was his sister but didn't know she'd died. 'But in the end, I kep' my word. Even when Debbie came crying to me afther, I said to

229

Rory, lie low. Stay away for a few months, let her get herself set-tled. I gave her a few bob to get the house on the go and then told her if Rory had gone, been killed, then she was bether off staying clear of all this mess. For the kids' sake. And tha' was tha'.' He looks to the side, where his minder is standing about ten-foot tall and as wide, black hoodie, black jeans and the latest Adidas trainers on his feet. Tyne had introduced him as Lights. He left me to fill in the blanks around where he got his nickname from and I'm gathering it's not from light-bulb moments. His arms are loosely clasped at his front, hands barely able to meet across his body, the muscles in his arms of cartoon-like proportions. He looks like if someone so much as looked at Tyne crossways, he could scoop the old fella over his shoulders while squeezing the life out of the other with his free hand.

'Do the girls know?' Magnus asks suddenly. 'About Rory.'

'Margot and Kristen? No, we don't think so.'

'Well,' he says. 'We kep' them safe anyways. Their father looked out for them. Didn't get the credit, I know, but it was bether for them this way.'

'We think Rory sent Debbie information,' I say.

He looks at me, surprised. I'm guessing of course, testing if he knows if there was any interaction between Rory and Debbie before they died.

He gives a little shake of his shoulder then: 'Debbie came to me a few weeks back. Hadn't set eyes on the girl for years, and afther Rory's death, I knew it couldn't be good. The fucker sent her a file. A bloody rat, he was.' He sniffs. 'And I don't mind saying he was good at his fucking job. Never suspected him for a minute. He named his handler, a Kathy Grant.

230

Said she was bent. Passing over all our business to that piece of shit, Vincent Conahy.' His eyes darken. 'He said he thought there was more. Someone else in Conahy's pocket. None of my business tha' now. I've wiped my side clean but if it helps Debbie's daughter's case then . . . ' he trails off. 'Why Nugent did what he did to himself, I'll never know.' He turns a foot to the side, slides it through the grass to remove a clump of muck. 'Useless cunt,' he adds, then raising his hand to his lapel, he unhooks the carnation and drops it into the ditch. He blesses himself. 'May she rest in peace.'

He looks at me expectantly. 'I didn't come up here for the air, Detective. And I'm not in the habit of talking to the pigs. If there's justice for our Debbie here and you say her daughter is in trouble, then start yapping.'

I try not to think about how many people Tyne has probably murdered or had murdered over the years. I make a mental note to check on Kathy Grant. His statement about wiping things clean can't mean anything good.

'Did Debbie know Rory was working for you?'

'In the beginning, yeah, sure. But not afther, not recently. Until a few weeks ago. Rory didn't want Debbie involved. She hated the family's line of work, but Rory couldn't give it up. Now I know why; thought it was ambition he had.' He laughs at that, then suddenly he's moving, a few steps away then back again, head bobbing like a pigeon's, fists tucked up tight in his pockets. 'He worked for me, right up until he blew his fucking brains out.' He stops walking. His face reddens.

Then after a while, he turns on his heel and walks away through the mulch and dirt down the narrow track, leaving me

231

standing alone at the side of the ditch. For a moment, I think he's going to confer with Lights on some kind of strategy, but when he gets to his minder he keeps walking and Lights gives me a final blank stare before following his boss.

'Magnus!' I shout after Tyne's retreating back. He doesn't turn but lifts a hand, signalling the end of our conversation, and I don't know if I imagine it but I think I hear the reply – 'I'll be in touch' – come floating up the incline towards me.

I stand, the sunlight squinting through the trees over my shoulder, the damp smell of earth rising up from the ground and the chatter of evening birdcall summoning the end of the day. I take out my phone, walk over and back on the hill to search for a signal. One bar appears and I hold still and call the Bureau. Helen answers.

'Can you do a search for me?'

'Sure.'

'Kathy Grant. Force records.'

I hear the tap of the keyboard on the other end of the line. Then a soft intake of breath. 'She worked in uniform on the Southside, Clondalkin.'

'Worked?'

'Her body was discovered in the lake near Blessington twelve days ago. Gunshot wound.'

I close my eyes, recall Keith telling me about the body they'd pulled from the lake. 'I remember. Is there a time of death?'

'Autopsy suggests mid-March.'

'Thank you.'

I turn away from the grave, away from the track, wanting to walk. The evening is clear. Wide peachy skies with a light haze of cloud. Goat's beard, my mam would call them, a sign of good weather. The breeze has dropped but occasionally the scent of pine, soil and decaying foliage lifts into my face. I step over a small patch of shale, find my footing on a clump of heather and turn to look down on the valley below; the dark tops of the trees, the sweep of greens.

Tired of the tangle of this case, I take off my coat, fold it beneath me and sit on the ground. I'm not sure how we'll get to the truth with every witness dead. Whoever has silenced Debbie has really cleared their tracks. I close my eyes, breathe in and try to empty my head. After a while, I give up and ease myself upright, shake out my coat and put it back on. The sky has deepened, tipped towards darkness, the sun now slipping below the line of mountains. I start back towards the track. The evening air has cooled. It's greasy underfoot. I glance at the sky, annoyed with myself that I've not kept a closer eye on the encroaching darkness. When the light finally goes, I know I'll have trouble seeing my own hand in front of my face, let alone navigating the undulating slope of the hill. I take out my phone. The battery at three per cent won't get me far with the torch on. I search for the silhouette of a couple that passed me earlier, but there's nothing but the quiet stance of the trees, the cool sweep of air rising up the valley. I pause for a moment, try to pick out the sound of birdcall but the silence is huge around me.

Another few steps, down through the trees, a hand out, trailing fingers against branches, bark, tree trunks and eventually the line of the track appears. Traversing the hill to get to it, I feel the wave of relief. When I look back over the valley, the sun is gone, the thin curve of the moon printed in the darkening sky, the first stars visible, watching from time past. Somewhere, above me, higher up the track, the soft click of a car door. A walker, perhaps, returning to their vehicle.

I move on, follow the track down. Miss my footing. My right leg shoots out, my heel hitting a puddle of stinking water, the shock juddering up my leg and landing me on my backside. I let out a short, sharp cry. Sweat rises on my forehead. Hands go to the scar tissue on my leg. When the stinging subsides, I wipe the moisture from my eyes, swallow dryness and peer down the road.

The familiar shape of my car is only metres away. I feel for my keys in my pocket, open the door and drop into the driver's seat. Resting my hands on the steering wheel, I take a few deep breaths, aware now of my thirst, the ache in my shoulders. I start the engine and pull away from the ditch; let the car rumble slowly down the track.

In seconds, the white glare of full beams fills my car. Another car, coming down the mountain. I squint into the rear-view. Try to make out its position. It's close but moving slowly. I have a brief thought that if Kathy Grant was killed by someone because she knew too much then I could be too. Magnus? I touch my foot to the accelerator. The lumpy surface of the road thumping up through the car. The car is too close. Bearing over mine. I push down on the gas. And the car follows, the roar of the engine trembles behind me, lights blinding in the mirror. Then a bang, it hits. The seatbelt snaps across my shoulder. My head jerks forward, teeth bite the edge of my tongue. I taste blood in my mouth.

My foot goes down on the pedal. I grab for my phone on the passenger seat, the steering wheel bouncing over and back in my other hand. I try to dial Baz's number but feel the car go, slide away from my control. I grip the steering wheel, manage to veer away from a tree, twigs and branches screech across the windscreen. I slow, move down a gear as I manoeuvre over another hump, the other car coming closer.

The junction is ahead. If I can get to it, I can let the car go, break free. I veer towards it and pray there's no other traffic. I've barely tipped the steering wheel for the turn before the car behind slams into me again. I spin. Lights cross my face. A loud crunch. I lift from the seat. The belt cuts across my chest. Then a jolt. The crunch and screech of metal bending. Then black.

CHAPTER 20

Eyes heavy. A toothache in my leg. The hum of pain magnifies, drags me to consciousness. My name.

Frankie.

A banging. A car door opens.

Chief.

Something warm on my face, down my neck. Salt on my tongue. I lift my head. Feel my bones groan as I try to push upright.

'Chief. Jesus. Fuck.' Clearer, louder.

I open my eyes. Timmy Morris' face is looking over mine. His giant frame filling the door of the car. He reaches across me, unclips my belt.

I stretch out my fingers, test them. Okay. I drag in a shaky breath. Turn my head slowly. My neck is stiff, muscle pain, no more.

'What happened?' he's asking.

The car. The lights. The hit from behind. Magnus Tyne?

'I was hit,' my voice rasps. I cough. I move my fingers over my chin, around my jaw. I touch a soreness on my cheek. The cut on my lips. Blood sticky. I try to turn my body and Timmy shuffles back, gives me room to get out, his huge arms ready to catch me if I fall. I grit my teeth against the pain in my leg. But it's okay, just stiff. Nothing broken.

'Christ. Who?'

I lean against the open door, survey the damage to the car. Wrecked, the front in a V. A tree standing in the way. Beyond that the rest of the hill, dropping away in a steep decline. The tree saved my life.

'I don't know.' I massage the base of my neck. Adrenalin or fear keeps me upright. Even through my daze, I wonder how Timmy knew I was here. 'How did you find me?'

He looks back up the road. 'This is the route I take home, Chief. I saw the car. Didn't recognize it was yours though until I got close.'

I turn back, look around for my phone on the seat. 'I need to get back to the hotel.'

'Don't you think it'd be good to get to a doctor's?'

'I'm fine,' I say. 'Just scratched and bruised.'

He hesitates, looks out behind him then to me again.

'I'm fine,' I say again. I see my phone in the footwell of the passenger's side. I climb back in, reach for it.

I pick it up and breathe a sigh of relief when the screen lights up. I go to call my partner but Baz is in Dublin. I look to Timmy. Swallow. Then call Alex.

'Alex,' I clear my throat, leave a voicemail, 'I'm on the Rathmullin track just west of the Nugent house, at the T-junction onto the R47. I've been driven off the road by another car.'

237

I close my eyes, try to make my brain pick out a colour. Was the car light or dark? 'The lights were high, maybe four-by-four territory. I think a dark colour but can't be sure.' I hang up, put my phone away. Straighten. Face Timmy.

'I need to get to the hotel.'

'I really think you should get checked out, Chief.'

'As I said, I'm fine.' I place my hands in my pockets to hide their shaking.

'Alright.' He waits for me to move first. I look over at his car, a Prius, no scratches. But I can't help checking the level of the lights.

'Thanks,' I say, and move ahead of him.

He puts a steadying arm around my back and I try not to shrink away.

The hotel receptionist looks up when we enter. She stands in a panic when she sees my face.

Alex is already in the lobby when we arrive. 'Jesus, Frankie. Are you okay?'

'Just a bit scratched and bruised. Any ID on the vehicle?'

He shakes his head. 'Nothing,' looks to Timmy. 'Did you see anything, Timmy?'

'No, only the lights of the Chief's car here. That's all.' He hovers at my side and I can sense he's eager to leave. His hand lifts to his hat and he tugs the brim down.

'You can go, Timmy,' I say. 'Thank you.'

'Right so, okay, goodnight,' he says, then turns, and I watch his wide shoulders retreat out of the hotel doors and into the night.

238

At my room, I step inside, then turn to face Alex. 'You didn't need to come out here, I just needed a check on vehicles in the area.'

He nods. 'I'll have someone pick up your car.'

I go to close the door but he puts a hand on it. 'What's going on?'

'I'm tired. That's all.'

His eyes are fixed on mine. 'You're scared of me.'

I don't trust anyone here, I think. I pull in a breath, think of my dad. His uniform transforming him to hero. We're the good guys. But what if the bad guys are wearing the same clothes.

He licks his lips, a note of urgency in his voice. 'Frankie, tell me what's going on? Someone has tried to hurt you—' he reaches out, tries to touch my face.

I turn away and walk into the room. 'Close the door,' I say over my shoulder.

He steps inside and I go to the bathroom. Run the hot tap, reach for a cloth. Wash my face, my hands. The skin over my knuckles sting from where they hit the dash during impact. I dry off my hands. Return to the room, go to the wardrobe, make a show of searching for a sweater as my hands reach into the shelves and find my gun. I turn, slipping it into the back of my waistband, then pull the sweater on, tugging the hemline down.

Alex stands awkwardly in the middle of the room, waiting for me to explain. I plug in my phone.

'Someone wanted Debbie Nugent dead,' I say. I watch his face.

'Her daughter,' he says.

I look at him. Wait for another answer.

'Someone else?'

'We think so. We think there might be someone in the Gardaí who wanted her dead.'

'What?' he laughs. 'But the . . . there's so much evidence. She killed her.'

I don't answer.

'But you thought so,' he says.

'Now I think different.'

His voice rises a little. 'Her trial is in six months.' He looks around him, sees the armchair in the corner. Goes to it and sits. 'Sorry,' he says. 'It's a bit of shock.'

I sit on the bed. Wait for the questions. It can be telling – the type of questions people ask in circumstances like this. Who they ask about, what they ask about. Are they testing our knowledge or trying to uncover the truth? Are they on our side or theirs?

'Who? I mean, who would want to hurt Debbie?' He presses a hand to his mouth, looks at me from over the top of his fingers. 'And why? She was a gardener, a mother, well liked in the community. What motive would anyone else have to kill her?'

'She had something. Information that could have been damaging to someone.'

His gaze lingers on mine for a moment as if waiting for me to elaborate. I don't. *Answer my questions by asking your own.*

His eyebrows lift. 'Hang on,' he says, his hand leaves his face. 'You think someone in our district is involved.' He frowns, hurt. 'You think *I* might be involved in this?' His breathing picks up, chest rising. I have a sudden memory of the scent of him, my nose pressed up against the curve of his jaw, mouth tasting salt from his skin.

I sit on my hands.

He steeples his fingers beneath his chin, head shaking from side to side over the tips. I wait for him to speak.

Finally, he stands. The sudden movement makes me jump. 'Okay,' he says. 'Okay. What can I do? What can I do to help or to at least get you to stop looking at me like that?' He sighs, tips his head back. 'Can you give me more? Context. Why would I want her dead?'

I look down, study the stiff weave of the carpet for a moment and consider what to share with him. 'Before Debbie moved to Wicklow, she lived in Dublin, Clondalkin. She was married to a Rory Nugent or McGrane. Rory was an undercover officer investigating organized crime. We think there might be a connection to her murder.'

Alex extends a palm as if the answer is clear. 'Well bring this Rory in. Question him.'

'We can't.'

'Why not? I know he's been out of her life for years, but there must be a way to trace him. Find out where he is now.'

'We can't bring him in because he's dead.'

He backs into the chair again. Sits. I watch him take this in, work through all the same avenues that I've worked through. His face, the lines across his brow deepen. 'I mean, I don't know anything about this guy, Frankie. You have to believe me. I don't know what you want me to say.' He looks up at me pleading. 'You can't think I'd anything to do with this? Or anyone here. We're a small-town outfit.' He waves a hand in my direction, eyes lingering on the cut on my lips. His hands tighten on the armrests of the chair as if stopping himself from getting up. His voice lowers. 'I would never hurt you.'

I swallow. I want to believe him. And he sees it. He eases out of the chair, approaches me slowly, his gaze steady on mine. 'You have to believe me.'

I touch my tongue to my lips. Dry. Sore. He sits beside me on the bed. Takes my hand. Raises it to his mouth, presses his lips to the bruised skin across my knuckles. 'Please. Question me, whatever. If you're sure this is what's gone down, let me help you.' His voice lifts. 'We could go to the station now. If someone here is involved, then there'll be something.'

I pull my hand away. 'As soon as this lead came on our radar, we searched every file in Ballyalann station.'

A look of betrayal crosses his face but he checks his emotions quickly, looks down at his hands, now balled in his lap. I hear the long draws of air in and out as he fights to control his frustration. 'Okay.'

'What do you know of the Tynes. The Conahys?'

He shakes his head. 'Not a lot. Big organized criminals, right? Wicklow has its drug scene but nothing heavy like you'd see in the city. We're small fry. I mean, if Debbie moved here to escape her family's background, there's a reason, right?'

I swallow. 'She thought she'd be safe.'

'Well, yes,' he replies.

'But she wasn't. Someone here knew what she was. When I think of it, the way Debbie's room had been wiped. The placement of the keys in Margot's pocket, but not a strand of hair or blood from Debbie on the coat itself. The blanket from Margot's bed found with Debbie's remains. How happy Debbie's killer must've been when Margot didn't report her missing, when she all but wrote herself into the role of her mother's murderer.'

242

I shake my head at the impossibility of it but the truth is people are not text books, there is no manual on what they should do in extreme circumstances. Our primary need is to survive and for some the only way to survive is to deny. To shut down and pretend that it's all okay. Red pill or blue pill.

Alex pushes a hand through his hair. 'Are you sure?' I hesitate for a moment and he sees it, pushes his question. 'Couldn't Margot have killed her and all of this is dirt coming out in the wash.'

'A coincidence?'

'In a way.'

'My colleague will tell you what I think of those.'

'They happen all the time in criminal cases.'

'Not in mine,' I say.

His face brightens. 'So Rory McGrane was assigned when?'

'Nineteen eighty-three.'

'Well, I hadn't even made detective then. I would have less clue about covert work than the man on the street.' I feel myself stumble mentally on this piece of information. He's right, he wouldn't have been in play at the time of Rory's assignment.

He points to my laptop on the desk. 'Can't you access Special Branch archives from that?'

I can. I study his face. His expression a mixture of desperation and hope. And I take a breath. The after-effects of the evening trembling through my fingers. The prickle of fear turning to numb exhaustion. Adrenalin seeping away.

'I have limited access,' I say. 'Intelligence files are on special request only. For a reason.'

'How can that be? You're a Chief Super, for Christ's sake?'

243

'Unfortunately, we're all of us on a need-to-know basis when it comes to surveillance.'

'Not exactly engendering trust in our colleagues, is it?' His attempt at humour falls dead between us.

'It engenders safety.'

He rethinks. 'Can't we cross-reference the areas the Conahys and Tynes operated in with garda who may have been eligible to run covert operations. Those at detective level?'

I see the energy in his eyes. The need to help, to prove himself. And I find myself hoping for the same thing. Maybe it's the violence of the crash, the aching down my neck and tiredness through my body, but I want him to be right. I turn away, open the computer. Log on. I bring up the lists, compare the geography. Pages of names come up. Hundreds of possible candidates for the murder of Debbie Nugent. I narrow the field again, this time ruling out officers that were not qualified and well into their career for the years Rory McGrane was active. I layer on the filters: arrests made on the Conahy side, arrests on the Tynes, drug busts, murders, arresting officers, what crime squad they worked on, and the list shortens to fifty officers.

Finally, I add the filter of Ballyalann, Wicklow. The list drops to one. The officer's serial number, and I feel something grip my insides. I look across the room at Alex, who is back in the chair, head bent over his knees, waiting for the results.

He looks up at the movement. Stands. 'Well?'

I turn back to the screen. And he's behind me. I bring the cursor over the officer's number and click. I take in the name on the screen and something sinks inside me. I recall the warmth of his wife's smile as she welcomed me into their home.

244

Then I think of his posture at the golf club the day I pulled Clancy away, ears straining like a dog's.

I stare at the screen and will the name to change. To some unknown person. But it doesn't change and I read it again and again to make sure.

Detective Sergeant (R.) Dennis Fitzsimons

Alex's hand rests gently on my shoulder. 'Christ,' he says.

The car lights flash again behind my eyes. I blink. Metal, glass crunch in my ears. The hissing whispers of a small town, fingers pointing behind palms. And I feel an unbearable loneliness at the thought that I was a target moving through the dark hollow of this area, picked out by my otherness. My breathing shortens, tightens to the small landscape at the base of my throat. Alex is quiet but the pressure on my shoulder increases.

'I'm glad you're okay,' he says, then leaves me alone in the room and I feel the tendrils of this case tighten, squeeze hard around my chest.

CHAPTER 21

The Dublin crime world may be a great unknown but it's my unknown. When I take my next step I know where to put my foot and where not to, or I've a better sense anyway. As soon I step onto the Bureau floor, I feel the tension loosen from my shoulders. I pause at the coffee machine, take in the clack of keys, phones ringing. Paul, a hand to his headset, the familiar frown between his brows, sweat on his forehead as he jots down notes or turns through files. Ryan is leaning back on his chair, as if he owns the joint, a stick of liquorice in his hand. He chews through another bite, picks up a pen and opens a folder in front of him.

Helen sees me first. A smile breaks across her face.

She smooths a hand over her hair, gets up and walks towards me. 'Everything's set up in the conference room.'

'The commissioner?'

'She's given the green light for the Surveillance Unit to share what they deem necessary.'

'No inquiry?'

Helen's face reddens. 'Not yet, at least nothing has been mentioned.'

I walk to the coffee machine. 'The commissioner wants evidence?'

Helen nods. 'Yes. Myself, Paul and Ryan have been working on ways to get that. We thought maybe bank accounts, but Detective Fitz shows clean.'

'His wife's.'

'Hers too.'

'Their house is worth a fair amount but they bought it close to ten years ago when, although tight, it would have been within his reach financially. His car is modest. No great outgoings.'

I select a coffee, wait for the cup to fill. Add milk. Check my phone to see if Clancy is on his way. But the battery has run dead. 'What about Kathy Grant?' I ask Helen.

'Autopsy confirms she's been dead for just under a month. Although it's difficult to get a clearer time of death because of the water.'

'Phone Jack again. We can't be late. And can you order me a new phone, this one's had it.'

She takes my mobile. 'I'll have a temp one ready for when your meeting is over,' she says. 'The McGrane files are on your desk.'

'Thanks, Helen.'

'You're welcome, Chief.'

I close the door on my office. Set my coffee down next to Rory McGrane's life as an undercover agent. The Surveillance Unit logo is on the top right corner. The stamp: *Highly Sensitive* an invitation to look. I sit, take a sip of coffee and open the file. Rory McGrane or working name Rory Nugent was given the

Tyne job out of the gate when he moved to covert work for the Drugs Bureau. I turn through the file. Only son of Liam and Kim McGrane. Grew up in Finglas, Dublin. Not the cleanest of records before entering the guards – joyriding, car theft, shop-lifting – but perfect for a life as a covert agent. He'd be able to walk the walk. His father returned from his teaching job one evening and attempted to help a student who was being kicked and beaten by a local gang. Liam McGrane got stabbed in the neck for his trouble and in Rory's notes he says it was the reason he applied for the guards.

Next page in the file is line after line of blackout. The next page the same. The only word visible is the header at the top telling me what I should be reading: the names and con-tact numbers of Rory McGrane's informants in the years he worked undercover in the bosom of the Tyne family. Any one of the names blacked out could be a person seeking revenge, Debbie's murderer. Any one of them could be Dennis Fitzsi-mons. The following pages contain summaries of operations that Rory played some part in or wherein his information led to arrests. But what the Surveillance Unit have given us borders on nothing. I read through the edited list of operations that Rory McGrane contributed to:

1986 *Operation Blue Sky* arrest of four men in foiled robbery of an armoured vehicle, money to the value of £750,000.

The next page blacked out.

1989 *Operation Alsatian* drug seizure, Clondalkin, cocaine to the worth of £25,000.

It goes on with some minor scores, arrests but no charges until the final page:

1993 *Operation Meringue* half a tonne of cocaine seized at Dublin Port. Worth £20 million.

I remember reading about that seizure, feeling a vicarious buzz of excitement at the size of the bust. I read on through the file. The rest of the details could be whittled down to fit on one page. There's a note on his marriage. Church name blacked out. Date given as 17 December 1985. There's a copy of the certificate. Debbie's signature bubbly and round on the bs and broad across the D, a tiny circle above the i. Rory's upright, sharp and fast.

There's a long spreadsheet, an expenses report. Receipts for wedding bands. Presents for their children. Rent for their home together all through the system. No address but we now know it to be Clondalkin. Close to the Tynes' main turf. Magnus Tyne is old-fashioned. He never did go for the down-the-country escape pad, running his enterprises from a distance through his sons and crew. That didn't mean he was a regular face on the street. Far from it. In 2007, he earned the nickname The Sheriff after the line in, *No Country for Old Men*, 'Oh Sheriff, we just missed him.' I think he's managed to wriggle out of every charge that's been brought against him.

I close the file, push it away. I'm thinking, like Magnus told me, the death of his sister, Evette, hastened Rory's decision to leave Debbie. And then, when it looked like the threat was coming for Debbie anyway, a public execution by his own hand might have seemed like the only way to secure her safety, to make sure everyone knew he was out of the game. It was stupid of him to send her information but I see his reasoning. Perhaps he thought it could act as her security. Leverage should she need it. Instead, he sent her a death sentence.

By the time I get to the conference room, my coffee's gone cold. Donna Hegarty, dressed in her usual garb, cashmere cardigan over pastel blouse, sits at the bottom end of the table. Her mouth arranged in its usual pose of, in Clancy's words, a cat's arsehole. And she looks at me with the same indifference. To her right is a man, older than me; long nose straight as a ruler, his forehead sweeping outwards over his eyes. Expensive suit: navy, complete with a white kerchief in a tidy triangle in his breast pocket to match the shirt that rises to his throat. Around his neck a lanyard, on which I glimpse the logo of the Surveillance Unit, his name and title, Chief Superintendent Detective Adrian Redmond, beneath it.

'Detective Sheehan. Come in. Sit down.' Hegarty indicates the chair at the end of the table. Her mouth gives a lopsided twitch that could be taken as a smile.

'Thank you,' I say.

'This is the head of Surveillance, Detective Chief Superintendent Adrian Redmond,' she motions to the suited man on the left. 'Adrian, this is Detective Chief Superintendent of the Bureau for Serious Crime, Frankie Sheehan.'

'We've met,' he smiles in my direction, 'you may not remember. At the annual awards ball. You were a bit,' he pauses, his smile widening, 'well, you were having a good time, shall we say.'

Hegarty enjoys this too much.

I give Redmond a cool look. 'I suppose those of us that work hard, deserve to play hard.'

'Any sign of the assistant commissioner on your travels?' Hegarty asks.

'I expect him here shortly.' I reply.

'Should we wait?' she asks.

'I think it would be advisable.'

She goes silent. Pretends to study the notes in front of her. Helen enters the room. She holds a coffee in her hand, sets it down in front of Hegarty.

'Thanks, dear,' Hegarty says. Helen flushes, nods, takes a notebook out of her pocket and sits at the table.

Paul shuffles in, takes a seat, followed by Ryan and Baz.

Hegarty checks the time. 'I think we'll start. Jack Clancy will have to catch up later,' she says. 'We have the head of Intelligence here. A busy man, no doubt.' She smiles indulgently at Redmond and already I'm exhausted by her leg-humping. But I join in with her smile; this meeting needs to go our way.

'I appreciate your time, Sir,' I make myself say.

He unhooks his leg, pulls his chair up to the table. 'Please, Adrian is fine. What can we do for you?'

Hegarty holds up a hand. 'Before we start, let me state clearly that because of the potentially sensitive material we are about to discuss our conversations here remain only between those who are leading or active in this investigation? Namely, those in this room. The assistant commissioner, Jack Clancy, included, of course.'

Hegarty already sweating a leak to the press.

Redmond dips his head in acknowledgement. 'Thank you, Commissioner.'

She offers him another smile then looks to me. 'Yes,' I say then continue. 'We need to access the files for one of your covert agents. Agent number 3540W. Rory McGrane. On paper, it says he stopped working undercover in nineteen ninety-three,

251

but as far as we can tell he continued in some vein with a different handler up until his death in February of this year. We need the names of all those who worked with him throughout his career.'

'I've read your report,' he says, flicking open the file in front of him.

'And?'

'We've already given you all the details we're prepared to give,' he says, referencing the mostly blacked-out offerings he's thrown our way. 'We don't disclose details of our Intelligence operations, Detective. Not even to you.'

'Your agent married and had children under his alias. You don't think that's a reason to share your information?'

'If that's the case, we will conduct our own inquiries.'

'If that's the case? Have you read your own file, Detective? It's there in black and white.' I reach for the folder, extract the right page from the file and smack it down in front of him.

He doesn't look at it. 'Our agents sacrifice a great deal in order to do the work they do. To secure the safety of our streets.'

'And what about Debbie Nugent? What work was she assigned to do?'

He looks to Hegarty, adjusts the cuff of his sleeve. 'She was a member of a serious criminal organization, as you are well aware.'

'Was she? Or did she just share their name? What intelligence did you gather to justify Rory McGrane's abuse of his position?'

'Agent McGrane may have made some mistakes in the eyes of the world we live in today, but at the time he did what was deemed necessary to ensure he had won the trust of his target so that he could procure the relevant intelligence for our operation.'

I bite down on the 'fuck you' that's on the tip of my tongue. The more I push, the further he retreats, the cooler he becomes. 'And what of Margot and Kristen Nugent, Debbie's children?' I ask. 'Rory's children. What criminal organization were they part of that deserved the attention of our nation's top Surveillance Unit?'

He laughs. Actually laughs. Then holds up both palms and looks to Hegarty: 'Am I on trial here?'

'Detective Sheehan, please,' Hegarty intervenes. 'Can we keep to the issue at hand?' she says. She looks at the door. 'And where is Jack Clancy!'

'Rory McGrane's wife was murdered a few weeks ago,' I go on. 'We have reason to believe that your agent was acting as an informant on a criminal organization and that his handler was passing that information into the wrong hands, and that our victim, Debbie Nugent, found out and was killed because of it.'

Redmond shares a look with Hegarty, a tolerant kind of humour in his eyes. He leans forward, talks slowly, as if explaining something to a child. 'Detective, if our agents act as informants on criminal organizations, then I would say it's a job well done. You are aware what Intelligence means in law enforcement?'

I feel the heat deepen in my face. Hegarty sniffs.

'Yes, Adrian, I am aware. I'm also aware that Intelligence is supposed to go one direction. Into our hands, no? That it's not something that should be whispered in a rival gang's ear. Am I understanding *that* right?'

He flushes. 'All our agents are clean. They have regular assessments. Our handlers feed back regularly.'

'That's all well and good. But what if the handlers are crooked? An agent who has married and had children with their target, that's a lot of leverage for the right person.'

'Are you threatening us, Detective?'

I feel the faces of my colleagues turn to me but I keep my eyes on Redmond. 'In fairness, I don't see myself as the threat here. A woman is dead. Your silence is keeping us from getting to her killer.'

He sucks in a sharp breath. 'We have our brief, Detective Sheehan. You have yours. From what I understand you've already charged someone for this woman's murder. In fact, she's awaiting trial, no? Now, if you need assistance in bringing this ghost in, then we'll be happy to oblige, but with regards to receiving any more information about our operations and this particular agent, I'm afraid our door is closed.'

I knew it was going to be an uphill battle against Redmond. We might have a name already but we need the evidence and it would be easier to get it from him. A solid link on paper – from McGrane to Kathy Grant to Dennis Fitzsimons – would be ideal, but Redmond's refusal to help makes me think that he knows there's more to it. But I hold on to his offer, limited as it is, that he may help in some capacity, even if it's on his terms. It's better than nothing and Clancy warned me that this could be how things would go.

He gathers up his papers. 'Come to me with something concrete then maybe we can talk but until then I would advise you find another tree to piss up.' He turns to Hegarty. 'Sorry about the language, Donna. It was good to see you again but I really can't spend any more time on this.'

254

Her hands are clasped below her chin, tips of her fingers pressed against her mouth. She doesn't look at him but nods and he leaves, shooting a red glare at me as he goes.

Helen is watching me, her expression a mixture of horror and stunned admiration. Paul is busy folding down corners of his file, trying to make himself small. Baz meets my eyes and I see my own frustration reflected in his gaze.

I cough, more to break through the tension than from any need. I glance at Hegarty who hasn't moved since Redmond left.

Baz gets up suddenly. 'Okay, well. We'd best be getting back to work.'

Hegarty looks up. 'Thank you, Detective Harwood.' She turns to the rest of us and gives us a nod as if to let us know that we're all dismissed.

The meeting was a long shot. Intelligence don't share. Not unless we have something concrete, like Redmond said, and without any records or details of Rory McGrane, with Kathy Grant dead and with no other in on who information was passing to, we have nothing behind us to pressure them into helping. The fact of McGrane's marriage and children was probably not something I should have rubbed in his face. Instead of succeeding in prising Redmond's mouth open, it closed him up like a clam.

I get up, my seat barely warm. 'Commissioner,' I say, by way of goodbye, and she nods again, head down in thought. Probably thinking of ways to yank me out of my job. I set my shoulders and follow the others out of the room.

'Frankie,' she calls out as I get to the door. I turn, wait for the verbal smack down. 'Wait a moment.'

A sudden wave of fear drops through me. I have an image of myself, sans work, dismissed from my role, and see the vacuum of my personal life around me.

'Close the door,' she says.

I do as she asks.

'Sit.'

I pull out the nearest chair and sit slowly.

'Do you know how many officers lost their lives while trying to combat gang crime in the last year?'

'No.'

'Four,' she tells me. 'It mightn't seem like a big number but it's not a number. These are people. People who put themselves before hardened criminals in an effort to make our lives safer.'

I don't answer. And she gets up, comes down the length of the room, sits her pastel-covered backside on the table next to me. 'You and I got off on the wrong foot,' she says down at me. And I think of the last time she asked me to work with her, hung me out to dry in front of the media. Or tried to. I remember who came out the worst because of it. Not me. Not Hegarty. But my family. Getting off on the wrong foot is a bit of an understatement.

'I wouldn't say that,' I reply.

She laughs, the sound surprising, a belter of a laugh, loud and hollow. 'However you want to frame it,' she says. 'But there's one thing we have in common.'

I wait for her to enlighten me.

'Neither of us likes to be told where we can put our noses. Not when it comes to getting our job done. We might come at different angles to this, but it's with the same aim.'

It's painful to admit the stirring of hope I feel at her words.

'Those officers that died. Some had children, one was due to get married a month after she was killed. Another was only twenty, an entire career ahead of him, stabbed like a dog when he approached the wrong vehicle.'

'We're stretched thin on the ground,' I say. 'Our unarmed officers can't always contain the violence, and our armed units can only be in one place at a time.'

'I'm not blaming you. The struggle is all of ours and I know that there'll be casualties. Deaths. Murders at the hands of these people. What I can't abide is that those murders might come, however far down the chain the links go, from one of our own. That is the ultimate betrayal.' She pauses, gets up from the table, and I feel like I can breathe again. She returns to her seat. Opens the files on Debbie Nugent and the few scraps of nothing we've put together on Rory McGrane. 'I see Redmond's problem. He needs to keep the walls up on his department. What use is security if everyone knows your business, right?'

'But—'

She stops me with a finger to her lips. 'But,' she says with some force, 'there are other ways to skin a cat. Or didn't you know that?'

CHAPTER 22

Dublin Industrial Estate is silent. All units cold and resting. The temperature has dropped again. The night sky clear and bathed in silver moonlight. A glisten of frost covers the ground. I drive slowly through the maze of broken roads, ridged concrete rumbling below the tyres. Baz is beside me. His eyes strain against the skyline, looking for the approach of other vehicles; headlights against the dark. His hand is on the radio clipped to his stab vest, ready to call forward the armed units, should we need them.

Ryan is in the back seat, a map of the estate in his hand. I can hear his mouth going; if not talking about himself, he's chewing. He leans through the driver and passenger seat, shoves the map out and taps a rope of liquorice against it.

'The next right, Chief,' he says, breathing aniseed into the air around us.

Baz pushes him back. 'Fucking stinks.'

Ryan has been with us in the Bureau for eleven months and, remarkably, still manages to wear his work lightly. He does

258

enough to fill his hours and does it well, so that I never really have a reason to pull him up on anything. He's a steady worker but all his showmanship is reserved for the cut of his suit and sculpting of his body. And Baz can't stand the clocking-off attitude he has, even if sometimes I suspect that the real reason Ryan gets under his skin so much is that he does seem to be able to have it all: social life, work, gym and ample sofa-scratching time on a Sunday.

He returns to the wedge of space between the front seats. 'Not as much as your mother.' Or it could as easily be that Ryan seems to irritate people just by his presence.

'Grow up,' Baz mutters.

I turn into a small empty car park in front of one of the units. To the right sits a row of bins, full bags of rubbish dumped up against them. The building itself is a small warehouse with three floors. The windows have long been smashed, the glass broken down to a few pointed shards behind rusted iron grilles. A red daub of graffiti down the front wall announces *Angel 4 eva* with a clumsy heart around the letters.

Only a small cluster of us know about this operation. Hegarty. A few select staff at the Bureau, Baz and Clancy. Hegarty managed to coax Adrian Redmond out of his hole to help us set up. Like he said, he'd help us in his own way but would only go so far. No one is above Hegarty's reach it seems, or at least that's the impression Redmond is willing to give us. We're all in uncharted waters. At least, I think we are. Fitz, our target, when we get him will be hanged, drawn and quartered in front of the nation. Hegarty will see to that. I have an uneasy feeling working with her this closely. But at the same time, I've to admit, it's nice to know that whatever happens, the powers that be are playing on the same side. For once.

I look out over the car park. A short wall holds back a sloping hill. It's a tight space. No other exit than the one we've just come through. I remind myself that we're armed, and more units await our signal should we need them, but if everything goes to plan no one should even know we're here. The plan being to get a shot of Dennis Fitz with the Conahys. Magnus Tyne did get in touch, put the scheme to us, a scheme that Donna Hegarty said she wanted to know little about but yet didn't shoot down. In other words, we were to do what was needed. She was prepared for sleeves to be rolled up as long as they weren't her own.

The plan is to lay down some nice, juicy bait to draw out our suspect. Thirty kilos of cocaine set for distribution in Dublin. Put up by us, but that Tyne would take ownership of, pretend it was his lot. It's taken days of planning. Days that we don't have. Clancy drip fed enough to Fitz over a game of golf at the weekend. A professional grumble about the escalation of gang crime in the city. How it was impossible to stay on top of it. That manpower on the ground would never be enough but no one seemed to want to get it under control. Hundreds of thousands of euro wasted and no one able to act for it. No show for the money. Even this week, Special had managed to intercept some information on another illegal import, but the pennies ran out so their entire operation was for nothing. Rumours that a shipment was coming in for Tyne but Harcourt Street couldn't get a hold on where and when.

The hope is that Fitz won't be able to resist gathering up the scraps of this information and presenting it on a platter to

Conahy. And in doing so hope that Conahy's greed will call him out to swoop in and take Tyne's pot of gold for himself, bringing Dennis Fitzsimons along with him.

Magnus knew there'd be eyes on the delivery. Conahy's men, or workers at Dublin port where the shipment was coming in – ready to answer questions for a few bob. We gave it a few days and now here we are, in an industrial estate in Dublin, waiting for either side to show. All we need is to get Fitz on camera in the midst of an exchange.

'You got the kit ready, Ryan?' I ask.

'Yep.'

'Good.' I wait for him to get out and open the large roll-up door of the building.

'What?' He looks to me not wanting to get out of the warmth of the car, then stares pointedly at Baz. 'He's in the front.'

I meet his eyes in the rear-view rather than turning. Baz passes him the keys and Ryan swears as he gets out. We watch him bend, breath clouding the air, and work the lock at the base of the door. He goes to the side, pushes the hydraulic system lever to open it, but it doesn't budge. This time I don't hear him swear but can see the flash of annoyance and the shape of the word 'bastard' on his lips as he squats down, slides his fingers beneath the door, wedges his shoulder against it and heaves it upright.

'Karma,' Baz says, smiling.

I drive into the blackness of the unit and the headlights light up the empty chamber. When the door goes down it clangs through the rest of the building. I check the time. We've got an hour before they're due to arrive. An hour to set up.

'Torch?'

Baz removes his from his pocket, turns it on and I kill the engine, turn out the lights and we get out of the car.

Ryan straightens, dusts himself off. He holds up the lock. 'What do I do with this?'

I nod to the base of the door. 'Lock it.'

'But what if we need a way out of here?'

'If we find we need a way out, we're fucked,' I say. 'Let's not get to that stage. For the moment, I'd prefer to keep them out. First thing these guys will do is search the perimeter. An open door here and they'll come in. One hand on the warm bonnet of our car will tell them that they've got company. So lock it.'

Ryan pauses for a moment as if set to object again. The seriousness of the operation finally registering on his face, he pales but turns back to the door and slips the lock on the latch.

'We're here for images. That's all. Clancy has confirmed that Fitz is on the move,' I say.

Ryan turns on his torch. I lean into the car, pop the boot. Take out our equipment. Baz and Ryan come to the boot, reach in and open the case that contains their firearms. Then check the guns over, load them and hook their holsters over their shoulders.

'Lets get into position.'

I turn, walk through the building, picking my way over discarded tools, beer cans and lumps of concrete broken free of the floor. We ascend to the third floor, where a broken window looks down on the car park below. I turn off my torch, wait for my eyes to adjust to the darkness, thanking the clear skies and the generous, wide moon that beams down on the estate. With dismay, I see our tyre marks through the frost-covered ground.

'Not much we can do about that,' Baz remarks from beside me, following my line of sight.

'No. The Tynes should be here first to sell to the distributors, it should cover them.'

'Do we know the players? The dealers they're selling to?' he asks.

'They wouldn't give us that. It's a non-issue.'

'Are we sure Fitz will come?'

'Yes. There's no way Conahy is going to take information from a source on this and attempt to intercept a competitor's shipment without having his man on the inside taking the risk with him. Magnus said it's what he'll do.'

Ryan looks up from fiddling with the settings on our camera. 'I'm not sure I'd go along.'

'No one would take you along,' Baz interjects. 'Unfortunately, we're stuck.'

I throw Baz a look telling him to lay off and concentrate.

Ryan settles down on the floor at the corner of the window. He fits the night-vision lens to the front of his camera then clicks a few shots into the dark. Studies the image. 'Nice,' he says to himself. 'Might need to get myself a piece of kit like this.'

'Keep your eye on the action,' I remind him. 'Film, not photographs. Something that we can break down later.'

'A photo would be clearer,' he says.

'We don't want to miss the shot.'

'Righto,' he says.

I rest a hand on his shoulder. 'This entire operation rests on whether you can capture Fitz on camera. You understand?'

His expression turns serious. I can see him mentally pulling back, his shoulders tighten under my hand. He nods. 'I'll get it.'

'Good.'

'Radios turned to silent,' I say. 'If you have mobiles, turn them off. Don't need the Trigger Happy theme tune fucking everything up. The Conahys will have men with them. I expect the entire ambush will be quick. They'll come in, show their muscle and take.'

'What if there's fire?'

A creaking fear stiffens my bones. The cold shapes of our victims appear in my mind's eye: Debbie, Rory. And others past when I've been here before. Hungry for answers or maybe, eventually, justice.

I sit down on the cold ground. 'We stick to our plan.'

I look out on the horizon, eyes scanning for the light of vehicles approaching. There's nothing. For a moment, I feel a terrible sadness for Dennis Fitzsimons, a man who at one time had wanted to protect. A man who somewhere along the way became disillusioned with the good fight.

Ryan lifts a hand. 'Here we go.'

I look at my watch. Still a half hour to go. 'They're early.'

Headlights send arcs of yellow across the empty estate. Two cars coming fast. A dark van following. I stand, move to the side of the window, wait for the beams of light to swim across the room. I press my radio.

'All units stand by,' I say into the speaker. Then turn the radio down.

The first car, a silver Beemer, pulls up, makes a U-turn and parks, lights off. The van follows, turns in, rear facing out.

The driver gets out of the van. A large man. Magnus Tyne's minder, Lights. He turns, leans back into the driver's seat and when he appears again, he's holding a rifle across his chest. Three men get out of the other car, an old red Vauxhall. The buyers. Can't be more than twenty-five, any of them. The youngest, weedy, a nervous excitement trembling through his limbs as he moves. Then the driver of the Beemer straightens out of his vehicle and I recognize the stiff, quick walk of Magnus Tyne. The white glow of his head as he moves around the side of the vehicle. I see the spark of a lighter and then the glow of a cigarette as he lights up a smoke.

Ryan has the camera trained on the men. They spend a few seconds shaking hands, mumbling words of greeting. Lights walks the perimeter of the car park. He goes to the piled-up recycling bins, peers around the area, prods the full plastic bags with the nose of his rifle. Next he approaches the unit. The rattle of the building door echoes through the building and I feel Baz and Ryan tense at the sound.

Magnus makes a twirling motion with his finger. There's a rumble of conversation. Magnus is anxious. Eager to get the exchange going. Every now and then he scans the horizon of the estate. One of the young fellas pops the boot of their vehicle, removes a bag and passes it to Lights. The money. Lights opens the bag. His hand searches the contents. After a while, he zips it again and hands it to Magnus, who directs the group of three to the van. I look out over the estate, worry for a moment that Magnus has fucked us over, that he's no intention of hanging around for Conahy's men, and that 30 kilos of cocaine are off to the streets of Dublin and beyond without a reward for us.

He shakes the hand of one of the men, nods over at Lights then gets in his car and skids off in the opposite direction he arrived from, away from the deal and from any chance of Conahy and his gang happening on him as he leaves.

Baz looks to me, eyes wide, mouths the word, 'Fuck'. I swallow, feel the pulse pick up in my throat, watch with a sinking feeling as the dealers are escorted to the van by Lights to move the merchandize to their own vehicle.

A screech of tyres causes all of them to freeze, look up. This time there are no headlights. And the weedy lad turns to the sound. He looks to Lights, his skinny body moving from foot to foot. He's wanting to leg it. Nerves strung tight, but stupidity or fear holds him to the spot.

Another two vehicles. A sharp Subaru. A silver that catches the moonlight. No shoddy car for Vincent Conahy. The dealers reach for weapons, stowed in belts and pockets, from what I make out, two handguns and a knife, which I know won't be enough to protect them if Conahy decides they're in his way. They stand, watch, wait and I find myself holding my breath. Lights trains his rifle on the approaching cars. Conahy has not come half-hearted. Another four men, at least, emerge from the second car, guns first. Doors open, ready for their escape. Then Vincent Conahy gets out. He smacks his hands against the cold and another two men get out of the back of his car. All armed. Lights and the dealers are grossly outnumbered. My breathing quickens. If we have a shoot-out before getting eyes on Fitz, it will all have been for nothing.

Ryan has the nose of the camera in their direction. His head moves up and down, adjusting the focus, the distance, trying to get an image of Fitz in the car.

'I'd drop your weapons,' I hear Conahy say. His voice is high-pitched, almost shrill. It rings out over the gathering.

Lights hesitates for a moment and I can see that, if he had his way, he'd give a good go of peppering Conahy's men with bullets. But Magnus has played this well and his man knows his boss has what he wants. A nice bag of money for his troubles. The drugs are as good as sold, not his to lose. I try not to think about where that money will end up but I have a flash of Mark and Gar stabbing each other on O'Connell Street in front of half the city.

Lights bends, lowers the rifle to the ground, Tyne's dealers follow suit before scrambling for their car. Conahy lets them go. It pays to let mouths live in Conahy's world. It pays to have someone distribute the truth of his power. Conahy waves his crew forward and, weapons up, they approach the van. They begin to unload the bales of cocaine then they place them in the boot of one of their own cars. Still no sign of Fitz. I share a look with Baz, hope that we've got this right. The men appear at the back of the van again, climbing down, give a brief nod to Vincent Conahy. Job done.

I see the glisten of sweat on the back of Ryan's neck as he turns the camera over the faces below us. Eventually, he stops. Fiddles with the focus a bit, pulls away from the lens then readjusts and sets his eyes against it again. He looks to me, rests two fingers below his eyes and points to one of the vehicles. He's got Fitz in sight. My heart tightens. Breath fast and short.

I will him out of the car. Let us get a clear look at you. And he obliges. He emerges slowly from the vehicle and, even in the dark and from this distance, I can see the distaste on his face.

267

His pallor a washed-out grey. He approaches Conahy awkwardly, like a green boy at a prom asking for a dance. Bitterness floods my mouth.

I watch as Vincent Conahy reaches back, claps a hand between Fitz's shoulder blades in a show of camaraderie. 'Good work,' I hear him say. 'Sorry for dragging you out here, old friend. I should have trusted you. Thought you'd wanted out and this was a set-up.'

Fitz laughed. 'Come on, Vinny, you know me better than that.'

Conahy smiles. 'I do. That I do.' He reaches out an arm, makes a sweeping gesture across the yard. 'Finish up, lads.'

He steers Fitz back to the car. Waits for him to get in. Then pauses, takes a moment to look around him. His gaze sweeping the cold, dark windows of the building until, I swear, he looks right at us. I glance down and I see the shake in Ryan's hand as he tries to keep the camera steady. But eventually Conahy looks away.

'Angel 4 eva,' he says, reading the graffiti. 'Ain't that the fucking truth,' he laughs again. He opens the door of his car, gets in and drives off.

We wait in the darkness for what feels like hours. Backs growing stiff along the cold walls of the room. When the last vehicle leaves, we peel ourselves from the floor and look out the window at the retreating tail lights; the sour metallic taste of exhaust thick in the air.

When we return to the Bureau, Steve begins to work on the footage, frame by frame. It's nearly midnight and the comedown

268

after the night's operation is creeping over our small team, an agitated exhaustion that makes me edgy.

Ryan has loosened the lever on his office chair and is leaning back on it as if it were a sun lounger. 'That was some buzz, alright. But can't say I'd jump to do it again, all the same. Bit fucking annoying that Magnus Tyne walks away with a payout though.'

Baz is quiet. He sits on the corner of his desk. 'We've got what we set out to do. We've got Fitz in custody.'

It was a struggle to get Fitz into the car when we did get to him. Winnie in the background, clutching the edges of her housecoat together.

Ryan yawns into his palm. 'Felt a bit sorry for him in the end. He sounded desperate altogether.' He stands, checks his watch. 'It's almost midnight, Cinderella. If we're finished here. I've got some z's to catch up on,' he says, and I wonder if Ryan has it right. Skimming along the surface of his work like a pebble on a smooth lake. Enough to move forward but never allowing enough of a hit to sink. I've tried that. I've tried to glide over the top but I'm not shaped the same way. Too many sharp edges and come the first ripple, I'm in deep.

He gathers his coat and bag up, shuts down his computer. He's gone in the space of a minute.

'You nearly finished with that, Steve?' I ask.

'Yeah. I'll be ready shortly,' he answers and reaches down to a large rucksack at his feet, checks over the contents, cameras, cables, various connections. He folds his laptop closed then slides it into the bag.

I look at the time. The night is slipping away. I think of what's on the other side of this. How fast our target might be moving and all there is left to do in the next few hours. I remind myself what's at risk. Debbie's justice and Margot's freedom. I imagine the brief moment of confusion Debbie must have experienced after that first blow, before the next strike landed. A betrayal. An attack from someone she trusted. Because she knew something. Had wanted answers.

'As Ryan says, we've enough to link Fitz to the gang. I only hope his desire to keep a lengthy prison sentence at bay is strong enough to make him talk. Because we know there's more to this.'

Baz looks at the door. 'I do feel a bit bad leaving Ryan out of the loop. I mean, the guy grates on me like sandpaper but he worked well tonight.'

'They should have Fitz in custody by now. We question him at HQ then see where we stand. Until we know who to trust, we don't know who we're risking. It's best that Ryan doesn't know what's coming next. This way he can go home, catch his sleep without risking one of Conahy's crew arriving at his house to thump information out of him.'

Baz stands. Sighs. 'You're right.'

Steve is waiting by the door.

'Come on, we'd better get going,' I say.

CHAPTER 23

My flat feels like a cold stranger. The space confined. Familiar, but as if I'm revisiting rather than returning home. Baz is on the sofa, scrolling through his phone, head down, hair falling over his forehead, knee jumping under his arm; trying to distract himself for a few moments.

We'd barely warmed our seats in the interrogation room before Fitz held up a small appetizer on what information he could furnish us with. No names. Yet. He wants witness protection for both him and Winnie before he gives us that. But it was enough to fill in some blanks. It's a gamble. He could be lying to save his own skin. His profile definitely suggests it's not above him. But he implied there was another tier. A protégé of sorts. A person who stepped in when Fitz decided he could finally afford to go part-time on his crooked side-business; the person on the other side of Rory McGrane's handler, Kathy Grant. The one who, even if we can't yet prove it, had the most to lose if the file Debbie had came to light. Kathy's name on that file meant she was a risk. She might talk to save her skin. And Conahy wasn't

271

about to let that happen. His chain of informants were much too valuable.

I spoon instant coffee into two mugs, stir in hot water and take them to the sofa. I pass one to Baz.

'Sorry, I've no sugar,' I say. I sit down next to him.

'What if Fitz is lying?' he asks. 'Hardly clean as the driven snow, is he? What if he's as far as it goes?'

I remember the confidence on Conahy's face as he surveyed the building we were hiding in tonight. Conahy knew. He knew we would be there. I remember the magpie below my window all those years ago, my shaking hand as I reached out to help it, thinking it was injured and my horror as it flew away, out of my reach, revealing the real victim, neck twisted, broken. And I'm back in that car, crushed up against the steering wheel. The deep black of the Wicklow mountains all around. The salty taste of blood in my mouth. And I remember that evening, after the accident, in my hotel room. Alex looking betrayed that I could doubt him. That I had to ask him if he was involved somehow. My question on how much he knew of the Tynes. The Conahys. The shake of his head before he replied. *Not a lot . . . We're small fry. I mean, if Debbie moved here to escape her family's background, there's a reason, right?* And I remember my struggle to keep the emotion from my face, to stop myself from moving away from him. He shouldn't have known about Debbie's family at that point. She'd kept that well hidden. And we kept our discovery from the local station.

I meet Baz's eyes and answer his question. 'He's not lying.'

Baz is silent, takes a drink of the coffee, grimaces then sets it down. 'I'm sorry. I'm sorry it had to be him.'

I feel my face flush.

'Look,' he continues. 'He had us all fooled, alright?' His hand moves over mine, a gentle squeeze of my fingers.

I try to smile. 'So much for not getting distracted by instincts.'

'Your talent is to follow your instinct. You should trust it. Alex saw an opportunity and abused it. Fitz too.'

And I could hear myself saying the same words to anyone who was in my shoes, telling them to put the blame where it belonged and that we can't all go through life with one eye looking for the devil in everyone we meet. And because I might say these things, I can't take them from Baz now. 'You weren't fooled. You didn't like him,' I say, fingering the bruise in my ego.

He frowns, waits just long enough to give his thoughts some room, the warmth of his arm resting along mine. 'Maybe I was being a man about it. Didn't like the feeling that he was taking my spot.' He shakes his head quickly. 'Not in that way. Just as your partner, you know?' He hangs his head. 'Pretty fucking basic, huh?'

'Yeah,' I say, and surprise myself with a short laugh. 'That's pretty fucking basic.'

The doorbell chimes and I get up. 'Here we go,' I say. I go to the door and press release.

In moments, Adrian Redmond is filling up my small flat. He stands awkwardly in the living room, his briefcase gripped in one hand, his eyes casting about, waiting for permission to sit or perhaps leave.

'Detective Redmond,' I say. 'You've met my partner Baz before?'

'Of course. Our meeting at the Bureau,' he extends a hand and

273

Baz shakes it. Redmond looks about again, his unease coming off him in waves.

'I know the location is a little unorthodox but we felt it was easier and safer to keep this meeting out of sight,' I say. 'Please, take a seat.' I indicate towards the sofa.

He slides in behind the coffee table. Sits down, places his briefcase across his knees, his hands resting on the black leather surface. 'The operation went to plan tonight?' he asks.

'Yes,' I reply. 'We got Dennis Fitzsimons but Alex Gordon never showed.'

He draws in a long breath. 'It can't be helped. We can set the traps but it doesn't mean our prey will walk into them willingly,' he says with a careless lift of his shoulders, as if he's just dropped a penny down the side of the sofa.

'We're at a stalemate,' I meet his eyes. We need more information from him.

'I told you, I can't disclose details of undercover operations. That's not how we work. Not without a significant inquiry and not without a valid reason.'

Baz utters a swear word under his breath and Redmond shoots him a glare. 'There's a reason why covert agents' identities are kept from general garda databases, Detective. It puts our agents, our operations, at risk.'

'But your agent, Rory McGrane, was already compromised,' Baz growls.

'And I assure you, we're looking into that,' Redmond counters.

I sit across from Redmond, thread my fingers together on my lap. 'Let's get back on track here. What have you got?'

Redmond puts down his case. 'Nothing much to add. We've two sets of eyes on Alex Gordon's place. He's not in, as far as they can tell. Car is in the drive though.'

'Someone's helping him out,' I say and I can't hide the accusation in my voice.

'It's likely,' he says with a semi-bored tone. 'I understand how frustrating this is. Believe me. But we have surveillance on the station, on Gordon's house and on Conahy's crew. He'll make contact, if he's involved. Bottom line, he'll want to get paid for tonight's gig. We need him caught in the act. Otherwise he'll walk. A court won't take anything less.'

Even if Alex gets done for organized crime, I can't help suspecting that he'll escape a charge for murder. I swallow. Try not to let my feelings of betrayal steer our investigation into the ground. But anger is churning beneath my skin. The heat of it crawls up my neck.

'Frankly, I think you're better off keeping to Fitz.' Redmond raises his eyebrows, his expression lightening. 'You've done good to bring him in. That was a nice piece of work. You should be happy with what you've achieved. If you're smart, you'll make a thing of it, get a bit of media coverage. It'll send a warning out.'

I see Baz tense at this.

'No,' I say. 'Alex Gordon will pay for the murder of Debbie Nugent.'

Redmond nods slowly, taking up his case again, his face regretful. 'Okay then. Well, as I said, our men are at your disposal, but I advise you to be very sure before you try to swoop in on Alex Gordon. Get your timings wrong and this looks good for no one.'

275

He goes to the door. Opens it and leaves quickly.

'That was helpful,' Baz mutters.

'Agreed,' I say. 'We had to try though.'

He looks at his watch. 'What now?'

'We head out to Fitz, start pushing him for Gordon's whereabouts.'

'He won't talk without a witness protection scheme on the table,' Baz says.

'Then I say we remind him what's at risk. He may be enjoying being babysat at a secret house presently but his wife is not tucked safely away and we can't offer her around-the-clock protection.'

'And if he still doesn't talk?'

'Then we hope that plan B pays off,' I say, taking out my phone.

I call Steve for an update. 'Has Kristen been in touch?'

'She's fine. At home. All is quiet. Clancy's on his way out shortly,' Steve says. 'Everything's going smoothly. So far.'

'Good.' I sigh. 'What's the feedback from Ballyalann station?'

'Nothing much happening yet. I've called in Helen and she's out there on the pretence that they need access to any old case files on Fitz. Garda Joe Kaminski is behind the desk. Quiet as a church. Three calls. None of them raising any alarms for us. I tried to run more checks on Gordon's phone but got nothing. His mobile is off, as far as I can tell. Or he's using another.'

'You'll stay on call?' I ask him.

'I'll be waiting here. I want to see this through as much as you do.'

'Thanks.'

CHAPTER 24

We drive from Dublin out towards Wicklow. Faster than we should but time is not on our side. It's coming up on two am. Baz fidgets in the seat next to me, he's not entirely comfortable with this plan. I think about what we're asking Kristen to do, put herself in the same position her mother was in, in order to draw Alex out. But we need to act quickly. The ripples rolling out from Debbie's murder will only grow. To some, police corruption is best hidden and if there's a way to tidy this up, maybe Adrian Redmond is already working out a different narrative, one that keeps him and his Surveillance Unit clean. I think of Fitz sitting in that house. A uniform who is clueless about what's going down minding him. The whole thing makes my skin itch.

I pull up a little way down the road from where Dennis Fitzsimons has been placed. It's a quiet cul-de-sac in Rathrum, about ten kilometres outside Ballyalann. Plenty of neighbours. Small, snug cottages sleeping in the moonlight. I turn off the ignition and we get out. A dog barks somewhere off in the distance.

The only sign of occupancy on the street is a string of golden garden lights on a lawn at the end and a soft light glowing dimly in the front room of one of the houses.

Baz closes his door gently. Looks at me from across the top of the car then stares down the street. A squad car. Parked up, the front wheel pitched up on the kerbside, like the driver got out in a hurry. It shouldn't be here. The hush of the breeze as it lifts through the trees behind us and the whir of my pulse starts up in my ears. I share a look of alarm with Baz and he opens the car door again to reach for the radio.

'No,' I hiss. 'Use your phone. Contact Helen.' He nods, and I reach into the back seat for my stabbie, pull it over my head. Slot my gun in at the shoulder. Baz sits in the front seat. Phone pressed to his ear. He squints out through the windscreen. Eyes on the number plate of the car in front. Then he goes silent. I watch his face change, his expression dropping from one of intent to confusion. 'What?'

'Hold on, Helen.' He gets out of the car, nods towards the squad. 'That's Timmy Morris. He reported a callout to this address ten minutes ago. Two bodies inside.'

'Fuck,' I say.

I'm running towards the house. I hear Baz behind me, still on the phone to Helen, his voice low but urgent, telling her to get a unit out here fast and no it doesn't fucking matter who knows. We're fucked.

By the time we get to the house, my gun is in my hand, my finger ready to move. Morris is standing in the open doorway. His face ashen. In the dim light, I can see his wide throat moving, swallowing.

278

He holds up his hands when we approach. 'They're dead,' is all he says.

I edge closer. Gun trained on his chest. 'Turn around. Hands where I can see them. Face the wall,' I shout.

He lifts his hands higher. Fingers shaking. He shuffles around until he faces the wall. His large feet scuffing the ground. A whimpering sound coming from his throat. I approach slowly. Pat him over.

'Hands together at your back.' He does as he's instructed and I reach for my cuffs. Snap them over his wrists.

'Turn around,' I say and he turns slowly. 'Who called it in?'

'I . . . I don't know. It came through the station. Mrs R called me. Deirdre. Said it was urgent. That there was a disturbance at this address. I . . . I didn't know. I just got here and the door was already ajar.'

'Where are they?'

He clears his throat. Tries to breathe through the nausea. He swallows again. 'First door on the right,' he manages.

I point the gun towards the door. 'Walk through.'

He closes his eyes for a moment but nods and turns into the hallway.

Baz finishes up the call. 'Forensics are on standby for when we're clear. I'll check the perimeter,' he says, and he crosses a short hedgerow and disappears around the side of the house.

I walk Morris slowly down the hallway. He stops at the first door. It's open, the room is warm. A welcoming light pink paint on the walls, two deep sofas, patterned in grandma floral. A small gas heater glows in the corner. A young blonde smiles out from

279

the TV, beckoning callers to place their bets as a roulette wheel spins black and red.

The uniform, a man, not more than forty, lies on his back, eyes fixed on the ceiling, a clean bullet wound through the front of his head. Fitz is facing the TV, his body thrown back on the sofa, his chin in the air, a corona of red on the wall behind him. The TV remote rests in his hand. I feel my heart sink. For Winnie. For Jack, whose friend is dead.

I take Morris by the hands, lead him out of the room then clear the rest of the house. The back door is locked. The windows in the kitchen shut. I open the door to the bathroom and the breeze snaking in through the open window cools the sweat on my skin.

Baz returns. 'Bathroom,' he says.

'Yes.'

'They knew. They knew Fitz was here,' Baz says.

I nod. Morris looks between us. If he has questions, he doesn't ask them. Never has a bloke looked more ready to go home.

'You'll have to come in to make a statement,' I say.

'Yes,' he says.

Morris in the car. I close the door on him, turn to Baz.

'We have to make a move. We have to trust that someone's on our side,' he says.

'How could they know where Fitz was?'

'Someone's talking,' Baz spits. 'And Conahy's men decided that Fitz was disposable, after all.'

My phone rings. 'Steve?'

'Chief, Kristen called from her mobile. She said she phoned through to the station twenty minutes ago. I told her to sit tight.'

280

I inhale a sharp breath. I throw a desperate look back at the house. We can't leave this crime scene. Plan B already in motion and already going wrong. 'Shit. Okay. We're on our way out. Is Clancy there?'

'He should be. But I've got nothing on the screen here.'

'Let's hope this works. Keep watch and move in when ready.'

'Yes, Chief.'

I hang up. Turn to Baz. 'We're up.' I uncuff Timmy Morris. 'Stay here with this scene until forensics arrive. They won't be long.'

The rest of the colour leaves Timmy's face but he manages a stiff nod of his head and I have to take that.

I remove my stabbie and get into the car, Baz throws himself into the passenger seat.

By the time we get to the Nugent house, Alex Gordon is already surrounded. He sits at the kitchen table, a bewildered expression on his face, as if this is all some peculiar misunderstanding that he can explain away with a smile and a calm conversation. Clancy is keeping his distance, braced against the sink. Anyone might think him calm but I can see the skin over his knuckles turn white where they are hooked on the edges of the draining board.

I pull out a chair, sit down across from Alex.

His eyes soften. 'Kristen phoned the station. I came out as soon as I could.'

'Do you have the USB?' I ask.

'What USB?' he replies.

Kristen goes to move forward and I put out an arm to keep her back. 'I gave it to you,' she hisses from behind me.

'You didn't,' he replies. 'You said it was in—' he pauses. 'The guitar. In your mum's guitar. I looked and there was nothing.'

Her voice hardens. 'I handed you that USB. You put it in your pocket.'

I wave a uniform over. 'Search him.'

They pull Alex to his feet. Pat down his body. And in each turning second the glee grows in his eyes.

Finally the officer stands back. 'He's clean.'

Steve appears at the door. Satchel over his shoulder. 'Where would you like me to set up, Chief?'

'The table is fine,' I say to him, and turn back to Alex in time to see his smile disappear.

'Have we got a time frame?' Steve asks, directing the question to Kristen.

'Shortly after I called. Maybe two-fifty.' The strain of the night is under her eyes. But she's alert. She folds her arms tightly across her chest, her fingers pinch and roll the fabric of her sweater.

'Thanks,' Steve replies. 'You've done really well.'

She gives him a tired smile.

'What's going on?' Alex asks.

'We're tidying up our investigation, Sergeant Gordon,' Steve replies.

'Tidying up? I haven't done anything.'

I point to the fruit bowl on the kitchen counter. It's not the most sophisticated of places to hide a camera but we were short on time. Steve reaches in, moves a bunch of grapes out of the way and extracts the camera from its hiding place. He sets it down in front of him. Then does the same for the two other cameras

282

that we've secured to the top kitchen units. He returns to the computer and accesses the feed.

Baz stands beside me. Eyes moving from Alex's face to the screen. We watch the recording. A playback of the last hour. Steve fast forwards until we see Kristen come into view. She's standing at the kitchen table looking to the door and I watch her steady her nerves, take a deep breath. She wipes her hands down the front of her skirt then crosses the room. I know there are officers outside. Hidden in the garden. Clancy with them. Armed and ready should she get into trouble. In her pocket a small alarm that, should she press it, will bring in the entire team. I see her reassure herself of its presence before she opens the door. Alex holds up his badge and she steps aside to let him in.

I see her turn to the kettle, extend a hand as if to offer tea. He shakes his head. Taps his watch. She nods, turns her back on him to go to a drawer in the sideboard. She extracts an envelope, passes it to him. He takes it. Opens it, shakes out its contents. A small silver object falls into his hand. His fist closes around it. He smiles at her. Puts it in his pocket. He reaches out, rests a hand on her upper arm. He says something to her and she nods. I watch, as on the screen, she moves away, out of the kitchen, out of shot, and for a moment – even though I know she's okay – I feel the sting of fear that she may not come down again, that somehow, he has gotten her, like he got her mother.

He watches her ascend the stairs then opens the Aga door. The flames light up his face. He removes the USB from his pocket and throws it inside.

When Kristen returns, she's holding her mother's guitar. He spreads his hands. A smile on his face. Extends his arms asking permission to hold it. She nods, passes it over. I see the pain cross her face as he turns the instrument to his chest and attempts to play it. I know what his game is, he's making sure Debbie didn't hide any other of his secrets inside the stomach of the guitar. But it's too late for Alex. On her short walk upstairs, Kristen had already pressed her alarm and we watch as in seconds Clancy and the team rush into the house.

Steve closes the laptop. We wait for Alex's reaction. He's silent. His eyes dark but I see the anger in them.

'It was just a USB. So what,' he says.

He's right, it was just a USB. We've nothing so grand as a file of information from Rory McGrane, but we knew if we put out the bait anyway, a decoy, Conahy's informant, Debbie Nugent's murderer, wouldn't be able to resist chasing it.

Baz keeps back as I fix the cuffs around Alex Gordon's wrists and bite out his rights along with a charge for murder. He comes easily. His smugness grating right across my nerves. I'm not someone inclined to thump a suspect on the back of the head when we have him in custody but never before have I struggled so much with that urge. I guide him out to the car, slowly. Mindful of my own intentions and the battle going on inside me. Remembering that this case is complicated enough without me adding dirt to the water.

We're halfway to the car when he speaks. Not able to keep his gob shut for the short time it will take to pile him inside. 'You'll never make this stick,' he says. 'It might look like a good idea now. But think of your career. You'll never be trusted again.'

I keep walking. At the car, I turn him around. And the confidence of his demeanour shakes me. At the same time, I can see he wants to talk. The gloat is riding on his face like a flag. And I can't help myself. I can't help wanting him to acknowledge that this is it. He's about to pay.

'Rory McGrane's handler was dirty,' I say. 'She threatened him. Told him that they'd make him pay. Through his wife and children. Kathy Grant told him this to keep him where he was, to stop him from speaking. She told him about you. Named you as Conahy's informant, as his protector. And if we've worked this out, a court will too.'

But he doesn't react. He looks at me as if he pities me. And I have the first tremor of uncertainty. Not in what I'm doing. Debbie Nugent was murdered by this shit. Murdered by Alex Gordon. Her body dumped in the mountains. How fucking happy both he and Fitz must've been when Margot Nugent practically volunteered herself as suspect. It must have felt like Christmas. The delay in reporting her mother missing. Living with that crime scene for so long. They could never have anticipated it, but it must have felt like a bloody gift. The well-placed forensic clues around the house. The hammer in the gutter, the weapon there to find – to help the case along but in a place that would wash it free of evidence.

He smiles. 'You don't know what you're dealing with. You think they're going to let this get out? It would make the force look like a fucking joke. In more ways than one. Do yourself a favour, uncuff me. Persuade Kristen that there's nothing here, that it all checked out as a legit covert op into organized crime, that it's a sad state of affairs her mother got caught up in her wee dad's pathetic life.' He strains against the cuffs at his back, leans up close. His breath hot on my face. 'Sooner or later, you're

285

going to have to learn to look the other way, Sheehan.' He moves back, keeps his eyes on mine, his voice coaxing, trying on a tone of decency. 'For the greater good.'

'Redmond,' I reply. He remains silent, eyes moving over my face as cautious as fingers testing a sharp blade. 'He's the one who fed you the information on Fitz's whereabouts.'

'I had nothing to do with Fitz,' he says. Whether he means generally or Fitz's murder, I don't know. And I don't buy either. He may not have been behind that trigger tonight, may not even have known what would happen, but between him and his allies Fitz's whereabouts got back to Conahy and they worked, they killed to protect their most powerful informant.

He meets my eyes, quiet. Then: 'You see what you're up against? Are you getting a wider view now? This is dirty crime, Detective,' he drawls across my title as if it's an insult. 'Fucking hardened criminals who'd blow your grey matter out the back of your skull as soon as look at you, and that's just the good guys.'

'Hardened criminals like you.'

He shakes his head, regretful that I don't seem to be following him. But I'm following him alright. And nothing he says will stop me from bringing him in.

'If that's your view,' he says. 'What I'm saying is, you've barely licked the sweat from the walls, is all.'

I turn him back towards the car. Open the door, but, before I push him inside, I lean in against his ear, let my lips brush his skin. My words driven out through gritted teeth. 'Trust me when I say you have no idea what I'm prepared to do to see you pay for Debbie Nugent's death.'

CHAPTER 25

I shift my weight on the hard wooden bench. Smooth the hem of my skirt along my knees, feel the scratch of a label against the skin of my lower back. I keep my face pointing forward, try to ignore the rumble of noise behind me as public and reporters trip and talk their way into seats. The sharp corner of something bumps against the back of my head and I duck a little in my seat, turning my head to look up at a photographer.

'Sorry,' he says loudly, his attention never leaving his comrade, who he directs on across the room so they can get a good view of proceedings.

Jack Clancy gives up on trying to look comfortable and loosens the tie at his throat, his thumb flicking open the button at the top of his shirt. He plucks the kerchief from his pocket and mops it across his forehead. He finishes by running it over his top lip then stuffs it back in his jacket again.

'Think they would've installed some fucking air-con in this room,' he mutters at me.

After the cold start to the spring, temperatures have risen to annihilation level, for Ireland anyway. Everyone hot and bothered, and a good lot of them hungover if the scent of stale booze coming from the mouth-breather behind me is anything to go by. To my right, Kristen Nugent and David Sutton angle themselves into their seats. David catches my eye; the corner of his mouth lifts in what could be a smile but it's gone quickly. He's wearing a suit, charcoal, the cuffs on the sleeves slip to his knuckles as he moves. Kristen is no longer in her loose skirts and blouses. A simple pair of cream trousers and a black tee. She's cut her hair, cropped it up by her ears. They're both thinner, their eyes with that hollowed-out look, like they've seen too much, shocked that the lives they thought they were living could treat them so cruelly.

Last night, I replayed my final interview with Margot Nugent. A chat to try and put to bed the last lingering doubt I had around her involvement in her mother's death. She looked tired. Her voice low and flat. And I got the sense that she'd given up. Knew that no matter how she framed it, she wouldn't be able to get her truth across. In the footage, she reaches up, scratches at a patch of inflamed skin below her ear. A round disc of eczema. Something that has flared up since childhood in moments of stress.

She feels trapped, she says. And somewhat deceived. Then there's the fear that's clawed at her insides for weeks. A fear that she's almost grown used to. She thought she was doing the right thing. Now, looking back, she can see how absurd it appears. To others. She knows people don't and won't understand it. And she's worried she won't be able to explain it clearly. But for as long as she can remember, both her and her sister's lives have been carefully curated. She wasn't always aware of that, but now – now that circumstances have dragged her out of that

288

world – she knows. She can look down, look back and see that any tentative interactions she'd had outside of the protective tower of her mother were managed. She was managed. Her sister got out, yes, but she was special. She knew that. Her mother told her often. Margot had to be more cautious. Because whatever was out there might just follow her home.

She recalls spraining her ankle while balancing on a kerb in town. There was no rush to A&E, even though she'd heard a crack, was sure it was through her bones. But her mother knew what to do, resting her in bed, propping up her foot, peeling away her sock to reveal the shapeless lump of her ankle. Debbie wrapped the swollen flesh, nursed her better. But her foot had never felt quite right since. A small click when she walked, an ache in the cold and she couldn't ever shake the feeling that she should have seen a doctor. But she'd never been to hospital, or a GP surgery. And now she thinks that might be strange. And then later, when items started to go missing. Things she knew she'd put away but then they were gone. Her necklace, her phone. Her mother telling her she'd lose her head if it wasn't screwed on, that she was hopeless and lucky to have her mother there to help her.

She's looking at her memories in a different light. She's beginning to think that maybe there hadn't been an intruder the night the rock went through the window. Or maybe there hadn't been a rock at all. Her mother didn't like it when she went out with David and they'd had arguments about it. Huge, teary, raging fights about Margot's work hours, her social life and her relationships. She'd put it down to her mother not wanting to let go, but suddenly she recalls her words, said so often they seemed

289

sewn into the fabric of her being. That people were not to be trusted. Other people. And even if bad things were to happen, they would sort them out themselves. Between them. That she should always wait for her mother's help first. *No matter what happens, wait and come to me first,* she'd been told. Over and again. So that when she'd opened that door and seen all of that blood, Margot had closed it again and waited for her mum to come home.

I hear the large oak doors suck closed. And with a general wave of sniffles, coughs, cameras beeping to standby and papers rustling, the courtroom falls to quiet. The side door opens and Margot is led to her seat. Her lawyer gives her a hopeful smile but she has learned not to return it. She looks beaten. Her red hair tied loosely at the base of her neck, greasy strings of auburn hanging down the side of her thin cheeks.

Judge Maeve Connor steps up to the bench, a quick survey of the room from above her glasses and she sits.

'Here we all are again. Another hearing,' she says, her mouth pulling down. 'Let's get this done, then.' She opens her files, looks over the contents, then fixes her gaze at the prosecution, Fintan McCarthy. 'Counsel, are you up to date with all witness statements?'

'I am, Judge.'

'Good, and Mr Devlin?'

'Yes, Judge.'

'Mr Devlin, you've submitted a request on behalf of Ms Nugent to have the charges against her dropped.'

'Yes, Judge.'

She turns over a page, her eyes scanning the documents, a

frown growing on her face. 'On what grounds, Sir?'

'During further investigation it appears that there may have been another party involved and that my client, Ms Nugent, has been set up, to put it in laymen's terms,' Devlin says, and I cringe on his behalf.

'Set up?' the judge says, her eyebrow looking fit to snap it arches so hard.

'The evidence submitted on behalf of the State is circumstantial at best. There are reasons to believe that the victim was, excuse me, the victim of organized crime.'

Judge Connor takes a deep breath. 'Detective Chief Superintendent Sheehan.'

I stand, find my balance on the handrail in front of me. 'Yes, Judge.'

'Would you care to elaborate further?'

I swallow. 'I'm afraid there is an injunction in place that prevents me from speaking about the nature of Debbie Nugent's past, only to say that there is a strong likelihood that she was murdered because of information she obtained around a police informant.'

'Likelihood?'

A hot flush spreads up my neck. 'Yes, Judge.'

She fixes her eyes on me. 'Has the evidence you submitted against Ms Margot Nugent in relation to her charge changed?'

My mouth dries. 'My interpretation of it has.'

She looks down again, sifting through papers with an occasional glance in the direction of Margot, who sits, head bent to chest, eyes staring blankly at her knees, unresponsive.

'This injunction pertains to another case?'

291

'Yes, Judge. First hearing in the coming weeks.'

'Yes, I'm aware,' she sighs. 'The evidence submitted against Ms Nugent has its flaws, as you know,' she says to me and I nod in response. 'Plenty of them,' she continues, 'the lack of concern for her mother's welfare, not a crime in itself, but does perhaps paint the picture of someone who doesn't share the same degree of compassion as the rest of us. The weapon found at her home, Mrs Nugent's blood in the defendant's bedroom. But within all that, not one piece of evidence places her directly in the crime scene at the time of the victim's murder with weapon in hand, is that correct?'

'That's correct,' I say.

'Cumulatively, I see where the connections were made,' she says. 'But I agree, in light of the case you speak of and the peculiarities brought to light through this new evidence, I'm happy to find Margot Nugent not guilty of the charges that have been brought against her.'

She collects up her papers. 'Court dismissed,' she says and I feel like someone's punched a hole through my body.

I sit back down, watch as Margot Nugent is led off again, the reporters behind me shouting questions at her back.

'I guess this is congratulations,' Jack says in a low voice next to me and I want to drop my head in my hands and cry.

When the courtroom clears, Jack and I walk out in silence and into the car park. As I open the car door to get in, Donna Hegarty steps out of a black Merc. I peer through the tinted windows and make out the shape of her driver. Of course, she'd bloody have one, couldn't be bending the leather of her shoes against a clutch.

'Detective Sheehan,' she purrs. 'Good news for Margot today.'

'Yes,' I say.

Jack swears and escapes into the passenger seat of the car, no doubt so he can avoid throttling the commissioner.

'It's a shame about this mess with Alex Gordon though, but I'm confident we'll get to the bottom of it all.' I put my hand on the door of the car, go to get in, but she continues: 'I wanted to thank you for all that you've done. You really put yourself out there. It will be noted.' Her body does a little shimmy under her jacket as if she wants to shake off something repulsive.

'Thanks,' I manage.

She goes silent, her eyes roving over my face, still trying to work me out. A sharp breath through her nose then she speaks again. 'Well, I must get back to the office,' she looks over her shoulder, in the direction of the Phoenix Park where the Garda Headquarters are situated. 'So much paperwork to catch up on today.' She gets in and closes the door. The car rumbles to life, rolls slowly out of the bay and out onto the road.

The inquiry into garda corruption in Ireland is being led by Detective Chief Superintendent Adrian Redmond. Alex Gordon has been advised to take a sabbatical for a few months. He won't work in the police force again but I have the sickening feeling, that despite everything we've done, justice will slither away from us and we won't have enough to charge him for Debbie's murder. There's no evidence placing him at the house, no prints on the murder weapon and, even with his connection to Conahy's gang, there's no clear motive. Our stunt at the Nugent house did not hit the mark.

When we interrogated him on why and how he responded to Kristen's call out, he waved the whole thing away as if it was

293

nothing. 'Okay, I'll admit it,' he said. 'I've access to the calls at the station. A call service where I can pick them up or listen in. I know it's not all above board. Data protection and all that. But we're a rural station, sometimes I switch off, flick the call diversion on and head home for a bit of kip. I just happened to see Kristen's call come in and picked up. Bad of me, I know but,' and he'd shrugged. 'There you are.'

When asked why he burned the USB – fake – but he doesn't know that, 'I made a mistake. In the heat of the moment, I thought it best to get rid of it. I mean, Debbie Nugent was likely killed because of that information. But I see now, it was a short-sighted and stupid thing to do.'

I watch Hegarty's car until it disappears, fighting the boil in my bloodstream. Then pulling open the door, I drop into the driver's seat.

'Christ, that woman,' Jack says. 'It must be woeful difficult having to view the fucking world through your own arsehole.' He glances at me. 'Ye alright?'

I stare at the steering wheel for a while, full of frustration, needing to do something but knowing there's nothing I can do.

'I'm fine,' I say. I reach out, turn the key and pull out of the park and drive in the direction of the Bureau in silence. Jack throws cautious glances at me the entire way. Here we are, back to our status quo: me determined not to let justice slip through my fingers and Clancy watching me nervously, thinking *What's she going to do now?*

The alert comes in on my phone. Another news update on the inquiry into Alex Gordon's involvement in organized crime.

It's been a week since Margot's hearing and with each day, the summary of statements from court becomes increasingly tepid. I'd gone for the first day, hoping, in the absence of justice for Debbie Nugent, it might make me feel better to see the law come for Alex Gordon another way. Only it became clear early on where the narrative was going and where there were holes in the case and how Redmond intended to fill them. Alex was right. This was dirty.

I balance the phone on the arm of the sofa and push myself into sitting position, go to place my feet on the floor then, remembering the scatter of my notes, pull them back. Debbie's case is all around me: transcripts of statements from the town, work colleagues, summaries of CCTV footage. Over the coffee table amid empty mugs of tea, coffee and a half-drunk glass of water, images of her autopsy, the crime scene. I rub sleep from my eyes, shove hair from my forehead, I need a shower. I've been wearing the same clothes for two days straight, a stain down the thigh of my jeans where I spilled my coffee yesterday, my eyes grainy, teeth furry. But I can't muster the motivation to get up.

Reaching out, I adjust a couple of pages. I need a clear view of everything. All strands. Somewhere in this mess of information is how we'll win a conviction for Debbie, if only I can see it. My mobile rings and I reach for it. Baz. I let it ring out, watch the screen change from calling to missed call. Seven so far. I wait for the accompanying voicemail but it doesn't come and I turn it off, leave it back on the side of the sofa.

I stand, reach for my laptop but my hand hits against a water glass. It pitches over my computer, bleeds water across Debbie's case. I drop to the floor, grab the notes, pat them with the end of my T-shirt. Then my computer. I open it, groan at the water running down from the keyboard, feel tears of frustration burn the backs of my eyes. I turn the laptop upside down on the floor then reach for more of the papers. Wiping them on any surface I can.

'Knock, knock,' a voice says.

I look up, handfuls of notes clasped in my hands.

Baz is standing in the doorway.

'Baz.' I look down at myself, dust off my T-shirt; get up slowly. He closes the door, puts a paper bag on the breakfast bar, along with a cardboard coffee holder, containing two cups.

'Sorry to intrude but you weren't answering your phone. I was worried.' Then he walks towards the sofa, looks around, the expression on his face bewildered, hands on hips, as if he was surveying a disaster zone. 'What happened?'

My fingers tighten on the pages. Try to keep my emotions under control. 'I spilled some water,' I say and hear the shake in my voice.

'Oh, okay,' he says, panicking. 'Well let's sort these out. Get them dry.' He goes to the kitchen, grabs a couple of tea towels. Then kneels, finding damp or wet photos, statements, patting them dry. Finally, he takes up the computer, wipes the keyboard. 'Not sure what to do with this but Steve will know,' he says, glancing up. He puts the laptop down. 'Frankie—'

'I failed,' I say. 'I couldn't do it.'

'You've done everything you could. We all have. The case isn't closed. Something will turn up.'

'He's gotten away with it.' I shake my head, hating the whinge of defeat in my voice.

296

'Right,' Baz says, his hands finding my shoulders. 'We'll look again. Ask some more questions.'

'There's nothing.'

'There's always nothing until there's something.'

And his tone, his positivity, grate on me. 'Where? We've questioned everybody. I've been through these files again and again.'

He can't think of anything. But he's trying.

'You see!' I say.

'Well, give me a fucking second, will ye.' He sulks. Arms drop away. Finally, he says: 'Victim first. That's what you always say.'

'Not helpful.'

'And who knows the victim better than anyone?'

I annoy myself by answering. 'Kristen. Margot,' I mutter.

'Margot,' he says. 'Margot knows Debbie better than anyone else.'

I sigh.

'We could talk to her again,' he says. 'We've nothing to lose.' He says it with a strained kind of hope and I know he's desperately trying to give me something to focus on. A goal. Even a hopeless one.

Despite knowing this, I find myself saying. 'No. No, we don't.'

Baz steps back. Checks my face for signs of a breakdown then, satisfied, nods. 'Right. You really need a shower.' He looks around him, lets out a low whistle. 'It's like a health violation in here. I mean, when you let the wheels off, you really let them go.'

'Fuck off,' I say. I walk towards the shower but pause halfway. 'How'd you get in here?'

He smiles. 'Justin. Says you owe him a pint.' He points to the bonsai at the window.

By the time I've dressed and dried my hair, Baz has cleaned up Debbie's case, slotted all papers into their appropriate folders, washed the dishes and opened a window.

'At least you look somewhat human now.' He checks the time, it's mid-morning, traffic will be the best it can be. 'Come on, they're expecting us.'

Kristen and Margot have returned to the B&B on the Wicklow Road. In the days after Margot's hearing they made the decision to put the family home on the market after all. Draw a line under their past. Under their parents' past. We sit in the front room, a tray of Rich Tea biscuits on a single nesting table between us and a pot of tea on another.

We ask Margot, like we did when we first spoke to her, to think back, to take her time, tell us as much as she can remember from around the week before her mother disappeared. She starts with St Patrick's Day, the Sunday, said they'd gone out to dig shamrock from the garden. They went to the parade together, her mum was helping with the float for the garden centre. Then Margot went on to the pub with Prissy. The next day, Margot was hungover but for Debbie it was business as usual and she went to work. She came home in the evening, they had dinner together and both went to bed early. The next morning Debbie stuck her head in the door of Margot's bedroom before she left to say she'd be late home. She was going round to Eileen's to do her garden, to plant some trees, as Eileen was away and it was her birthday. She said that she'd pick up a Chinese takeaway for dinner on the way home. Wednesday, Margot got up, her mother had already eaten breakfast, they talked briefly over a tea then her mother kissed her cheek, said goodbye and left for work. The last Margot saw of her was that morning.

We settle back in the car.

'Sorry,' Baz says quietly. 'We could try some of the neighbours again. Show them a picture of Debbie's car, see if anyone noticed it on the road that night.'

But I'm barely listening. I'm thinking of Debbie. Thinking of her leaving work on that Tuesday afternoon. Reversing her car up to the garden centre's doors where she's set out six small trees she'll later plant along the entrance of her friend Eileen Carty's house. The trees are already in bloom. Beautiful globes of small white flowers, with a light pink hue, dusty with pollen. Flamingo Willows. She opens the boot, lifts the pots inside, sliding them well into the trunk. Carefully, she lets the boot close on them, relieved that they just about fit, although some are pressed firmly against the glass of the rear window. But she doesn't worry overly about damaging them. She doesn't have far to go.

She dusts herself off. Smiles. Pleased that she can do this for her friend. She waves a goodbye to the staff who are busy closing up the centre for the evening, then gets into her car and drives off.

I dial Steve's number, put the car in gear, pull away from the B&B.

'Hello?'

'Is the Nugent vehicle still in auto?'

There's a small pause then. 'It was released last week.'

I take a breath. 'Were there swabs taken from the rear window?'

'Hang on.' Another pause. And I try to wait patiently as he searches the files on Debbie's case.

'Well?' I ask.

299

'Got it. The boot and rear window were divided into grids, swabs were collected from all grids, fingerprints over handle and internal components of the handle. And samples taken up from the interior carpet. It looks pretty extensive.'

I let out a mouthful of air. 'Good. We'll need them pulled please.'

'Righto, Chief.'

I hang up.

Baz frowns at me. 'You mind filling me in?'

I hold up a finger. 'In a minute. I've one more call to make.' And I make this call as insurance. I may have a new lead, but if that doesn't work, I need to find another way to expose Alex Gordon and all those connected to him.

Shelley Griffiths answers quickly but her voice is steady when she speaks: 'I thought you'd call sooner,' she says.

CHAPTER 26

The viewing room at the Bureau is dark and cool. It's a busy Monday morning in the office, days after our last visit with Margot and Kristen Nugent. The staff are already consumed with our new cases. The conveyor belt of crime does not stop, does not recognize that we're possibly on the cusp of a charge. If all goes well. There is no pause, no collective intake of breath. But we've done everything. Worked the crowds up into a fever. This time in our favour.

Shelley ran the article on Alex Gordon. No direct finger-pointing at Debbie Nugent's murder but enough to keep the public's eyes and ears working for us, to keep voices shouting for justice. A grand unveiling of Dublin's underbelly with the delicious whisper of garda corruption, of undercover agents marrying to get close to their targets.

I move up to the window that looks in on the interview room. The window is a double-sided mirror; where I'll be able to see our suspect but he won't see me. Instead, all he'll see is his reflection. *If Looks Could Kill.* On the table beside me, a set of headphones and two screens that hook up to the video feed in the room, should I want a closer look.

Steve opens the door, steps in beside me, sets his notebook down. 'Not a bother on him,' he says referring to Alex. 'Cool as a summer's day in Dublin that fella.' There's a triumphant sourness in his voice that tells me he's looking forward to the end of this as much as I am.

He reaches for the screens, adjusts the contrasts, checks the audio. Then gets up, shuts the door on the Bureau and the buzz of the office is immediately silenced behind the specialized acoustic doors. We both fall silent. Eyes on the door inside the interrogation room. Finally, it opens. Alex Gordon is the first to enter, followed closely by his lawyer, Fintan McCarthy. My arms tighten across my chest. Baz lopes in afterwards, he directs them to their seats and both men settle down, share a smile. This will be over soon, they think. And it will. I make myself breathe out. Try to hold on to my nerves. Hope that we've prepared enough.

Helen is the last to enter the room. She closes the door and I see her pull in a quick breath. Her eyes go once to the mirror, then she sits down next to Baz.

Suddenly, the room seems very crowded.

Baz scans the small congregation. 'Are we ready?'

Alex doesn't answer.

'Can you say your name for the recording, please?' Baz asks.

'Alex Gordon.'

'And your age?'

'Fifty.'

Baz makes a note on the form in front of him then looks to Helen who dives straight in.

'What's your involvement in the murder of Deborah Nugent of Rathborne Road, Ballyalann, Co. Wicklow?'

'No comment.'

'Can you tell us what your connection is with the late Garda Rory McGrane?'

'No comment.'

'Did he work for you?'

'No comment.'

Fintan McCarthy is following the interview through his notes. He will have predicted most of these questions, will have advised Alex Gordon not to answer any of them. But it's amazing how tempting it can be to provide an answer when you know it. Some deep human drive to be right. To get something right. To correct a wrong. And for someone with an ego like Gordon's that temptation must be gnawing at his very bones.

'Were you aware that Rory McGrane was Debbie Nugent's husband?' Helen asks.

Alex leans back, draws in his chin. 'No comment.'

'Did Debbie Nugent approach you with information on her late husband?'

'No comment.'

'What was contained in this information?'

McCarthy shakes his head.

'No comment.'

'Were you worried it might implicate you in organized crime?'

'No comment.'

A short pause, then Helen continues. 'She came to you as a trusted member of the Gardaí. A face she knew. You abused that trust.'

Alex tips his head. 'Is that a question?'

Helen, momentarily shaken by Alex's response, pulls back. A flush creeps up her neck, reaches her hairline. It's awkward but she's doing better than she knows. McCarthy looks up. I think I see a flash of concern in his eyes. Lawyers do not like it when their clients go off-script. Helen's fumble has gotten Alex to speak and, in my experience, that's the first hurdle cleared.

'Do you have anything to say about that?' Helen asks, finally.

Alex throws an exasperated look at his lawyer then stares back at Helen. 'No comment.'

Baz passes Helen a document, which she turns around and places on the table before Alex and McCarthy. 'Showing suspect exhibit 26D. The image is of a hammer that was found in the gutter of the victim's house.' She takes a quick breath. 'Mr Gordon, would you look at this picture, please. Do you recognize the item photographed?'

He looks at the image but answers, 'No comment.'

Helen pulls the photograph back and Baz returns it to the folder. She continues, more photographs; the living room, the carpet, the window. All met with, 'No comment'.

'Did you hit that hammer against the window in anger? Is that what you did?'

'No comment.'

Another pause. She's drawing out his memories of that evening. Painting them slowly in his head. Coaxing any tiny morsel of remorse he possesses forward. 'Did you use that hammer to kill Debbie?' she asks.

'No comment,' he whispers.

She lays out more photos. Debbie's autopsy pictures. Debbie's remains, cold, partially covered in a damp ditch. She gives Alex a second. Lets the effect of the image descend on him like thick smog.

'Did you drag Debbie Nugent's body from her home and dispose of it in the mountains using her car?' she asks.

He leans against the armrest of the chair. Swallows a dryness from his mouth. 'No comment.'

'Can you tell us about your activities on the day of the twentieth of March 2013?'

'No comment.' He gives Helen a frustrated glare. 'Is this it? Are we nearly done here?'

McCarthy stays quiet.

Baz passes Helen another photo. She lays it down on the table and I see Alex glance first then look again. The tension clicks down my spine.

'Showing suspect picture 6AF, a photograph of the boot of a Ford Focus. Interior,' Helen says. Then to Alex. 'Do you recognize the car in the picture?'

His eyes don't move from the image and the police officer in him almost appears. He opens his mouth and I can see the shape of the word 'Yes' on his lips. Can almost hear him thinking, *Yes, that's the victim's vehicle, Ma'am.* So hard not to reply when you know the answer. But he pulls himself back, runs a hand over his face. Breaks the spell. Then he folds his arms over his middle as if he can hold what he wants to say inside.

'This is the victim's vehicle,' Helen answers for him. 'Debbie Nugent's car. Did you place her body in the boot of this car?'

He tips his head back, blows air at the ceiling. 'No comment.'

Helen looks rattled. But I know it will make her more determined to pace herself. There's no surer detective at playing the slow, careful game.

She takes the next photo, lays it down. Another image. This time a different car. 'Do you recognize this vehicle, Mr Gordon?'

He sighs. Impatient. But when he looks down, he stills. Stops fidgeting. The mask slips. He reaches out, picks at the corner of the photograph and I see the panic spread on his face, his eyes widening, the colour dropping away like a curtain.

'That's mine,' he murmurs.

My fist is in my mouth, teeth on my knuckles.

Helen keeps calm. 'The suspect has identified the car as belonging to him. Mr Gordon, we have a receipt from a local garage for a valet and car wash, dated 17 March 2013. Do you remember that?'

'That was before all this,' he stops himself, waves a hand through the air. 'Go on. Next question.' I can't tell if he's annoyed at himself or desperate to know where we're going.

Helen goes back. 'Is this the car you used to drive to Debbie Nugent's house on the evening she was murdered? On the evening of the twentieth of March 2013?'

'No comment,' he answers quickly.

McCarthy keeps his attention down on his notes but I see his eyebrows go up.

'After leaving Debbie Nugent's body in the Wicklow mountains using her car, you returned to your home in your own vehicle. Is that correct?'

'No comment.'

306

'We have evidence to suggest that you drove this car directly or within hours of murdering Debbie Nugent and disposing of her body.'

He sucks in a sharp breath. Irritated. Angry. 'I'd like to hear it then so.'

McCarthy gives Alex a warning stare that he ignores.

Helen rests another photo down between the images of the cars. This picture shows a row of small trees. Almost a metre in height and in full bloom.

'Do you recognize these trees, Mr Gordon?'

'No.'

'This image is of a section of Eileen Carty's garden. Debbie Nugent planted these trees on the nineteenth of March. The evening before she was murdered. We found pollen specific to these trees coating many areas on the inside of Debbie's car but particularly heavy in the rear elements, including over the rear window.'

Alex rolls his right shoulder. Places his hands on the table and frowns. 'There must be pollen all over her house, she was a gardener. And I was in that crime scene.'

'These trees were ordered especially for Eileen by Debbie. On their delivery, Debbie drove them straight to Ms Carty's house where she planted them.'

His tongue works the inside of his cheek. 'Is there a question here?' he snaps.

Helen is calm. 'We found pollen, that shared the same bio-markers and profile as those collected from the rear window of Debbie Nugent's car, on the driver's headrest of your car, Mr Gordon.' She pauses, meets his eyes. 'Can you explain that?'

307

I see his rage travel down his arms, his clasped hands tighten. Through gritted teeth, he replies: 'No comment.'

'We believe that as you were placing Debbie Nugent's body in the boot of her vehicle, pollen from those trees transferred onto your hair and from there to the headrest of your own vehicle. Have you anything to say to that, Mr Gordon?'

I see his throat working; the colour heighten over his face. For the first time, he looks over at the window. He knows we have him. 'No comment,' he says.

CHAPTER 27

Jack has taken his place in front of the fire, the leaves of his newspaper spread out over his knees, although he's given up looking at it, his cheek turned towards the heat, his eyes drifting closed. Enda, the landlord, has stacked the wood high on Jack's command, waving away any mention of the rise in temperature from outside. The bar is nicely full; not packed, but enough punters to send out a gentle lull of chatter around the room. Baz walks carefully towards us, three pints of lager balanced between his hands – his eyes intent on them, as if he could will them into not slipping from his fingers.

'Your age is showing, Jack,' he says to Clancy's half-sleeping form.

'So is yours,' Jack mumbles, eyes still closed, a smile lifting the corner of his mouth.

'I have to say, it's nice to be back.' I smile. Clancy, I know, is feeling similar; the rush, push and adrenalin over the past few weeks, now receded, has left behind a bitter kind of success.

Baz bends over the table and lowers the drinks slowly into the

309

centre before reaching back and removing three bags of roasted nuts from his pockets. He drops a packet each in front of us then sits, reaching eagerly for his pint.

Clancy rouses himself enough to pick up his, the paper crumpling on his lap. 'That it is,' he agrees, raising the full pint to his lips and slurping at the white foam. He sighs, his face softening with pleasure. 'That's the stuff,' he mumbles.

I open a packet of nuts, tip a few into my hand, push further back into the armchair, curling up my legs and tucking them beneath me.

'The papers have eased off her, at least,' Jack says after another drink. 'Her suing half of them helps.' He says this with a satisfied smile.

Jack, when we come to the end of an investigation, peels himself back slowly, away from the case, as if he is easing a plaster from his skin. Victims are reduced to pronouns or 'yer man, yer woman', when talking out of the office. I've no doubt all the details are there, that he could remember with absolute clarity the delicate gold-faced watch Debbie wore; black leather strap. The colour of her eyes, the clothes she was wearing when we found her. He could lead you up the steep pine trails of the hills behind Debbie's home to where we found her body in the ditch. I know that when he closes his eyes at night, Dennis Fitz's face is the first thing he sees, a flare of red blood spattered on the wall behind him.

I take up a few more of the nuts, drop them in my mouth, then lean forward to my pint. Baz passes it to me and I smile my thanks.

'The headlines are certainly reading differently these days,' I say.

'Too right,' Jack says. 'It will be good to see him stand trial.' He puts out his hand, makes a cup of his palm and I tip some nuts into his hand. I know he's still feeling the sting of Fitz's betrayal. Know that there must be a bittersweet feeling to our success. I think of Winnie. Alone. Dealing with the aftermath of Dennis' involvement in all of this. 'Well,' he says, 'it's certainly upset the applecart. That's for sure.' He dusts off his hands, folds the paper closed and throws it on the table.

DETECTIVE SHOT DEAD IN GANGLAND KILLING

Article by Shelley Griffiths

I can pick out a few phrases in the text. The names, *Conahy*, *Tyne*, *Nugent* and *McGrane*. The words *corruption, informant. Gordon. Fitzsimons.* A false marriage, the links to an anonymous man who shot himself in a Dublin park on a warm February day. The slow coercion of a troubled covert agent by fellow colleagues. The money, the drugs and, eventually, the murder of Debbie Nugent. The article hit news channels throughout the country, the Gardaí Ombudsman Commission scrambled to secure all files necessary for an inquiry. Adrian Redmond's voice from the radio, stammering to explain his unit's involvement, the cool satisfaction of Donna Hegarty at a press conference assuring the public that all those involved will be thoroughly investigated and that already there have been great strides forward in creating new policy to ensure this kind of thing can't happen again, including new legislation that allows historical cases handled by Intelligence units to be viewed when deemed *necessary* to active cases. Necessary according to whom, would be my first question.

I sit quietly, Baz and Jack strike up a conversation on Clogherhead, the potential for a holiday home, if they ever

311

saw the money, or whether it would pay to have a house somewhere hot, or would it be best simply to save for more holidays? At some point Jack mentions Baz's love life and they both fall into an awkward silence for a bit before they settle on the safer subject of cars. I half listen, my mind dipping in and out of their banter.

The ghosts of the case are still around me, Debbie Nugent's in particular. Her eyes look out from newspapers, work bulletins. The investigations into the murders of Kathy Grant, Dennis Fitzsimons and Garda Robert Matthews, the uniform who was shot along with Fitz, are ongoing. It's looking likely that it was one of Conahy's crew who was responsible for their deaths but on whose orders? Alex Gordon is keeping quiet on all fronts. Fintan McCarthy wanted a big case. Now he's got more than he can handle – and this time the public are on the right side. They are crying for blood and McCarthy won't be able to stop them having it.

I finish my drink and refuse an offer for another, telling Baz and Jack I've a date with the folks.

'Court tomorrow,' Jack says.

'I'll be there,' I say.

'Then we'll be back to business as usual, whatever that is,' he says.

Baz gives a short laugh.

I stand in the living room. The morning sun is bright at the window and warms one side of my face. The smell of toast and butter drifts out from the kitchen. Beyond the door, there is the soft crackle of a newspaper, my brother's laugh as he teases

Mam about the strength of her tea, the slide of cutlery drawers, the rush and bubble of the kettle.

Looking in the mirror, I push the final brass button through its eye, draw the thick black belt around my waist and fit it through the buckle. I lift a hand to my throat, adjust the pointed knot of the navy tie. I pause at my reflection in the mirror. Look for the person I'm supposed to be, but the person I am stares back: flesh, bone, fear and faults. Far from a hero but human and in this job, I'll take that. I bend to the table beside me, pick up my hat and fix it on my head. I brush my hands over my shoulders, tug the bottom of my blazer down. When I turn, he's behind me, in the doorway. The dream of a smile on his lips or maybe its just where the sun's light has cast a pleasing shadow around his mouth.

'Hi, Dad.'

His eyes move over the uniform and I wonder who he is seeing. He nods as if answering some question to himself and then he does smile. 'I can drive you, if you like.'

I smile back. Take in a steadying breath, then follow him out the door.

ACKNOWLEDGEMENTS

To everyone who has supported and read the Frankie Sheehan books – thank you!

Thank you to all my publishing team at riverrun: to my editor Richard Arcus and copyeditor Anne Newman. Thank you to the publicity and marketing teams, in particular Milly Reid and Laura McKerrell, and to Dave Murphy and the sales team.

Huge thanks to my wonderful agent, Susan Armstrong, and to all the rights team at C+W Agency and to Zoe Sandler at ICM.

Thank you to friends and family who have supported my writing over the years. Special thanks to my sister, Ann, and to all those writers who have given me advice and friendship.

Thank you to those members of law enforcement and law professionals who have answered my questions patiently when researching this book. In particular, solicitor Brian P. Doyle, author and barrister Tony Kent and detectives within the Thames Valley Police and An Garda Síochána. Any inaccuracies in procedure are my own.

And thank you to Matthew for always being excited on the highs and encouraging on the lows. Thank you to Grace for your smiles, love and for asking all the important questions.